New Horizons

Wings Press, Inc.

Michael Embry

New Horizons

"I'm so excited about this trip," she said, looking in the vanity mirror on the visor and touching up her cherry-red lipstick. "Budapest should be fun. It's the heart of Europe and a new adventure for us."

"If you say so."

"Oh, John, stop being that way." Her brows furrowed. "You sound like a grumpy old man."

A wry smile crossed John's face. "Maybe I am a grumpy old man."

"Try to be positive."

John glanced at her. "I'll try."

"We'll be back before you know it and you'll probably complain about that."

"I don't think so."

"Admit it...you don't like all the drama with Brody and Mother."

"You don't either."

"That's why I'm looking forward to getting away for a week and a half. You make it sound like we'll be gone forever. You should be thankful the travel agency allowed us to split your retirement gift rather than take the whole twenty-one days."

John shrugged. "You're right. It's just the idea of being out of control of things going on back here."

"Just let go and relax." Sally beamed. "New horizons for us."

"You sure like that phrase 'new horizons.'"

"Because it's part of growing and exploring new things in our lives. You always complained about not wanting to be one of those folks who sit around in a rocking chair all day watching TV.”

“Point taken.”

Sally leaned over and pecked his cheek, leaving a faint red imprint she wiped away with her thumb.

What They Are Saying About
New Horizons

This novel has such a realistic feel to it. It's not of the thriller genre, but I found myself turning those pages, wanting to know what was going to happen next. Even when John and Sally (Ross) return to America from their exciting trip, the suspense is still on, and problems are there to be overcome. These characters handle the difficulties with grace and are to be admired. The issues they tackle are important as well, and the process is entertaining to read about.

—Lara MacGregor
Author of *The Secret Mask of Truth* and *The 12th Kiss*

For retired baby boomers John and Sally Ross, following through on a wish to experience "new horizons" means a vacation in the beautiful city of Budapest. Complications arise when they must manage their fun time against the demands of a possessive and boorish couple seeking friendship. That, and continuing family complications back home, make this getaway a little less than ideal. Author Michael Embry leaves us both laughing and crying with his flawed but recognizable characters.

—Steve Flairty
Author, columnist, and *Kentucky Monthly* reviewer

"The best Michael Embry yet. *New Horizons* continues the John Ross Boomer Lit saga as John and Sally Ross go on a whirlwind tour of Budapest. In *New Horizons*, his latest novel, Embry honestly addresses many of the issues so many boomers face today—adult children who need help, parents who need us more than we need them, drugs, memory loss, and a longing for a simpler, better America. Honest, accessible writing that keeps you turning the pages."

—Chris Helvey
Author of *Snapshot*

New Horizons

Michael Embry

A Wings ePress, Inc.
Boomer Lit Novel

Wings ePress, Inc.

Edited by: Jeanne Smith
Copy Edited by: Rebecca Smith
Executive Editor: Jeanne Smith
Cover Artist: Trisha FitzGerald-Jung
Cover photo: Michael Embry

Wings ePress Books
www.wingsepress.com

Copyright © 2019 by Michael Embry
ISBN 978-1-61309-616-1

Published In the United States Of America

Wings ePress Inc.
3000 N. Rock Road
Newton, KS 67114

Dedication

This novel is dedicated to the memory of my sister, Carolyn Embry Jones, 1957-2017

Loving mother to daughters Sierra and Dominque; doting grandmother to Jonah; beloved sister to Sheri, Marilyn, Paul, Julie and me and kind, dear, and sweet friend and nurse to many others.

"No one is truly lost when they remain in the hearts and minds of those who love them." —American writer Kirsten Beyer
Star Trek Voyager: Children of the Storm

One

"Do you think this is a good idea?" John Ross glanced at Sally before backing the SUV out of the driveway. His lips pressed together. His muscles tensed as he buckled his seatbelt.

She reached over and tapped his forearm. "John, we've talked about this over and over. We've made the decision. We're going to Europe for ten days and we're going to enjoy our trip. Now relax. Okay?"

John shrugged and let out a deep breath. "I'll try."

"Thank you."

John maneuvered past pedestrians, cyclists, and cars moving in and out of busy side streets in the Garden Springs neighborhood for the short drive to Blue Grass Airport. On most days he'd be antsy dealing with the traffic but not today. In less than three hours they'd be boarding a small commuter plane to Atlanta, then hop on a jumbo jet for the trans-Atlantic journey to Budapest, Hungary.

John gripped the steering wheel as if preventing the vehicle from turning around on its own. He avoided flying, and the thought of being in the air for more than eight hours and four-thousand miles didn't make matters any easier for him. And what he was leaving behind in Lexington troubled him.

Sally smiled. "Honey, everything's going to be okay."

"If you say so."

But John couldn't get the domestic state of affairs off his mind. Whoever said being retired was like taking a stroll down easy street must have been intoxicated or living in la-la land. Every age has its set of hurdles.

John groaned.

Sally peered at him. "Something wrong?"

"Just thinking."

Sally shuffled in her seat, gazed straight ahead, and didn't respond.

An unstable situation on the home front, especially with their son Brody, occupied John's thoughts. Brody had spent two weeks in a rehabilitation facility after the Christmas holidays for an opioid problem. While Brody attended three-times-a-week recovery classes for the addiction, counselors cautioned John and Sally about the chances of a relapse. They knew it was a real threat and something could reemerge because of their son's vulnerability to drugs.

Brody appeared on the road to recovery, at least on the surface, but John remained skeptical because looks could be deceiving, especially when it came to Brody. John and Sally hadn't had a clue about Brody's drug habit until John paid a surprise visit to his apartment in Chicago. He learned that Brody's use of pain pills following a back injury playing flag football had evolved into a dependency, resulting in losing his job and depleting his bank account. Brody was on the brink of homelessness, or worse. Perhaps becoming another casualty in what had become the nation's scourge.

The situation didn't improve after bringing Brody home to Kentucky. He ended up in the hospital for overdoses. He was arrested for a public disturbance involving drugs. And there was a perilous episode with a local dealer after John found a pouch in his car containing heroin that Brody had inadvertently misplaced. Now John hoped Brody realized the seriousness of the problem. Only time would tell.

Four months had passed since that family nightmare. Brody reassured them about his drug-free commitment when he assisted John in loading luggage in the vehicle for their week-and-a-half trip to Europe. He promised to attend classes, watch over his grandmother Geraldine, and take care of Whiskers, the family pooch. John had heard Brody's empty promises to turn things around before, usually denying there was a problem. He knew Brody's previous pledges were paper thin. He had come to realize there would be ups and downs over time. Maybe a long time. Or a lifetime.

"You think your mother can keep him in line?" John asked as he turned on tree-lined Man 'o War Boulevard and headed to the airport.

"Mother promised me that she would make sure he attends all his meetings," Sally said. "You know how persistent she can be."

"I'm not so concerned about that. It's what he does in his free time."

"Please, John, quit fretting about everything. Even when we're here we can't control everything he does. You know that. Try to relax. Let's enjoy our vacation. We've been putting this off for several months. Don't you think we deserve it?"

"We deserve it." John drummed his fingers on the steering wheel. "I just don't know what to expect while we're gone. I'm not sure we deserve that. Anything can happen. That bothers me."

"Mother's getting around better now. And we've told her what to do or who to call if Brody gets out of hand."

"Leaving Brody with your eighty-eight-year-old mom doesn't seem like the best thing to do. Or leaving her with our self-centered son. It's a recipe for disaster, in my humble opinion. Just sayin'."

"Our neighbors will keep on an eye on them. Everything's taken care of."

"If you say so," John said as he pulled the SUV into the long-term parking lot at the airport. He found a spot under a tree and turned off the ignition. They sat while Sally made sure their tickets and passports were easily accessible from her purse.

"Mind if we sit here a minute while I get my head straight?" John said.

Sally nodded.

"I'm so excited about this trip," she said, looking in the vanity mirror on the visor and touching up her cherry-red lipstick. "Budapest should be fun. It's the heart of Europe and a new adventure for us."

"If you say so."

"Oh, John, stop being that way." Her brows furrowed. "You sound like a grumpy old man."

A wry smile crossed John's face. "Maybe I am a grumpy old man."

"Try to be positive."

John glanced at her. "I'll try."

"We'll be back before you know it and you'll probably complain about that."

"I don't think so."

"Admit it...you don't like all the drama with Brody and Mother."

"You don't either."

"That's why I'm looking forward to getting away for a week and a half. You make it sound like we'll be gone forever. You should be thankful the travel agency allowed us to split your retirement gift rather than take the whole twenty-one days."

John shrugged. "You're right. It's just the idea of being out of control of things going on back here."

"Just let go and relax." Sally beamed. "New horizons for us."

"You sure like that phrase 'new horizons.'"

"Because it's part of growing and exploring new things in our lives. You always complained about not wanting to be one of those folks who sit around in a rocking chair all day watching TV."

"Point taken."

Sally leaned over and pecked his cheek, leaving a faint red imprint she wiped away with her thumb.

John grabbed sunglasses from the visor and put them on. "I know this is silly, but I worry about Whiskers. I'm not convinced your mother and Brody will take good care of him. Maybe we should have put him in a kennel."

"I can't believe you, John. Never in my life would I've ever thought you'd be that concerned over a dog. And you know he wouldn't be happy in a kennel."

"I told you it was silly. But I'll miss the little bugger. Did you notice his sad eyes when we left the house?"

"Yes, and I saw you dab your eyes when you walked to the car." She pushed out her lower lip.

John cleared his throat. "I had something in my eye."

Sally rubbed his shoulder. "Mother and Brody will keep a watchful eye on him. Brody promised to walk him every day. And you know how Whiskers likes to tag along with Mother. He'll be fine."

"You're right, as usual. I shouldn't worry about that. There are bigger things I should be concerned about than Whiskers—like Brody and your mother."

"John!"

"Let's get started on our new horizons." John opened his door and went to the rear to remove their luggage. The adventure was about to begin, whether he wanted it to or not.

Two

John and Sally clutched their carry-on bags as they rolled their suitcases through the gray concrete parking garage to the terminal. They checked in with the airline for the first leg of their flight. After clearing TSA checkpoints, which included a pat down of John, they took the escalator to the second level and sat in the nearly vacant boarding area.

"So far, so good." John tapped a foot on the floor. "If only the rest of the trip goes this well."

"We can only hope." Sally fetched her cell phone from her blue-and-white checkered carry-on.

"Checking back with your mom?"

"I want to make sure she doesn't have any questions."

"Can't you relax? We've only been gone forty-five minutes."

"Quit being a smarty. You know how Mother can be."

John shifted in his seat and stretched out his legs. "I'm going to the restroom. Let me know if everything is relatively calm. I don't want to know if things are bad."

Sally smiled as she punched in the phone number as John walked away. After going to the restroom, he stopped at the automated flight display on the wall to make sure nothing had changed on their schedule before returning to his seat.

"Looks like we'll be boarding on time." He stood next to Sally. "How's everything with Geraldine?"

"She's a bit peeved because I called during the middle of one of her soap operas."

"Heaven forbid."

"And Brody went to the store and Whiskers scratched at the door to go outside."

"She can't let Whiskers outside for a few minutes?"

"I guess she wants Brody to take him for a short walk, like you always do with your little buddy."

"Brody promised me he would."

"That's what I told her."

"Have you talked to Chloe?" John asked.

"I called this morning, but she was at work. I'll try again when we get to Atlanta."

John jiggled his shoe on the floor.

"Something the matter?" Sally asked.

"I wish we'd get the show on the road. I don't like this waiting. Reminds me of my Army days. Hurry up and wait."

"Relax, honey." She touched his knee. "That's what I want you to do for the next ten days. That's what this vacation is for."

John sighed. "I'll try to remember that."

"Now would you sit down and take it easy? We'll be flying off into the wild blue yonder in no time."

"You didn't need to say that."

~ * ~

They ate at the Blue Moon Brewhouse in the sprawling Hartsfield-Jackson Atlanta International Airport, taking their time since they had three hours between flights. They walked down the corridor to their gate as travelers whisked past them in all directions, several giving them annoyed looks for their unhurried pace.

Sally stopped at the women's room while John sat near the boarding podium. She tried once more while standing in line to reach Chloe but got voice mail. She called home and Brody answered.

"We're about to leave." She raised her voice in the restroom, contending with the announcements about arrivals and departures and the continuous flushing of toilets. "Want to make sure everything's okay."

Brody laughed. "You haven't been gone that long. And where are you? I can barely hear you for all the racket."

"Restroom."

"What are you doing in there?"

"I'm not going to answer that."

"Uh, no problems so far."

"I hope it stays that way."

"Don't worry."

Sally squeezed the bridge between her eyes. "I'm serious, Brody. You've done so well the past few months."

"It's gonna stay that way."

"Love you." Sally wiped a tear away.

"Have a safe trip, Mom," he said. "Tell Dad I hope everything goes well."

"One other thing. I tried calling Chloe, but she didn't answer. Would you mind getting in touch with her later and telling her that we're on our way to Europe?"

"Will do," Brody said.

"Please get in touch with us if you need anything. All the contact numbers are on the refrigerator."

"I know, Mom," Brody said. "You've only told me twenty times or more."

"I want to make sure."

"Anything else?"

"I can't think of anything right now," she said. "Just behave yourself. We'll see you next week."

After ending the call, Sally located John in the waiting area, reading an *Atlanta Journal Constitution* newspaper. Her cheeks dimpled as she sat on the cushioned chair.

John folded the newspaper and placed it in the empty seat next to him. "How's Chloe?"

"She didn't answer. I hope everything's all right with her."

He patted her hand. "Chloe's the least of my worries. She can take care of herself."

"I'm concerned about her and Whitney, especially after the problems she and Sam had during the holidays."

"But hasn't everything been going somewhat well since then?"

"I hope so." Sally crossed her arms. "I'm not sure she'd tell me if there were problems. You know she's always been a problem-solver and prefers to take care of things by herself."

"I assume you called home?"

"I talked to Brody. Everything seems to be okay."

"That's a relief. I'm glad he's at the house rather than running around the minute we're gone. I hope he remembers to mow the lawn. I don't want the yard looking like a jungle."

"I'm sure he will."

"Really?"

"Now don't start worrying about Brody. He's been on his best behavior the past few months."

"And you know all too well how fast that can change with him." John leaned forward, resting his forearms on his legs. "Don't try to deny it."

"Let's not talk about the past right now. Let's focus on our trip."

"A new horizon."

"Yes, dear," Sally said. "*Our* new horizon."

An announcement blared from the airline clerk's microphone to begin boarding the plane. They grabbed their carry-ons and stood in a line that moved at a snail's pace. After locating their seats near the back of the economy section and placing their carry-ons in the overhead bin, Sally sat next to the window and John by the aisle.

He clasped her hand. "Are you sure this is a good idea?"

Three

After landing at Amsterdam Airport Schiphol for a layover, John and Sally meandered to a crowded commons area and didn't speak for several minutes. Their feet dragged not only from the long flight but because of the attentiveness of the saccharine-sweet stewards. They showed up about every hour delivering snacks, meals, handing out water, or picking up leftovers. And with passengers bobbing up and down like fishing lines, taking short walks in the aisles, going to the restrooms or standing next to their seats and stretching their arms and legs, there was hardly any time for napping.

"You know, flying is for the birds." John chuckled at his remark. "Why I ever agreed to this trip to Europe is beyond my comprehension. I hate going through security and customs. I hate being in airports. I hate being six miles in the air. I hate—"

"But we're in Europe," Sally said, almost breathlessly. "We'll be in Budapest soon."

"We're at another damn airport. This could be Peoria, Salt Lake City, or Cincinnati. They all look the same."

"Oh, John, settle down." She placed an arm around his shoulder and squeezed. "You're going to make yourself sick."

John inhaled and exhaled several deep breaths to soothe his nerves. He noticed signs printed in different languages. He listened to people as they hurried by chatting in various tongues. Armed guards in black uniforms and blue berets stood at various strategic points, on alert for any suspicious behavior, or worse, a terrorist attack. He knew he had tourist written all over him.

John snorted. "You're right. We're in Europe. This definitely isn't Peoria, Salt Lake City, or Cincinnati."

"Can we finally start our vacation?"

"I'll give it my best shot."

"I sure hope so. You're beginning to sound like a skipped record."

"Oh, thanks."

"Well, you are. That's all I've listened to since we left home, complaining about this or that. Driving me nuts."

He grinned and nudged her with his elbow. "I'll try to be a good boy."

She pecked him on the cheek. "Thank you."

"I wonder how Chloe and Brody are doing?"

"There you go again," Sally said.

"It popped into my head because you mentioned home. It's all your fault."

"I'll call after we get to the boarding area." She glanced at her watch. "We'll have some time to eat before our flight to Budapest."

"Let's find our gate first so we won't have to make a mad dash at the last minute. I don't like feeling rushed."

"And to think you worked on deadlines at the newspaper."

"That's history," John said. "I've grown accustomed to not having them in retirement. Unless it's one of your honey-dos."

"You've got it made, John."

"I won't argue with that unless—"

"Don't go there!"

"I wasn't going to mention—"

"Stop."

"Let's go to our gate then."

They lifted their carry-ons and merged into the traffic going toward their gate. While the pace was brisk, it actually felt good as their bodies began to revive after the hours in cramped seating on the airliner.

After finding gate five, they couldn't enter because it was on the other side of a long plexiglass wall. They walked to several points before John took Sally's advice and asked an airport guide for directions. They first needed to go through immigration and customs at gate sixty-one. By the time they completed the necessary passage for entry into Europe, their KLM flight to Budapest beckoned them over the loudspeaker to gate five with little time to spare. No time for a laid-back lunch. Not even a bathroom break. And the momentary spring they had in their legs had sprung.

They sat among the other passengers waiting to board the flight. Sally pulled out a packet of cheese crackers from her carry-on. "Want some?"

"I've lost my appetite," John said, a corner of his mouth lifted. "I'll wait until the flight to Budapest."

"We're almost there." Her bouncy voice belied her fatigued face.

He closed his eyes and leaned back on the hard, plastic chair. "That's what you keep telling me."

Sally took out her phone and called home but ended the call when she realized the six-hour time difference. She'd wait until later in the day, after getting settled in Budapest, to check in with their children.

Four

When the bumpy two-hour flight ended without snacks being served, they stepped into a narrow passageway from the plane at Budapest's Ferenc Liszt International Airport terminal. Twelve hours from home.

John clasped Sally's hand as they walked to the baggage-claim area. "Believe it or not, we finally made it."

"Isn't it exciting?" A weary smile merged with the shadowy circles under her eyes. "We're in another part of the world. It even feels different. Don't you think? Budapest, Hungary."

"Did you say hungry?"

"I still have a packet of cheese crackers in my carry-on."

"I think I'll pass," John said, even though he experienced some hunger pangs on the flight. "By the way, I was trying to be funny."

"I know," Sally said. "That's why I ignored it."

They located their tour group at the far end of the baggage area. A middle-aged woman held up a bold red and white Here and There

Travel Tours sign and a clipboard. Several travelers around her stood clutching suitcases, leaning against posts, or milling about the small area. They all looked glassy-eyed and exhausted. John recognized two couples from their flight from Amsterdam.

"We're still waiting for a few more," said the woman with a British accent as John and Sally approached her. "After they arrive, we'll board the bus and go to the hotel. It shouldn't be much longer. I hope. In the meantime, you can go to the restrooms right outside the door or to one of the nearby shops for something to drink or eat."

No one moved.

John studied Sally for a few seconds. "I'm bushed. I don't think I'm up to much of anything today."

The woman with the sign apparently heard him, smiled, and spoke loud enough for everyone to hear. "My name is Pauline Shaffer and I'll be your guide in Budapest. We'll get checked into the hotel, rest a bit, and then have a welcoming dinner. That's all that's planned for today. I know everyone's tired because it's been a long day."

She glanced at John. "We'll have a full day of activities tomorrow."

"That's fine by me," John shook his weary head. Several in the group bobbed their heads in agreement.

Pauline checked off his and Sally's names on her clipboard as well as the other two couples from their flight.

Four couples from South Carolina showed up in the next twenty minutes to complete the group. John wondered if they experienced a rough flight because of their grim expressions. The women had some similarities such as light complexions and prominent noses, giving the notion they were sisters although in different shapes and sizes and ages. Their male companions lagged behind. All in all, there was a haughtiness about these travelers as if this were their tour and everyone else was simply tagging along.

John turned to Sally. "Did you ever call Brody or Chloe?"

"When have I had time?" Sally grimaced.

John's shoulders shrank. "Just asking."

"I'm sorry. I'm just tired. I didn't mean to snap at you."

John gave her a conciliatory peck on the cheek.

John took a quick survey of the group, noticing it was primarily white and ranging in age from fifties to seventies among the twenty-five or so travelers. While most were couples, a few were single, especially the younger ones, maybe in their twenties or thirties.

Everyone boarded the private luxury bus, and despite being the last ones to arrive at the airport, the South Carolina couples somehow took the first eight seats behind the driver, a burly man named Andras. John and Sally sat in the rear. They stared out the window, almost lulled to sleep, as the bus whisked down the four-lane highway the thirteen miles to Budapest, the anointed Pearl of the Danube.

They arrived at the hotel, located in the heart of Budapest, a few blocks away from sophisticated Andrássy Avenue. Pauline told everyone to gather in the hotel's dining room at seven, giving the tired trekkers three hours to recuperate from their long journeys from different points in the United States.

"It looks like we have WiFi in the room," Sally said, glancing at her cell phone from the dresser.

"It's not like we're in a Third World country," John said, lying on the bed in his sock feet with a pillow curled under his head.

"Quit being a smarty. I know that. I was only making a comment."

"I'm sorry."

"Apology accepted."

John closed his eyes and dozed off within five minutes, letting out a few snorts. Sally sent text messages to Brody and Chloe, not expecting a quick reply because of the time difference. Chloe should be a work and Brody in rehab class. She kicked off her shoes and slipped into bed, nestled under a puffy navy comforter. Within a few minutes, she was asleep as well.

A shrill-ringing phone roused them from their slumber. Sally grabbed it on the nightstand as John blinked bug-eyed at the ceiling as if jolted by an electric shock. Pauline Shaffer wanted to know if they were coming down for the dinner. Sally apologized and said they'd be there in fifteen minutes.

"We overslept," Sally said as her feet touched the thick carpet. "Let's get moving."

John rubbed his eyes. "Overslept for what?"

"The welcoming dinner," Sally said as she lifted her legs off the side of the bed. "Don't you remember?"

"Do we have to go?" he muttered.

"Yes, dear. I told her we'd be there in a few minutes. And we don't want to be rude, so hurry up."

"Can you go by yourself?"

"John, you get up now!"

John stretched his arms with a wide-mouth yawn. "Only kidding, sweetie." He yawned again and took a deep breath.

Sally headed toward the bathroom. "Kidding or not, we need to hurry. I can't believe we overslept on the first night. This is embarrassing."

"I look and feel like crap. I don't have time for a shower?"

"If you can take one in three minutes."

John slipped out of his clothes next to the bed and dashed butt naked to the shower. Moments later, Sally stood next to him under the warm spray. John did a double-take, surprised to see her.

"Now this will wake me up." He cupped her breasts.

"Not now, silly man," she said, pushing away his hands. "Three minutes. We need to get clean, dressed, and down to the dining room. We don't have any time to spare."

"Shucks."

They arrived in the dining room with damp hair as Pauline addressed the tour participants, looking more like cardboard cutouts with their fixed expressions as they'd probably prefer being in bed as well. A buffet dinner of Hungarian dishes as well as several American and European sides sat on a long table against the wall.

John and Sally hurried to the first table they spotted with two vacant chairs. Before they could sit, Pauline asked them to introduce themselves and where they were from to the rest of the group. Pauline welcomed them as the only travelers from Kentucky. A minute later, another couple crept into the room, identifying themselves as Frank and Dorothy Finsterwald from New Jersey.

"It looks like we have people from South Carolina, California, Texas, Louisiana, Wisconsin, Kentucky, New Jersey, Wyoming, Indiana, and Ohio," Pauline said. "That's quite a cross-section of America. We have lots of places to see and things to do in Hungary. Please feel free to ask me anything about the tour."

There was silence.

"I know everyone's exhausted from the flights," she said. "To be honest, I'm tired as well and I only came here from London. I want to let you know I'll be posting our travel agenda for each day's activities on a poster board near the elevators in the lobby. So please check that each day."

John glanced at their tablemates' nametags: Phil and Edna Deat from Indianapolis. They appeared to be about their ages. Phil sat upright, slender and balding with an introspective demeanor, almost aloof. Edna appeared contemplative, sipping on tea, a pretzel-thin physique as well as thin lipped, with gray hair with red highlights in a bun. An odd, perhaps quirky couple. Other than hurried smiles, the Indiana couple didn't utter a word to them the entire meal.

As they devoured their dessert of chocolate mousse cake, Pauline went over the next day's itinerary and highlights of the tour. John looked around at some of their fellow travelers as she spoke. She had an audience, but he wasn't sure how attentive it was by their languid eyes. He stifled a yawn or two when Pauline turned in a different direction.

When dinner ended, Phil nodded and Edna smiled, leaving the table without saying a word.

"What a scintillating dining experience." John tilted his head. "Let's make sure we spend a lot of time with them."

Sally covered her mouth and snickered. "I don't think I've ever felt so uncomfortable. Did we say or do something to offend them?"

John took a whiff of his underarm. "I don't see how. I've never seen them in my life. And I did use deodorant."

"Quit being silly," Sally said. "At least we know who to avoid."

"That shouldn't be a problem. I bet they'll be avoiding us."

On the elevator, John held the door open for an approaching middle-aged man.

"Thank you very much," the man said. "I think I saw you in the dining room. My name's Tyrone Lewis but I go by Ty."

John shook his hand and introduced him to Sally. "Are you as tired as we are?'

"I'm from Wisconsin," Ty said. "Madison. It took me nearly fourteen hours to get here. You?"

"Twelve hours from Lexington, Kentucky, so I guess you could be a tad more exhausted than us," Sally said.

Ty stepped off the elevator on the third floor. "It's a pleasure meeting you. I'm sure we'll see a lot of each other over the next week or so."

"No doubt," John said. "See you in the morning."

John and Sally got off on the sixth floor, their room two doors from the elevator.

As they undressed, Sally asked, "Did you bring all your meds, hon?"

"Yes, dear, and then some," John pulled back the comforter and white linens on the queen-sized bed that filled most of the room.

"I didn't see them when I unpacked. Are you sure? We don't want to have any kind of episode with your heart."

"They're in my carry-on," he said, easing into bed. "Safe and secure. Experts recommend doing that in case luggage gets lost."

"I wanted to make sure." Sally slipped next to him and placed her arm across his chest. He turned his head and kissed her forehead.

"I hope everything goes well. It's like being in another world. It's so different than home. Even the air feels different. I'm really looking forward to everything. The castles, churches, monuments."

"Hey, don't forget about the castle on Versailles Road," he said with a light laugh.

"That's not the same thing," she said. "These castles in Europe are hundreds of years old. I can't wait to walk through Buda Castle and see all the art and learn about the history."

"Me, too," John said. "By the way, did you ever hear back from Brody and Chloe?"

"I received several texts from Brody while we were at dinner. He and Mother are doing okay. And he said that Whiskers has been watching the front door, like he's waiting for us to return."

"I miss that little guy," John said with a wistful expression. "But nothing from Chloe? That's unusual"

"I know. I'm a little concerned but I'm sure Chloe has a good reason. I'll try again tomorrow."

They closed their eyes and were fast asleep.

Five

"Sleep well last night?' Sally asked as she lifted her legs out of bed. "I know I did. I was beat."

John turned his head on the pillow, watching her stretch her arms. "I was beat as well. Still a little beat. But as they say, the beat goes on."

Sally smiled. "Let's make the most of it while we're here."

"I'm sure we'll reenergize. At least I hope so."

"We can rest our weary souls after we get back home."

"Amen."

After getting dressed, they headed to the hotel's restaurant for the buffet breakfast. They each poured a cup of coffee at the beverage-dispenser counter and looked across the room. John noticed the Deats and steered Sally to a vacant table twenty feet away. They recognized several travel companions and nodded and exchanged pleasantries as they sat down.

"We're going to Heroes Square this morning," Sally said. "From what I've read, that's a good place to start the tour. We'll learn something about Hungary's past."

"And tomorrow's itinerary looks interesting." John perused a sheet of paper Pauline handed out the night before. "I've never heard of the House of Terror."

"Me neither." Sally took a sip of coffee. "From what I remember, Pauline said it was about the communist rule in Hungary during the Stalin era and beyond."

"The thermal spas look inviting as well," he said. "Did we bring any swim wear with us?"

"Sorry." Sally's lower lip protruded. "I didn't think to do that. Would you want to buy swimsuits?"

"Let's think about it."

John winked. "I wonder if they have nude bathing."

"You can forget about that."

"Mind if we sit here?" A man and a woman, both appearing to be in their 70s, stood next to the table holding breakfast plates. The man had bushy white hair and a matching moustache while the woman's hair was salt-and-pepper in a neat bob and gentle smile lines from the corners of her eyes.

"Oh, please do," John said, removing travel sheets from a place setting.

"I'm Chester Wilson," the man said as he set his plate on the table and hooked the handle of a cane around the back of his chair. "And my wife, Penny. We're from Ohio."

"A pleasure to meet you," John said.

"I'm Sally. We're from Kentucky."

"We're practically neighbors," Penny said as she unwrapped her silverware from a napkin. "Where from?"

"Lexington," Sally said. "You?"

"Green."

"Green?" John asked. "Don't believe I've ever heard of it."

"We're up toward Cleveland," said Chester, whose hands quivered as he stirred his coffee. "A small community."

"First time to Europe?" John asked.

"Heavens no. We've lost count," Penny said. "We've been doing this since Ches was in the service, back in the late fifties."

"Wow," John said. "I'm impressed. First time for us."

"I think you'll like Budapest," Penny said. "It's such a gorgeous city with so much history. It's one of our favorite places."

"I think we'll like it unless something crazy happens," Sally said.

As they ate breakfast, Chester shared that he retired as a hospital administrator while Penny spent her career as a nurse. They had five children who inherited their parents' wanderlust, sometimes traveling with them to exotic locations around the world.

"We plan to travel until we can't get out of bed." Chester raised his shaky hands. "Or until this Parkinson's sidelines me. I'm sure my odometer is reaching its limit."

"Odometer?" Sally asked.

Chester laughed. "The miles I've racked up on my rickety body. It's too bad I can't trade it in on a new model."

"Don't we all wish we could do that," Sally said, grinning.

"We can get new hips, knees, even hearts and lungs," Penny said. "Who knows what the future has in store for us?"

"For me, it's time to get moving," Chester said, pushing his seat back. "I'm not going to sit around and wait for a cure."

Chester and Penny sauntered to the front lobby, holding hands, where several travelers were gathered near the entrance. At Sally's urging, John made a pit stop in the restroom, taking longer than expected after waiting in turn behind three men who apparently had prostate problems as they took more than the standard time to urinate. John had learned to be patient because he knew someday it could be him holding up the line.

Sally was sitting at the end of a couch, talking to a couple, when John returned to the crowded lobby. More guests were bunched near the front door as if they feared the tour bus would leave without them.

"I hope we don't have a stampede to the bus," John said, standing next to Sally.

"Like school children on a field trip," Sally said. "Everyone's excited."

"I don't think the bus will leave without everyone. At least I hope not."

"Pauline said the bus should be here in a few minutes. She said he got caught in a traffic jam a few blocks from here."

"Hurry up and wait."

"Please forgive me for not introducing my husband John," Sally said, glancing at the couple who appeared to be in their late fifties. They were short; the woman had a pudgy, round face and a graying, fluffy pixie hairstyle while the man was thin, long-faced, and slightly stoop-shouldered.

John nodded and smiled. "Pleasure to meet you."

"Sebastian and Claire Hebert," the man said in a slow Southern drawl as he rose from the couch and extended his arm to shake hands. "From Baton Rouge, Louisiana. Nice to meet ya'll as well."

"First time to Budapest?" John asked.

"First time out of the country," said Claire, the tips of her purple tennis shoes barely touching the floor.

"Same for us," Sally said.

"We thought this would be a safe place to vacation. Right, Seb?"

"Haven't heard of any them terror attacks here," Sebastian said, looking up at John. "You know what I mean?"

"I think so," John said. "I believe it's relatively safe." He paused a few seconds. "But you never know."

"Now don't you say that!" Claire said, grinning. "I want to feel safe."

"Sorry 'bout that."

"Don't give it any thought," Sebastian said, letting out a snort. "She frets about everything."

"It doesn't hurt to be careful," Sally said. "Regardless of where you are."

"She's right, Seb," Claire said, nudging Sally with her elbow. "Better safe than sorry."

The crowd began moving, or more like pushing, toward the revolving front door as squeaky brakes signaled the bus pulling up next to the curb.

"Looks like our ride has finally arrived," John said, looking toward the window.

Claire bounced up from the couch, reached down and grabbed an oversized tote bag, and dashed toward the congested doorway.

"Hey, wait for me," Sebastian said with a bewildered expression as he followed her to the door, glancing over his shoulder for a moment at John. "We'll see ya'll later," he said before clutching his wife's hand and entering the mini-logjam.

"Stay safe," John said, lifting his hand.

"I would say they're excited," Sally said as she took John's hand. stood and watched the Heberts disappear through the door.

"Ready to join our fellow travelers?"

"You lead the way."

As the group boarded the tour bus, hovering dark gray clouds threatened rain. Heroes Square was a short drive from the hotel. Pauline mentioned other places to consider that were not on the overall itinerary to visit on their own in the afternoon.

"There are many brilliant places to see, all within walking distance of the hotel," she said on the microphone. "I know some of you are a bit knackered from yesterday so pace yourselves because we have a lot to see and do in Budapest."

Despite an intermittent drizzle, the eager travelers stayed semi-dry for the most part with plastic ponchos and mini-umbrellas they had tucked in their bags. John donned a khaki Tilley while Sally wore a blue baseball cap with "UK" on the front.

"I don't believe what I did," John murmured as they followed Melinda, a local guide, toward the monuments.

"What?" Sally creased her brows.

"I forgot my damn camera." John gritted his teeth. "Shit!"

"How did you do that?"

"I guess because I left it at home. What do you think?"

Sally pursed her lips and stared at him for a moment. "Can you buy another camera?"

"I don't want to, but I suppose I can this afternoon. It's not an expense I was expecting. I sure didn't come all the way to Budapest to buy one. I can't believe this."

"Now John, don't get riled up. It's not that big of a deal."

John clenched his jaw. "Maybe it's not a big deal to you."

"Why don't you buy postcards instead?" she asked.

"How in the hell can I put you in a postcard?" Several in the group looked in his direction. John lowered his head and fumbled with the zipper on his jacket avoiding eye contact after his momentary—and embarrassing—outburst.

"Calm down, John. It was a thought, honey." Sally bit her lower lip.

John walked a few steps ahead of her, a signal she had learned from their forty-plus years of marriage when he needed to cool down, and especially in front of temporary travel companions. It was rare for him to lose his cool in public, perhaps stemming from his days at the newspaper when his job included being the stalwart sports editor keeping everything under control at all times. There wasn't supposed to be that pressure in retirement. He had discovered there were other demands, even the adjustments to being retired.

John stopped and took several deep breaths before taking Sally's hand and following the others. They strode past the tall columns and bronze statues featuring the seven chieftains of the Magyars, the early settlers of Hungary in the ninth century. As Melinda explained the country's glorious and violent past, John thoughts drifted to the camera back home, sitting on the dresser in the bedroom in clear view.

"It's on the dresser back home," John leaned over and whispered in her ear.

"How do you know?" Sally twisted her head.

He grinned. "No pun intended but I have a photographic memory."

Sally elbowed his side. "Silly."

When the short talk was over, Pauline asked everyone to remain near the square since the bus would be departing in fifteen minutes. She suggested using the time to take photographs.

John glanced at Sally with a crooked face.

"Sorry," he said. "I didn't mean to take it out on you back there. I'm upset with myself. I can't believe I was so stupid to leave the camera at home."

"I understand." Sally tucked her arm inside his arm. "It's my fault too. I probably should have had a checklist. There's always something."

"Now don't start blaming yourself. I should have remembered to bring it. I'll take your suggestion and buy postcards. Those images are probably better than what I could take."

"Or you could use our smartphones."

"Damn!" He looked around to see if anyone was listening. "I completely forgot about that."

John snatched the phone from his inside pocket, towed Sally in front of the tomb of the unknown soldier and clicked several images. He took a selfie of them in front of the Millennium Monument. Sensing time running out, they scurried to the center of the square for a panoramic view as the drizzle turned to a steady shower.

At the bus door, Pauline waved a small purple-and-white tour flag, motioning for everyone to return.

"We'd better get going or they'll leave without us," Sally said, stuffing her hands in her side pockets.

"I'm glad you mentioned the phones," John said as they scampered to the bus arm in arm. "We can use yours as well."

"I wish I'd said something earlier."

"Me, too, but it's not a big deal. I should have thought about it. It just never occurred to me. I don't use my smartphone much for photographs unless they're of Whiskers or Whitney or something going on during my neighborhood walks."

"We can still buy another camera if you want to," Sally said as they sat in middle of the bus.

"I'll think about it," John said. "I don't want to spend time shopping for a camera when we came here to take in the sights."

"It's your decision."

Several minutes passed as the South Carolina contingent, drenched to the bone, dawdled to the bus, even showing chagrin on their faces when four other couples were sitting in the front four seats. Pauline, usually displaying a pleasant disposition, seemed nonplused by their tardiness as the bus pulled out of the parking area.

"Still no word from Chloe?" John asked on the quiet return to the hotel.

Sally shook her head. "I didn't call this morning because of the time difference. But I thought I would have received a text from her. That's just not like her. I'll try again when we get back to the room."

Six

"Oh, my god!" Sally placed a hand over her mouth as she sat at the small writing desk in the corner of the hotel room.

John stepped out of the bathroom, holding a toothbrush. "What is it?"

"Chloe's been in the hospital the past few days. I got a text from Sam. She said Chloe had been feeling nauseous before she went to the ER with stomach cramps. They're still running tests on her. She didn't want us to know because of our vacation."

John's jaw tightened. "What? I don't believe that girl. What should we do?"

"Let me get back with Sam."

"I'm ready to go to New York right now."

"C'mon John, let's not get carried away. I think if it were serious, Chloe would have told us. At least I hope so."

"Me, too."

"I'll call Sam in about an hour," Sally said. "I've got her cell number. It's about six in the morning there. We can find out more about what to do then."

"Why don't you get in touch with Brody and see if he knows anything?"

"I'll call him after I get in touch with Sam."

John sat with his arms crossed on the corner of the bed. "Call now."

Sally crinkled her forehead. "But you know he's still in bed."

"It's his sister. He needs to know."

"John, it's early back home. We can wait."

"No, we can't!" John grabbed the hotel phone on the nightstand. The phone rang five times before the answering machine clicked on. John left a message for Brody to call as soon as he could.

He glanced at Sally, putting a hand over the mouthpiece. "Anything else?"

"You might as well tell him Chloe's in the hospital." He could tell Sally was perturbed by her steely stare. "Isn't that the reason you called?"

"You're right." He passed on the information and put down the handset.

After an hour, sitting in stifling silence, they hadn't heard from Brody. Sally dialed Sam's number. She answered in Chloe's hospital room.

"I got your message about Chloe," Sally said in a measured but friendly tone. "We're in Budapest. Can you tell me anything else?"

"They thought it might be food poisoning but ruled that out after bloodwork," Sam said as if reading from a script. "Now they believe she has some kind of virus."

"How does she feel?"

"She's better than she was a few days ago," Sam said, sounding more natural. "I begged her to go to the ER then. She was so afraid that you and Mr. Ross would cancel your trip if you found out."

"Should we return?"

"I don't think so. Like I said, she's better than she was yesterday. It could be a flu bug. You know how those things come and go. I hope we find something out later today, so we can go home. She's getting restless being here in the hospital. You know how she likes to be on the move all the time."

"Where's Whitney? Is she all right?"

"A close friend's watching her. She's doing fine. I'll see her later this morning."

"Please promise me that you'll let us know what the doctors find out as soon as you hear something."

"I will, Sally. I know it has to be difficult for you right now, being so far away. But if there's any change, I'll let you know. Promise."

Sally passed on the spare details to John as she went about removing clothes from her luggage, refolding and placing them in a dresser drawer.

"Still upset with me?" John asked.

"No," she said without looking at him. "Why would you think that?"

John walked over and placed a hand on her lower back. "I didn't mean to upset you by calling Brody. I knew he wouldn't be up. I'm just exasperated by everything. Let's not fuss. Okay?"

Sally turned around with a pensive face. "You're forgiven. We're both concerned about Chloe." She smiled and kissed his cheek.

Instead of venturing out to explore the city, they stayed in the room and waited to hear for an update on Chloe's condition. As John flipped through a Hungarian tourism magazine, Sally dozed on the bed. The phone's piercing ring startled them for a moment before Sally answered.

"Mother?"

"I got your message," Geraldine said. "Why were you calling so early? Don't you know we have to sleep around here?"

"We have a six-hour time difference."

"Well, you should take that into account before you call."

Sally held her breath for a couple seconds. "Is Brody there?"

"Don't you want to talk to me?"

"Mother, we're concerned about Chloe."

"Then why are you calling here? She doesn't live here. How would I know? Why don't you call her?"

"Mother, please," Sally said in a strong, deliberate voice. "Didn't you listen to the message? Chloe's is in the hospital. We wondered if you or Brody had heard from her."

"I haven't. I'm not sure about Brody."

"May I speak to him?"

"He didn't come home last night."

"What?" Sally raised her voice. "He didn't come home?"

"He spent the night with a friend and left me here all alone with John's little mutt," Geraldine said. "I don't know what's got into that boy."

John cocked his head at Sally.

Sally mouthed, "Brody's not at home."

"Did you say something, Sally?" her mother asked. "I could barely hear you."

"When do you expect Brody to come home?"

"I hope very soon because the little mutt is bothering me about going outside. I don't know why you couldn't have put him in a kennel. He's so much trouble."

"Please tell Brody to call as soon as he gets home," Sally said. "Is everything else okay?"

"Yes," Geraldine snapped. "And thank you for asking. I was beginning to wonder if you cared."

"Please, Mother, you know better than that. We'll talk later."

After ending the call, Sally closed her eyes and took a deep breath. "My dear mother."

"What's going on?" John asked, rising from the bed.

"You know how she rants." Sally spread her fingers over her face. "Drives me crazy. I almost feel a migraine coming on."

"Don't let her do that to you."

"You know how she can be. Or maybe I should say, how she is."

"I understand. What did she have to say?"

"Brody spent the night with a friend. That's the reason we haven't heard from him."

"What in the hell does he think he's doing?" John slapped an open hand on the mattress. "We told him in no uncertain terms to stay at the house and be with your mother."

"I know, John. I don't know what else to say. So you calm down, too."

"And she didn't know anything about Chloe?"

"No."

"This is exactly why I didn't want to go on vacation." John paced back and forth at the foot of the bed. "We're away for two damn days and Brody's already up to no good. Unbelievable."

"Now, John."

"Don't 'now John' me."

"We don't know if he's in any trouble."

He stood in front of her. "That's beside the point. We told him to stay at home. He should only leave for his rehab classes, or heaven forbid, a job interview. Is that asking too much of him?"

"Please calm down."

"What if he—"

Sally reached and touched his hand. "Let's take a walk."

"But what if Samantha calls?"

"I'll call her back. Let's wind down a little. We both need a break. Okay?"

A bright mid-afternoon sun engulfed them as they stepped out of the hotel on to Teréz Boulevard. They donned their sunglasses and glanced up and down the busy thoroughfare.

"Which way?" Sally asked.

"Let's start walking and see where we end up." John took her hand and they veered right into the flow of pedestrians. A light breeze brushed against their backs as they strolled into new and foreign surroundings. They stopped several blocks away and stared at life-sized statues of a disheveled man in an overcoat with a small dog.

"Is that who I think it is?" Sally's brows furrowed.

John chuckled. "If you think it looks like Columbo, or should I say Peter Falk, then you're right." They walked over and read the plaque about the late American television star.

"I never knew he was from Budapest."

"Same here." John rubbed his chin. "I may have to Google this when we get back to the hotel."

They crossed the Margaret Bridge, connecting Buda and Pest, over the wide and serene Danube. Vehicular traffic was light. They followed other walkers to Margaret Island, a tranquil islet in the middle of the river. They observed locals riding bicycles, strolling along paved pathways, and children playing in open fields. They sat on a bench across from the spiral Centennial Memorial for a few minutes, taking in the peaceful setting without saying a word, before walking deeper into the park. They discovered a small zoo populated with animals indigenous to Hungary.

"This is quite a treasure." Sally peered through a chain-link fence at a fallow deer. "I'm glad we went this way."

"Part of the adventure of being urban hikers," John said. "You never know what you'll discover."

They wandered the perimeter of the zoo before moseying over to a path parallel to the river, leading back to the bridge. They were in no hurry, stopping on occasion to observe people on the banks and boats on the river.

"You know what I like about being here?" John asked.

"What's that?"

"We're in a foreign country, but you realize the people here do much the same things we do back home. We may have language barriers but we all share common activities and interests. This could be Jacobson Park in Lexington with a petting zoo."

"Only at a slower pace. Or at least it seems that way."

"You've got that right," John said. "It makes you wonder if Budapest is as Americanized as other cities."

"Honey, we've only scratched the surface."

"I guess we'll find out over the next few days. And I did see a McDonald's along the way."

"Maybe we'll get lucky and see a KFC," Sally said with a laugh.

"I wouldn't be surprised."

"We'll have to make plans to visit other places and see. I bet the Wilsons have seen a lot in their travels."

"We may have to do that," John said. "If things ever settle down back home."

"Let's try to savor the moment we have now. These are going to be our memories."

"You're right." John put his arm around her shoulder and pulled her close. "Try to live in the present."

"And keep Chloe in our thoughts."

John chuckled. "And perhaps your mother and Brody and Whiskers."

"I know. But I'm concerned about Chloe."

"As much as I hate to admit it, there's not much, if anything, we can do right now," John said. "And I'm not sure there's much we could do if we were back home."

"We could provide support."

"I would hope our children know we support them, regardless of where we are. Even Brody."

"And Mother."

"I'm not sure she'd realize it," John said. "But that's fine. At least we know."

"Let's head back to the hotel." Sally shivered. "It's getting a little chilly. Maybe we can reach Sam."

When they opened the door to their room, John noticed a light flashing on the telephone. He dialed the number to the front desk and was told that Samantha Berry had left a message for Sally to call her. John wrote down the numbers in case Sally didn't have them.

Sally took the note and called Sam. She answered on the second ring.

"It's nothing serious," Sam said in a soothing tone. "I want to let you know what's going on with Chloe."

"What is it?"

"Chloe has an ovarian cyst," Sam said. "That's what was causing her abdominal cramps."

"Anything else?"

"Well, they did a biopsy.'"

Sally sat on the bed. "Please don't say it."

"Stay calm, Sally. It was, uh, benign."

Tears trickled down Sally's pallid cheeks as she covered her mouth for a few seconds. John tried to figure out the course the conversation as he stood staring out the window, unaware of Sally's watery eyes.

"What?" he asked, turning around. "The tests are back?"

"It's benign." A smile lined Sally's lips as she covered the mouthpiece on the phone.

John craned his neck. "Benign? What's benign?"

"Hold a second, Sam," she said. "I need to tell John."

"What?" John asked, stepping next to her, his forehead furrowed.

"Chloe had an ovarian cyst. They did a biopsy and it came back benign. It wasn't cancerous."

Her words forced John to retreat to the easy chair in the corner, dropping his head and running his hands over his thin scalp.

"Did you hear me? It's benign."

"Hon, I'm just letting it all sink in," John said, shaking his head. "But thank goodness."

Sally turned her attention back to Sam. "Thank you so much for letting us know. When can we talk to her?'

"She's sleeping now. I'll call back when she's awake. Will that be okay?"

"That's fine, Samantha. Just tell her we love her."

After putting the phone on the receiver, Sally scooted on the side of the bed and squeezed John's hand.

"That's enough excitement for one day." John let out a deep breath. "Especially when we didn't know what was going on to begin with."

"I don't know what I would have done if Sam had said it was cancerous." She released John's hand. "My heart may have stopped beating." Tears welled again in her blue eyes.

"I thought I was going to quit breathing listening to you talk to Sam."

"Do you think we can get back to enjoying our vacation?"

"You forgot something."

"What?"

"We haven't heard from our prodigal son."

Seven

John went to the lobby to read Pauline's notes about the next day's events on a large poster board near the concierge's desk. He was amazed when he saw other travel companies with notices tacked on it as well. His group would be going to the House of Terror in the morning, a few blocks from the hotel. A trip to historic Buda Castle followed in the afternoon.

When he returned to the room, steam seeped from under the bathroom door as Sally showered. He thought about joining her but decided against it. A desirable distraction but dinner was calling, and they needed to get a bite to eat. John laughed to himself that it must be another sign of growing older. But then he thought it wasn't so funny. Maybe more practical, or mature, but certainly not humorous. That was something he'd have to give more thought.

John walked inside the bathroom to brush his teeth. He watched a few seconds as water flowed from the overhead shower down Sally's slender body that had become more delicate with age.

He marveled how she had taken care of herself, especially when he thought about the various shapes and sizes of some of the women on the tour. Not that it mattered because he loved her regardless of her shape. At least he hoped he wasn't that jaded.

Sally stepped out of the shower and John reached out to hand her an oversized white towel. She turned around. "Honey, could you dry my backside?"

"My pleasure. And the front, if you so desire, my lady."

She laughed. "Let's see how well you do the back first, my knight in shining armor."

"Okay." He rubbed a little harder between her shoulders to the small of her back, eliciting gentle moans from her.

Seconds later, she turned around and faced him. "Okay, you did good, Sir Lancelot."

John patted her chest and breasts, then her soft, flat belly. "I can take it from here," she said, taking hold of the towel. "I don't want you to get carried away."

"Are you sure? It won't be a problem."

"I don't want you to go to any more trouble. You might strain your back by bending down."

"How thoughtful of you." He grinned and handed her the towel.

The phone rang. John nearly slipped on the damp bathroom floor as he left to answer it. He braced against the door jamb for a second before proceeding to the phone.

"What a surprise," he said, grimacing with a hand on his lower back. "Finally get home?"

"I'm sorry, Dad," Brody said. "I know I promised to stay home but a gal in the rehab session invited me to her place, and one thing led to another, if you know what I mean."

"I didn't think that was allowed by the facility."

"Well, Dad, if you saw her, you'd break some rules, too."

"I don't think so, but we can discuss it some other time." John eased down on the side of the bed. "Do you know about Chloe?"

"That's a reason I'm calling. I talked to her a few minutes ago. She told me about what happened to her. She says she's doing fine now. But I thought she sounded a little weak. I tried to get her to tell me, but she said everything was okay so I just dropped it."

"We'd like for you to call her every day or so until we get back."

"Are you serious?"

"Damnit, Brody. She's your sister. I shouldn't even have to ask you to do it. You know if it were reversed, she'd be checking on you every day. Probably several times a day."

"Okay, okay, I get your point."

"We haven't talked to her yet. Mom will probably call her in a few minutes since you've been able to reach her."

"Anything else?"

"How's your grandmother? You know you had no business leaving her at the house by herself."

"Come on, Dad, she's been around a long time. She can take care of herself. She knows her way around the house."

"Damnit, Brody, she's eighty-eight and not fully recovered from the fractured hip. You should know better than to leave her alone. What if she fell again?"

"I never thought about that."

"Then start thinking."

"Don't go ballistic."

"I'm concerned, Brody. I'd like for your mother and me to have a nice vacation, one that you and Chloe paid for. She's housebound and dependent on you. Is that asking too much for you to stay at home?"

"No. I'm sorry. Okay?"

"How's Whiskers?

"He mopes around the front door most of the time, like he's waiting for you guys to return."

"I hope you're taking him out for short walks."

"I try to."

"And how's the rehab coming along?"

"Good as ever. Drug free. Clean as a whistle."

"Let's keep it that way." John paused. "And the job search?"

"Nibbles."

John knew better than to ask for more details. Brody had mastered the technique for making excuses about the lack of interviews. Brody had expressed his desire to return to Chicago or move to another large city, counteracting any motivation to search for positions in Lexington.

"Anything else going on that we should know about?"

"I don't know. Kinda boring for the most part."

"Sometimes boring can be good."

"Hey, there was a mass shooting in Florida this morning. That's about all I know."

"How many people were killed?" John asked.

"I didn't pay that much attention, but I think quite a few. There was breaking news about it on TV, but I didn't catch it all. I know it pissed off Grandma because she couldn't watch her shows."

"Now that's really tragic."

"What do you mean?"

"Nothing, Brody. Forget what I said. I was just being sarcastic."

"About Grandma?"

"The way some people react to them. But it's still shocking that it happened again."

"Yeah, maybe," Brody said. "They've been going on for a long time. It's not such a big deal anymore. Kinda commonplace."

"What?"

"You know what I mean."

"No, I don't know what you mean but we won't talk about it now."

"Whatever."

"Call if you need anything," John said.

John slammed down the headset and clenched his teeth.

"That had to be Brody." Sally stood barefoot at the bathroom door with the towel wrapped around her body.

"How could you guess?"

"You look upset and your face is red. He seems to have a knack for bringing that out in you."

"Oh, really?' John shook his head. "You're so observant."

"Now calm down, John."

"He said there was another mass shooting."

"Oh, my goodness. Where?'

"In Florida. He didn't have any details. Acted like it wasn't a big deal."

"That's just Brody."

"What in the hell does that mean?"

"John, try to relax while I get dressed. You know how Brody is."

"I know how he is, but that doesn't mean I have to like it."

"Accept it."

John found CNN International on the TV as it finished an update about the shooting that claimed at least fifteen lives and wounded more than a dozen. "How can Brody be so nonchalant about something like this? This is horrendous."

"That's just Brody."

"Damnit, would you quit saying that?"

"What?"

"That's just Brody. It's like you're making an excuse for him."

"I'm just saying that's the way he is. You should know that by now."

"But I don't have to like it. And you don't either."

She turned her back to him. "I'll be dressed in five minutes; then we can go eat."

John recognized her declaration as a signal to stop ranting about their son. When Sally didn't want to discuss something, she would completely change the subject or walk away without saying a word.

John stared at the screen for several more minutes, nothing registering in his head as news headlines flashed from various parts of the world. He clicked off the TV and tossed the remote on the bed. "I almost wish he hadn't said anything about it."

"I know what you mean," Sally said as she put on a pair of black denims. "It's like you can't get away from all the evil in the world. It follows you everywhere. There's no escape."

"Maybe we should just go to Disneyland next time to get away from it all."

"I prefer reality."

"I hate to admit it but maybe Brody's right."

"How so?" she said, buttoning an off-white blouse.

"It happens so often that a lot of people don't give it that much thought. They send up their 'thoughts and prayers' and go on about their daily business. If those 'thoughts and prayers' were effective, we wouldn't be having more shootings. And people are getting so damn complacent about what's going on in our society. Unless, of course, it happens to them."

"I know what you mean, honey. I don't want to sound complacent but there's nothing we can do about it here."

"I can't help but verbalize my thoughts when something like that happens. You know that. I know you probably get tired of hearing my outbursts but I need to vent once in a while."

"Maybe you need to keep a journal and write down what you're thinking."

"Not a bad idea. At least it would spare you my tirades."

"It should be easy for you because of your journalism background."

"You're going to make it sound like work," John said. "I don't need that."

"It might be better than getting worked up over things."

"I'll think about it."

"One more thing."

"What?"

"If it makes you feel better to let off some steam occasionally, I don't mind hearing it. You've done the same for me, especially when it comes to Mother."

"Oh well, let's go grab a bite to eat," John said with a tight-lipped smile. "I saw a buffet-style restaurant a few doors down the street. At least it looked like a buffet. My Hungarian is more of a guessing game."

"Pauline said Hungarian is one of the most difficult languages to learn," Sally said as she slipped on black walking shoes. "It's supposed to be a combination of Finnish and a western Russian dialect. It's difficult to learn and pronounce. Even for non-English speaking Europeans."

"She should know," John said. "By the way, we're going to the House of Terror in the morning. I thought we left one in the Lexington."

"Now, John. That's not nice. But I understand what you're saying so let's not go there right now."

He angled his head. "House of Terror?"

"No, silly. I'm talking about our home."

They got on the elevator to take them down to the lobby. The other occupants were the Deats, the couple who didn't have anything to say. John nodded and Sally smiled. They smiled back.

"Enjoying Budapest?" John asked, lifting his brows.

Phil shook his head in the affirmative. He turned toward his wife and used sign language to communicate with her.

Stepping out of the elevator, the Deats headed toward the hotel's dining room. John and Sally darted through the crowded lobby to the street.

"I guess that explains a lot," John said as they turned left when leaving the hotel. "No wonder they didn't speak to us."

"I'm embarrassed about it because I thought they were being rude."

"We'll know better from now on."

"I noticed something else about them," Sally said as they stood in front of the hotel. "Their nametags don't say 'deat.' They say 'deaf.' The 'f' looks like a 't.'"

"Now I really feel foolish." John's forehead puckered. "We definitely need to apologize when we see them again."

"We didn't know."

They strolled, hand-in-hand, to the restaurant in the fading sunlight without saying a word. A note written in Hungarian, English, and other languages was tacked at the entrance, informing customers that credit cards were not accepted because of a computer malfunction.

"Shit," John said. "Can you believe this?"

"I have some forints. Don't you?"

"A few. I hope we have enough."

They walked up to the cashier, who didn't speak English and apparently hadn't learned how to smile. She ignored them for a few seconds while flipping through paper receipts. She waved her hand to a man who came over, and in broken English, told them how much the buffet would cost. He led them to a table, motioned toward the buffet table and took their order for drinks.

"Now that wasn't too bad, was it?" Sally asked.

"I guess not," John said. "But do I have bad breath or something? That gal wasn't very friendly."

"It could be a cultural thing."

"I don't think so. The man was polite. Others have been cordial. She wouldn't even make eye contact."

"It only goes to show you can run across rude people everywhere you go."

John chuckled. "I thought that was only supposed to be in France."

"Maybe we'll find out someday."

They filled their plates at the buffet table, trying to sample as many Hungarian dishes as they could even if they could only guess at the ingredients. They ate in relative silence, serenaded by the sounds of clanging dishes and silverware from the kitchen and the buzz of lively conversations, and the occasional outbursts of laughter from distant tables. It was almost like being at a hometown bistro.

Stepping out on the sidewalk after dinner, they walked several blocks past the hotel toward Margaret Island and sat on a bench near a flickering nineteenth-century ornamental street light. Night began to fall on the city. Pedestrian traffic dwindled, and most shops were shuttered for the day. Several public buses drove by, packed with passengers probably heading to their homes after work.

"It doesn't look like we'll get any sightseeing in this evening," John said. "They roll up the sidewalks at dark like we do back home."

"Were you looking for something to do?" Sally asked.

"Nah. Just an observation. Kinda nice just sitting here and resting my feet."

"It is relaxing."

"Reminds me of being back home, sitting at the park while Whiskers chases after ducks at the pond. Not a care in the world."

"I remember seeing a small café on the way here. Would you mind if we stopped there on the way back to the hotel and get a nightcap?

"I'd like that. And it's getting a little chilly out here."

John placed his arm around her shoulders as they headed toward the restaurant. They sat at a table and ordered *Gere Villányi Syrah*, a balanced red wine recommended by the server. As they waited for their drinks, John sensed someone was staring at them. He glanced at the adjacent table and saw a couple from their tour, talking softly to each other, and looking in their direction with friendly smiles.

"Oh, hi there," John said, nodding. "I'm sorry; didn't see you sitting there."

"Mind if we join you?" the man asked in a deep voice. "I think we're the only Americans in this joint."

"Please do," John said. "We thought we'd come in for a drink before calling it a night."

The man, tall and lanky with a thick moustache, pulled out a chair for his wife and sat across from John. He introduced himself as

Rodney Johnson, and his decidedly younger wife, Tiffany, from Sheridan, Wyoming.

"Are you having an enjoyable time?" Rodney asked.

"Can't complain," John said. "You folks?"

"So far, so good. We've been stoked about this trip."

"We're on our honeymoon," Tiffany blurted, twirling her ring finger with a luminous diamond for everyone to see.

"Your ring is beautiful," Sally said, backing off as Tiffany held it about twelve inches from her eyes.

Rodney leaned over and kissed his wife on the cheek. She blushed, her face nearly matching her shoulder-length deep red hair.

"Congratulations," John said. "Can I order some wine for a toast?'

"Oh, that's okay," Rodney said. "We've been living together for a few years so it's not that big of a deal."

"Rodney!" Tiffany pouted.

When the server returned with John and Sally's wine, John went ahead and ordered two more to salute the tablemates after seeing Tiffany's sullen face. Minutes later, with wine glasses held high, John wished the couple many years of wedded bliss.

"I hope it works this time," Rodney said. "Number four for me."

"Wow," John said, grinning. "Number one for me."

"That is so wonderful," Tiffany said. "My parents have been married for more than forty years."

"So have we," Sally said.

"How did you meet?" John asked, turning toward Tiffany.

"I worked with Rodney's daughter at an optometry shop. He came by one day to take Mindy to lunch and invited me to come along. I guess it was love at first sight."

"How charming," Sally said, glimpsing at John. "I guess it's nice being friends with Rodney's daughter."

"She won't speak to me now," Tiffany said.

Rodney chortled. "My little Mindy seems to think that she has to call Tiffany 'mom' now. Hell, there's not much difference in their ages. Isn't she only two years older, Tiff?"

Tiffany nodded with a tiny smile.

"What's your line of work, Rodney?" John asked, channeling the conversation in a new direction.

"Coal mining. I do pretty well."

"We have some where we're from Kentucky."

"We got the cleaner stuff out west. Those eastern states have the dirty, high sulfur kind."

"The mines have been struggling."

"Because of natural gas. Cheaper and cleaner than coal."

"That's what I've heard," John said.

"You in the energy business?

"Retired from a newspaper."

"Kind of struggling, too. Right?"

"Might even say that it's that way because new technology that we know as the Internet is cleaner and cheaper."

"Everything's a changin'."

"One thing that's changed and that's the time zone," John said, leaning back. "And it's time for us to head back to the hotel."

"Don't rush off," Rodney said. "The night's still young."

John grinned. "Maybe for honeymooners."

The server returned with small cups of coffee and mezeskalacs, or Hungarian honey cakes, for Rodney and Tiffany.

"Look what you're missing," Tiffany said before taking a bite of the icing-covered dessert.

"Tempting but we need to run," John said as he and Sally pushed back their chairs and stood. "We'll see you tomorrow."

~ * ~

After returning to the hotel, John took meds from his travel bag and went to the bathroom sink. Sally put on her long satin nightgown and climbed into bed.

"Are you going to sleep?" John asked, peeking out the door.

"There sure isn't anything I want to watch on TV and I really don't want to know more about the shooting," she said. "I don't want to know what else is going on back in the U.S. It's kinda nice being several thousand miles away from it. I know I sound complacent. But maybe ignorance is bliss."

"I hear ya." He walked back into the bedroom wearing a white T-shirt and checkered boxers. "And I bet when we return, things haven't changed hardly one iota. Maybe another shooting."

"Unfortunately."

"A sad state of affairs."

"I may read from my Kindle. I downloaded several books before we left home."

"Go ahead. I'm not that sleepy yet."

Sally retrieved the Kindle from her carry-on bag and returned to bed, positioning the pillow to prop up her head.

She turned and faced him. "Did you get your physical before we left?"

"What brought that on?" he said.

"It just crossed my mind, that's all."

"Well, yes, dear, I got my annual physical about two weeks ago. The doctor said I was in great shape for an old fart." He flexed his biceps. "Wanna feel?"

"Why didn't you say something about it earlier?"

"Because there was nothing to report. If there'd been a serious issue, I would have said something. I never question you about your physicals."

"That's because I always volunteer the information before you can ask."

"Oh."

"And you're not an old fart." She elbowed his side, causing him to flinch.

"Just smell like one?"

"John Ross, can't you ever be serious?"

"Serious?" He tilted his head. "Not to change the subject, but do you have any more thoughts about our children?"

"What can we do about it now?"

"I agree. Let's make the most of our time together. We haven't had much for that in the past six months or so."

"Hardly any alone time either." A tender smile crossed her face.

John slipped out of the bed. "I need to go to the bathroom. I'll be right back."

A minute later, he cuddled up next to her, putting an arm across her belly and kissing her cheek.

Sally set the Kindle on the nightstand. "What's that all about?"

"Don't you like physical attention once in a while? And are we alone now?

She turned on her side, their mouths meeting in a passionate wet kiss, a spontaneous moment they hadn't experienced in a while.

Sally let out a wispy breath. "That was nice."

John felt himself getting aroused. From the look in Sally's eyes, he knew she sensed it as well.

"Can you hold that for a minute?" she asked.

"Of course." John grinned like a confident attorney sure of a decision. "A lot longer."

Sally slipped out of bed and found her toiletries pouch. For some reason, maybe it was intuition of things to come, she had brought a small bottle of lubricant. She removed her gown and got back into bed.

John began kissing her neck and breasts before easing between her slender legs. They moved in a quiet but robust rhythm until reaching orgasm.

John rolled over on his back, unable to suppress a wide smile that seemed to take years off his face.

"I don't know what to say," Sally said. "It's been so long."

"Long?"

"You know what I mean, naughty man."

"The doctor gave me some magic blue pills," John said.

Sally raised up on her elbows. "You asked Doctor Riley?"

"I felt a little uncomfortable talking to him about it, but he assured me that things sometimes go south for men as they get older. Especially those under mental stress. And I have been under some stress lately. Wouldn't you agree?"

"How about your heart?"

"That concerned me as well. But he said my heart could tolerate it. He warned not to overdo it, like take two pills." John puffed his chest.

"How long will it last?"

"Several hours. Why?"

Sally lifted her brows and grinned as she moved to straddle him. "You want to do it one more time?"

Eight

John awakened early the next morning, rejuvenated from the best sleep he'd had in ages. He'd almost forgotten how lovemaking put the body and mind at rest. He wondered if Sally, curled in peaceful slumber next to him, felt the same. If her stress-free face, with a hint of a dreamy smile, was any indication, she did. Maybe lovemaking is contagious, especially for those in love.

Easing out of bed, John glanced at his renewed manhood. It brought a grin. Nothing like having the old sidekick back in working order for the first time in a long while, even if on a temporary basis. He looked forward to using it again, tempted for a moment for an early riser. But they had about ninety minutes to shower, get dressed, and eat breakfast before departing to the House of Terror. Furthermore, Sally might not be in the mood. And what if he didn't get the positive response he was anticipating? That would be a downer. Pun intended.

He leaned over and kissed Sally's cheek, stirring her from her serene sleep. She responded with a sleepy-eyed smile.

"We need to get moving," he said. "We've got things to do and places to go."

She stretched her arms wide. "I had a wonderful night's sleep. How about you?"

"My thoughts exactly," he said, massaging her bare thigh.

"We could do it again."

"I'm not so sure about a quickie, although it sounds inviting."

"How come?" She pushed out her lower lip in a mock pout.

"I'd have to take another one of the magic pills and I don't think I want to spend the morning with an erection. What would our fellow travelers think? And taking another one so soon isn't something I believe Doctor Riley would recommend. But don't think it's not tempting." He kissed the tip of her nose.

"Okay."

"I'm acting like an old goat rather than a young stud," he said. "To be honest, I thought about waking you up and making love again but wasn't sure we had time. And I wasn't sure if you'd want to. I didn't want to force myself on you because I never have. I hope that makes a little sense."

"You're off the hook then," she said. "But you were wrong."

"Can I get a rain check?"

"Always, darling," she said in a sexy inflection, flipping the back of her short hair with a swipe of her hand.

John could feel a stirring in his loins from their suggestive banter. Maybe he didn't need a pill after all. He escaped to the bathroom and turned on the shower, hoping to quell his unanticipated desire for her. A minute later, she stepped in the shower and pressed her body against him. He was unsure if the steam filling the glass cubicle was coming from the shower or their bodies—or both. He pulled her against him, planting a long passionate kiss on her inviting mouth.

"I don't know if I want to leave the hotel today," he whispered in her ear.

"I know," she said, pecking his neck. "This is something we can look forward to this evening."

"That's what I was thinking." He squeezed her butt cheeks as she rested her head against his chest.

Sally giggled.

"What is it?"

"We haven't acted this way in years," she said. "Back when we were newlyweds."

"Those were the days."

"It seems like only yesterday."

"Remember when we would do it in the shower?"

"And a few other places."

"Maybe we should explore new places."

"You don't sound like an old goat," she said.

"Maybe a horny goat," he said before another lingering wet kiss.

Seconds later, they snapped out of their erotic embrace, showered, and got dressed for their busy schedule that included an afternoon excursion across the celebrated Chain Bridge to legendary Buda Castle. In the crowded restaurant, John and Sally found a vacant table in the corner of the room.

Pauline walked over from another table, where she had spoken to several travelers, clutching a brown clipboard and checked off their names.

"Did you bring an umbrella?" she asked with a luminous smile. "Some rain's in the forecast today. It's a little misty again this morning so we'll take the bus instead of taking the short walk to the House of Terror."

"We have our plastic ponchos," Sally said.

"That'll work."

"It looks like an interesting day for us," John said.

"At the House of Terror, our guide is a woman born in Hungary during World War Two," Pauline said. "She lived here during the

Communist regime. She's quite an authority. And Buda Castle is breathtaking. So historical. It's one of my favorites in Europe. Have you enjoyed your trip thus far?"

"Every single minute," John said, bumping his knee against Sally's.

"That's good to hear. We're going to be busy the next few days. Please let me know if I can be of help in any way."

"We appreciate that, Pauline."

"I hope you have a scrummy breakfast."

After she left, John got coffee from the beverage bar while Sally filled a plate with four croissants, butter patties, and jellies. Only ten minutes remained before the bus departed the hotel, so they hurried through their light breakfast. They flashed smiles and "good mornings" to others in the group as they eased their way to the rear of the bus as the last ones to board.

"No hanky-panky," Sally cooed as they scooted to their cushioned seats.

John shook his head and muttered, "Would you cut it out."

She wiggled her brows, then pecked his cheek.

Sally got over her friskiness after entering the House of Terror. Eerie music and sound effects hovered through the stark museum and memorial housed in a stone building used by Nazis in the Second World War. It possessed a sense of foreboding. A three-story wall of grim black-and-white images of Hungarians killed during the communist regime caught the attention of the visitors. They studied the sad, bleak expressions in silence or whispers, paying homage to those who had the courage and determination to stand up to cruel dictatorships. John noticed a few people wiping away tears, wondering if some of the older ones may have been looking at relatives, loved ones, and friends from a perilous era not that long ago. He couldn't help but think about America's "greatest generation," those men and women from his father and mother's age group who fought and sacrificed their lives as well against the forces of evil in World War II.

They walked through the building in hushed tones, viewing interrogation rooms, different forms of propaganda, torture devices, and enlarged black-and-white photographs that recorded those dire times in Hungary's history. John felt a lump in his throat. He glanced at Sally, whose watery eyes exposed the impact the encounter with the cruel past was having on her.

Sadness saturated John's soul as they stepped back outside in the light drizzle, a dreary way to begin the day in more ways than one. Passengers on the bus had little to say as many read House of Terror pamphlets or sat with meditative expressions from what they learned about man's inhumanity to Hungarians. Any conversation was in hushed tones. Glancing out the window, John noticed several from the South Carolina contingent holding up selfie sticks, smiling in front of the building. They were the exception.

"I suppose they saw some humor in the museum," John said, staring out the tinted window.

"Don't be so harsh, John," Sally said. "Maybe it's something else."

"I hope so."

The bus stopped in a commercial district where everyone could get lunch, walk to various shops, and experience another part of the extraordinary city. The drizzle abated, leaving a gray glow in the sky. John and Sally wandered off to a side street and found a small café. They ordered cappuccinos at the counter and sat at a table by the front window. They watched the locals on the avenue going about their daily business. Sunshine finally streaked through the clouds, a marked contrast to the gloom and doom of the House of Terror. A waitress brought their hot drinks, breaking their momentary silence.

"The House of Terror makes you thankful for what we have in America," Sally said.

"In a way," John said.

"What do you mean?"

"Look at our history, even during our lifetime. Discrimination and persecution against blacks, Muslims, Native Americans, gays, or whatever group. Even the gun violence, especially mass shootings at schools, businesses, hotels. Things could improve back in the good ol' U.S. of A. We're not immune to hate and cruelty. It's part of our national fabric."

"I guess we need to revisit the Muhammad Ali Center in Louisville or the National Underground Railroad Freedom Center in Cincinnati," Sally said.

"Those places put things in perspective."

Sally sipped on her hot drink for a moment. "I guess we're often blind to what is happening in our own backyard."

"Or, if it doesn't affect a person on a personal level, they don't care so they turn their head in the other direction. Like Brody's response to the shooting. Some people internalize those things while others simply view them as just another day. Time marches on, through the good and bad and it doesn't seem like there's a damn thing we can do about it. Maybe they're right but I don't want to believe that. It just takes time, usually a lot of time."

"We need to get more involved when we get back home."

"That's fine by me." John touched the top of her hand. "We ought to find a cause that's right for us. Something that has meaning or purpose."

"Let's give it some thought."

"When we were younger we thought about joining the Peace Corps." John sat back, crossing his arms. "One of my life's great regrets is that we didn't."

"We're still not too old."

"You're right but we still have other responsibilities. Maybe excuses, too. It's difficult to just pack up and leave everything behind for a couple years. We've accumulated a lot of personal baggage and possessions through the years that we'd have to liquidate."

"Maybe our situation will change."

"That could happen as well. Maybe Brody will have cleaned up his act and no drama from Chloe. And your mother, well, who knows about her? She's liable to be around for another ten years. Maybe longer. We need to keep our options open for her."

"There's so much to consider."

"And another thing—Whiskers."

"You and your dog," Sally said with a light laugh.

"I just can't go off and leave him for two years. I'd have to take him with me but I'm not sure they'd let me."

"I guess we'll have to keep the Peace Corps on the back burner then."

"My excuse."

"We can still do things in Lexington. Sometimes people need to look at what's around them and help others."

"Right again."

Sally noticed Pauline and several others heading toward the bus. "We need to go or we're going to miss our ride to the castle."

"I almost forgot we were on vacation," John said.

It took less than fifteen minutes to cross Chain Bridge and go up a narrow road behind the impressive structures of Buda Castle. By the time they stepped off the bus, dark and threatening skies supplanted the sporadic sunshine of the past hour.

As they trudged up the steep steps to a rear entrance, John shook his head in disgust. "Damn."

"What's the matter, hon?" Sally asked.

"I forgot to buy a camera."

"We still have our smartphones," she said, raising her brows.

"Did you charge yours last night?"

"No."

"I didn't either. I hope we have enough juice to snap a few photos."

"John, does it matter that much?"

"What do you mean? Don't you want photographs of our first and likely only trip to Europe?"

"That'd be nice, but don't you think the memories we're sharing with each other are as important?"

"You're right." He shrugged. "As usual. I need to chill."

"We'll be going to other places so you have time to buy another camera," Sally said. "And we can always come back here during a free afternoon."

"I'll think about it." He shrugged. "Anyway, I didn't come all the way here to take photos."

"What do you mean?"

"I came to be with you."

She squeezed his hand. "John, you can be so sweet at times it melts my heart."

"I know it's a rare occurrence, but I try."

They followed Pauline and the others across the cobblestone walkway, past several statues, to the wide courtyard next to Matthias Church.

John looked around and saw people with digital cameras and even a few throwaways snapping photographs in all directions. As they approached the majestic church with the diamond-pattern roof tiles, someone tapped his shoulder. He turned around and Phil Graybar nodded with a expressive eyes. Phil held out a small point-and-shoot camera.

Phil handed him a handwritten note: "Please use this camera," and mouthed the words.

"Oh no, I can't," John said, shaking his head and holding up his smartphone. "I can use my phone. We're good."

Phil pushed the camera into John's hand. He mouthed, "Please."

"Are you sure?" John asked, brows furrowed.

Phil pointed to the large, expensive dSLR camera strapped around Edna's thin neck. He gave a thumbs up.

John took the camera and shook Phil's hand. "Thank you, very much, Mr. Graybar," and returned a thumbs up.

Phil and Edna smiled, then headed toward the entrance of the church, turning around once to wave.

John gave Sally a perplexed look. "Can you believe that?"

"How sweet. They must have noticed you being upset about not having a regular camera," she said.

"I must have made a scene for them to figure that out."

"Uh, no comment."

"You're right about that."

John clicked away at historic statues and buildings as they explored several areas in the vast complex. He posed Sally next to the King Stephen statue and took a couple selfies with the Danube and Pest side of the city in the background. He noticed the Graybars exiting the church and dashed over and snapped several photos of them.

As John and Sally returned to the bus, the clouds unleashed a torrent of rain. They pulled their ponchos over their heads to avoid getting soaked. Several passengers weren't as fortunate, sitting drenched in their seats as the vehicle departed to the hotel.

Pauline, her hair damp despite wearing a poncho, stood in front holding a microphone. She announced they would tour the Parliament building the next morning and the departure time. She suggested they bring rainwear just in case, resulting in a few moans from the passengers.

"Maybe we should bring swimwear," a passenger shouted.

"Let's hope it doesn't get that bad," she said. "At least we'll be inside."

~ * ~

As they stepped off the bus in front of the hotel, a clock in the distance chimed four times. The rain let up as quickly as it had begun, with clouds parting and thin rays of sunshine glistening off the surroundings.

"We have time to do a few things before it gets too dark if you're up to it," John said as they walked into the lobby.

"Why not," Sally said, tugging his arm to go back outside.

They hurried down sidewalks, dodging numerous puddles and pedestrians in their spur-of-the-moment exploration. They strolled around the Hungarian Opera House, studied statues and monuments of famous citizens that dotted the area. And John remembered to use Phil's camera to capture those spontaneous moments of discovery.

Along the way, they stopped in front of a camera shop showcasing several brands and types in the window display.

"Should we?" John asked.

"I don't mind," Sally said.

John clenched his jaw for a few moments before stepping toward the entrance. "Okay, let's do it. Nothing fancy or expensive. Just a simple camera."

The clerk spoke English and recommended a pocket-size Nikon camera with basic functions and battery recharger. John also purchased two memory cards, one to give to Phil for lending him a camera.

They continued to the Danube, near Chain Bridge. They sat on a bench by the banks, observing several tour boats create light ripples on the calm river. Buda Castle sat high on a hill, lights illuminating its grand location like an enchanted fairytale fortress.

"We'd better get back to the hotel before it gets too dark," Sally said. "Do you remember the way?"

"No problem," John said.

Sally gave him a wary look. She heard those words before with opposite results.

"I kept it simple coming down here," John said. "We need to follow this street back to the square and turn left to the hotel."

"If you say so."

"Trust me."

"I hate that phrase."

They walked on Attila Avenue in the direction of Andrássy, but somewhere took a wrong turn. They found themselves in the dark in the foreign city in more ways than one.

"John, do you know where we are?"

"It sure looks familiar." He stopped and stroked his beard, looking in several directions. "But I'm not sure."

John asked several people along the way, but to no avail since they didn't speak English, most shaking their heads, shrugging or spreading their arms without saying a word. They eventually found themselves in the rear of the Hungarian Opera House.

"We're okay now." John breathed a sigh of relief. Sally did the same.

"We better be." Sally nudged him with her elbow.

"There's one thing I noticed while we've been walking."

"What's that?"

"The dogs."

"Are you serious?" Sally angled her head. "What about them?"

"Haven't you noticed the dogs walking with their masters without a leash? I wouldn't dare do that with Whiskers. He'd be chasing every bird, squirrel, or anything that moved."

"Come to think of it, you're right," Sally said as a young woman and unleashed hound approached them. "They're trained to do that."

"The mind of a trained journalist. Always observing things."

"So much that he ends up watching the dogs instead of where he's going and gets us lost," Sally said. "Thanks a lot."

John laughed. "But we're safe and sound now. Hungry in Hungary?"

"A little."

"Want to go to the buffet we went to yesterday?"

"Something lighter?"

As they approached the hotel, John motioned to a well-lit Subway restaurant between two dark buildings. "At least we can point to what we want if they don't speak English."

"Suits me fine."

They ordered sandwiches, potato chips, and drinks and carried them to their room. After unwrapping their food and eating for a minute, Sally noticed the call light flickering on the phone.

"Why didn't we see that when we came in?" She dialed the front desk. She was told Chloe Ross had called.

Sally dialed Chloe's hospital room. An operator informed her of Chloe's discharge an hour earlier. Sally called the apartment, but got Chloe's chirpy voice on the answering machine. She tried her cell phone but got voice mail. Sally left short messages, asking her to call when she got a chance.

Sally frowned. "She's not home."

"You know how New York traffic is," John said. "And it could have taken some time for her to check out of the hospital. You know how those places are. Maybe she had to pick up Whitney and they went out to eat. Knowing our daughter, it could be anything. I'm sure we'll hear back from her soon."

"I hope so."

"I hate to admit this, but I'm beat." John took a small bite from his veggie sub. "I bet we walked ten miles today. Or at least it seemed that far. Would you mind if I retire early?"

"My knees and hip are sore from walking up and down the steps. And we probably took some extra steps as we wandered in the darkness."

"You'll never let me forget that."

"It's always an adventure with you. I never know where we'll end up."

"I try to make things interesting."

"And unpredictable."

John placed his hands on his lower back and twisted back and forth several times, producing several pops. "I used muscles I haven't used in years."

"I can imagine how some of the older folks on the tour must feel, especially that woman with a cane. She makes faces every time she moves around. But I give her credit because nothing gets in her way. She'll run over you."

"A couple of those overweight folks were huffing and puffing at the castle," John said. "And sitting down quite a bit to catch their breaths."

"I could have done that a few times," Sally said. "At least we paced ourselves."

"Have you noticed one of those women from South Carolina, the Amazon type? She seems to do calisthenics whenever get off the bus. Stretching her arms and doing knee bends. I even saw her pushing up against one of the walls at the castle."

"I think her name's Moretta," Sally said. "At least that's what it looked like on her nametag. She's certainly fit. I wonder if she realizes she does it so often."

"Maybe a nervous habit. Looks kinda goofy though."

"Her sisters aren't as fit."

"Yeah, and the puny one smokes."

"I think that's Noretta. I'm not sure the names of the other two."

"Interesting. I've never paid that much attention to the nametags. I don't even know the names of their spouses."

"I'll check them out tomorrow." Sally said. "Maybe introduce myself."

"Good luck with that. They seem rather standoffish and cliquish."

"We'll see."

"Oh well, would you mind if we sleep tonight?"

Sally tilted her head. "Huh?"

"I mean, I'm too tired to take one of my magic pills."

Sally laughed as she rose from the side of the bed and hugged him. "Oh, honey, you should know better than to ask me that. That hasn't even been on my mind."

"You seemed that like you wanted to this morning."

"That's your imagination." She hugged him tighter. "I was having fun with you."

"We can do it again tomorrow, if you like."

"We haven't done it that way since we first got married. We've been spontaneous, and I want it to stay that way."

"Spontaneous doesn't always work."

"Let's say then, that when you're in the mood, I'll be ready because I love making love to you."

John pecked her cheek. "You're too sweet."

"I know." She lowered her head with a teasing grin.

They finished their sandwiches and chips. John turned on the TV and found the CNN International channel. There weren't any updates about the shooting nor major scandals or other catastrophes back in the States. It was another news cycle. Time to move on until the next catastrophe. But no news was good news as far as he was concerned.

Startled by the phone, Sally grabbed it on first ring, expecting it to be Chloe. John muted the TV with the remote.

"It's so wonderful to hear your voice," Sally gushed. "How are you, sweetie?"

"I'm feeling a lot better," Chloe said. "Just a little sore."

"Sam said you had an ovarian cyst. I've heard they're very painful."

"You've heard right, Mom. The pain's excruciating. I thought I was going to die."

"Do you have a follow-up with your doctor?"

"Next week," Chloe said. "So how's the vacation. Is Budapest as beautiful as it looks in photographs?"

"We're having a lovely time. We've seen so many things. We went to the Buda Castle this afternoon. Tomorrow we're going to the Parliament Building."

"I wish I could be there with you. Be sure and take lots of photos."

"Your dad has taken quite a few," Sally said, glancing at John with a smile. "I'm sure he'll take quite a few more. You know how he is with a camera."

John puffed his cheeks and exhaled.

"Oh, almost forgot," Chloe said. "I talked to Grandmother a couple hours ago. She seems to be doing fine and in a good mood."

"Brody wasn't there?"

John looked at the ceiling.

"Grandmother said he was at one of his rehab meetings."

"That's good," Sally said. "That's where he should be on most days."

"How's Dad?"

"He's doing fine. A little tired from all the walking but he's enjoying the trip as well. Hold on a sec."

Sally handed the phone to John.

"Hi sweetheart," John said. "I hear you're doing better?"

"A little sore but feel a thousand times better than I did before I went to the hospital. It's going to take time."

"How's Whitney?"

"Doing great. She loves school. She's made lots of friends."

"That's good to hear," John said. "I'm giving the phone back to Mom. Great hearing your voice. Now get well. Okay? Love ya."

"Love you too, Daddy."

"I suppose we should be getting off here," Sally said after taking the phone from John. "You let us know how much this call costs and we'll reimburse you when we get back home."

"Please, Mom," Chloe said with a light laugh. "I think can afford it. And it's worth it to hear your voices and know you're having a great time."

"You let us know if we need to do anything."

"I will, Mom."

"Love you, sweetie."

"Love you, Mom."

After putting down the handset, Sally gazed teary-eyed at John.

"What is it?" John asked. "Did she say something?"

"It's what she didn't say." Sally dabbed her eyes with a napkin. "She's holding something back. She didn't sound like herself."

"She has been through a lot in the past few days. She's tired. Don't cha think?"

"I don't know. It's a feeling. A mother's intuition. But I hope you're right."

They undressed without saying another word and got under the covers. John snuggled next to her back, placing an arm around her waist, then kissed the back of her neck. They were asleep in no time.

Nine

After breakfast they boarded the bus for a short drive to the Parliament Building. Located on the banks of the Danube, the imposing Gothic Revival structure, the largest in Budapest, was even more spectacular inside. Ornamental staircases, sixteen-sided central hall, more than 200 sculptures, and frescoes adorned lofty ceilings. No expense was spared in the construction and maintenance of Hungary's government edifice.

"It's a bit more elegant than what we have in Frankfort, Kentucky," John said to the building guide as they completed the tour.

"You have something like this where you live?"

"Pulling your leg,"

"What do you mean?"

"Oh, never mind," John said. "I was trying to be funny."

"I see now. Very funny." The guide gave a whimsical grin and walked away to greet another group of visitors.

John and Sally followed Helga, another local guide hired by Pauline, on a walking tour with a handful of other travelers to various sites, leading back to the hotel. A clear blue sky contributed to an ideal day for strolling and listening to someone impart information about a city she loved. Walking across Liberty Square, they were surprised to see a life-size statue of President Ronald Reagan, in a smiling pose. John took a photo of Sally holding Reagan's hand and posing to appear walking in step with him. Others in the group lined up for similar shots, asking John if he would do the honors with their smartphones.

"This has been very interesting," a petite woman said in a cheery tone as she walked next to Sally. "It reminds me of visiting the Reagan museum back home in California."

"I never expected to see these sights," Sally said. "I'm glad we took this optional side trip. I may have to go to California now when we get back home."

The woman's slender husband, wearing a blue LA Dodgers baseball cap, said, "You should. It's well worth the trip."

"We'll put that on our bucket list," John said. "I haven't been to California in years. And the Reagan memorial hadn't been constructed then."

"Where are you from?" the man asked.

"Lexington, Kentucky," John said. "No presidential libraries but we do have Abraham Lincoln's birthplace in our state."

"Interesting," the man said, nodding.

"I'm John Ross and my wife, Sally," John said, reaching out and shaking the man's hand.

"Pleasure to meet you, sir. George Chen, and my wife, Lei. We're from Cat City, California."

John's forehead creased. "Cat City?"

"He means Cathedral City," Lei said. "People there call it Cat City."

"Is this your first time in Europe?" Sally asked.

"Yes it is," Lei said. "Our children bought this for us an anniversary gift."

"How many years?" John asked.

"Fifty," George said with a wide grin.

"Our son and daughter did the same except it was for John's retirement," Sally said.

"How nice," Lei said.

After the cross-town hike ended, John noticed a café with several tables out front on the sidewalk. "Feel like resting your feet?" he asked. "Maybe a cappuccino?"

"Sounds good to me," George said as they wandered over to a table and sat down. A waiter came out of the restaurant and took their beverage orders.

"Are you folks retired as well?" John asked.

"I retired from the postal service nearly ten years ago," George said. "I still work part-time for a delivery company. It costs so much to live nowadays that it's almost impossible to completely retire from work. At least in California. The cost of living is so high."

"I can imagine," John said. "It's not quite so bad in Kentucky."

"So you don't have to work another job?"

"So far I haven't had to," John said with a short laugh. "I got a nice retirement package from the newspaper where I worked, and Sally retired as a teacher so we have her pension as well. But you never know what the future holds. Anything can happen."

"We have a special needs child," Lei said. "She has cerebral palsy. We love her dearly, but she requires round-the-clock care and supervision. She's with one of our daughters while we're here."

"I suppose this has been a nice break for both of you," Sally said.

"I guess, but sometimes I feel a little guilty because we've never been away from her for more than a few days."

"Is she young?"

"Oh, no, she's thirty-seven. She suffered brain damage when she was born."

"At least you know she's in good hands."

"We've been blessed with caring children." George said. "Three boys and three girls."

"It must be nice," John said.

Lei, holding her cup, smiled. "And we have been blessed with four grandchildren."

"Are you enjoying the trip?" Sally asked her. "I know I could spend several days at Buda Castle."

"It's been wonderful. Everything. We've also met some interesting people on the tour."

"Same with us," John said. "Some we'll probably remember for a long time."

Lei let out a giggle and covered her mouth.

"Did I say something wrong?" John asked, his brows furrowed.

"Oh, no. It just made me remember someone asking me if I was Japanese, Chinese or Filipino. They even said Oriental."

"Really?" Sally asked, tilting her head. "That's so rude."

"Lei laughs about it now but she was a bit peeved when it happened," George said, turning toward his wife and grinning.

"What did you tell the person?" Sally asked Lei.

"I told him I was an American." She raised her head in mock defiance before a broad smile emerged.

"What did they say to that?"

"He just shook his head and said, 'excuse me,' and walked away."

"I hope he was embarrassed," John said.

"I felt a little bad after I said it," Lei said. "I usually don't get mad about things like that because maybe those people don't see others of different nationalities that often."

"Well, they should," John said. "Unless they live in a cave."

"I hope it wasn't someone in our group," Sally said.

"I believe he was European because of his accent," George said. "He probably thinks we're rude Americans now."

"Anyway, we had a good laugh about it in the hotel room after I cooled down," Lei said. "It's not worth getting all riled up about.

George and I were born in America and we're American as apple pie."

After finishing their drinks, George and Lei said they needed to get back to the hotel to check on their family back home. John and Sally headed toward Andrássy Avenue, taking their time as they decided how to spend the remainder of the sunny afternoon.

"What a pleasant couple," Sally said. "I'm glad we got to spend some time with them."

"You have to admire folks like them who are totally dedicated to their family," John said. "Sometimes you don't realize what people have to deal with in their lives."

"I believe we all have some secrets and skeletons that we don't share with others."

"Oh well, let's go relax."

Sally crinkled her nose. "Huh?"

"The thermal baths. That's one thing Budapest is noted for."

They purchased swimming attire at a department store along the way to wear at the Szechenyi Thermal Bath, the largest in Budapest. Before long, they were submerged up to their necks in the steamy pool, savoring the warmth of the well-known hot spring along with locals and tourists.

"Now this is relaxing." John spread his arms out across the water. "I can feel my tensions melting away. We should have come here sooner."

"I've read that they have medicinal properties," Sally said. "Everything from joints to gallbladder."

"They should include mental health."

"I know what you mean. I'm so relaxed right now. Makes me think of those Calgon commercials. Just take me away."

"Maybe we should buy a hot tub when we get back home."

"It's not the same, John."

"Maybe we can travel to a hot spring in Georgia or Arkansas."

"That's something to put on our bucket list."

They closed their eyes for several minutes, relishing the tranquil water, their heads appearing as fishing bobbers on still water.

"Any more thoughts about Chloe?" John asked.

"Sometimes I overreact." Sally pursed her lips. "But something didn't seem right. The tone of her voice, like she was keeping something from us. But like you said, she's tired and I'm probably reading too much into it."

"I hope so," John said. "I didn't pick up anything when I talked to her."

"Like I said, it's a mother's intuition," Sally said. "It's something you wouldn't understand. But there's nothing we can do about it. Especially here."

"You're reminding me of my mother," John said. "She always seemed to have a sixth sense about things, especially when I wasn't forthcoming about something I did or didn't do."

"John, I know when you're holding back about something. I can read it on your face or your mannerisms."

"So it's a wife's special power, too?"

She flicked her brows. "One of many. But they're secret powers."

"Oh, that's great," John said, grinning. "I don't know what I'm up against."

"And you never will."

"I don't think I have any secret powers."

"That's because you're a man."

John broke out laughing. "Somehow I knew that was coming."

"Getting back to Chloe. I'm happy she's independent but wish she'd be more open."

"Brody isn't open."

"Chloe's that way because she doesn't want us to worry about her. Brody because he's hiding something. There's the difference."

"Maybe we'll go see her after we get home," John said.

"That'd be nice."

"Of course, it depends on what's going on with Brody and your mom."

"Please, John, let's not go there right now. Let's just relax for the time being."

"Like those folks over there?" John said, motioning to the left with his head.

"You've got to be kidding me."

The South Carolina couples were propped against the edge of the pool, arms outstretched, and eyes closed in dream-like states, the women wearing identical red, white and blue bathing suits. John could only imagine the men wearing similar swimming trunks as he could see only heads and tops of their shoulders. Please, no Speedos.

"Maybe we should go over there and join the fun," John said.

"Yeah, right," Sally said. "They're probably saving that side of the pool for themselves."

"I'm sure they are."

"You know what they used to call people from South Carolina."

"South Carolinians?"

"That's what they call them now."

"Gamecocks."

"That's the mascot of the university."

"What then?"

"Sandlappers," Sally said.

"Sandlappers? I never heard of that."

"I've heard it refers to those who live near the coastal areas. Kind of makes sense."

"They kinda look like sandlappers, don't you think? Maybe fish out of the ocean?"

Moretta treaded away from the family, cracked her fingers behind her head, and began twisting her body back and forth in some sort of aquatic exercise, creating small ripples. The others remained in their lolled positions, like seals on a pier.

"Is there a place she doesn't exercise?" John asked.

"Apparently not."

John and Sally spent another hour in the soothing spa, moving as far as they could from the South Carolinians. They opted for gentle massages to end their special outing. As they were about to leave, John's mouth dropped open when he noticed the South Carolina contingent marching single file toward the dressing rooms. The men were wearing Speedos, their paunch bellies protruding in full display.

"You don't want to look," John said. "Close your eyes."

Sally glanced in the direction of their fellow travelers. "Oh, my goodness!" she said, covering her mouth.

"I warned you."

John and Sally considered walking back to the hotel but decided against it in their relaxed state of body and mind. Instead, they cuddled in the back seat of a taxi.

They glimpsed at the message board in the quiet lobby before going to their room, but nothing had been posted. John was pleased that the phone's red message light wasn't blinking. Sally puckered her brow.

"I thought Chloe would call," she said, removing their swimming attire from a plastic pouch. "Or someone." She took the wet garments and draped them over a towel bar in the bathroom.

"No news is good news," John said. "Let's continue to relax."

"I'll try." Sally slumped in the easy chair. "But I'd still like to hear from Chloe again. I'm worried about her."

"When do you want to go out for dinner?" John asked, sitting on the corner of the bed. "There's plenty of places around here."

"Let me change clothes and freshen up a bit," Sally said. "I'm open to anything that looks good to you."

"Up to doing something later?" John couldn't suppress a wicked grin.

"Now what do you have in mind, John Ross?"

"I could bring a magic pill along with me to take with my meal. But only if you're in the mood."

"Can I give it some more thought?"

John creased his brows. "More thought?"

Sally giggled. "I thought about it."

"And?"

"Only if you're up for it."

"Trying to put pressure on me?"

She leaned over and kissed his cheek. "It didn't stop us the last time."

"How about now?"

"How about it."

~ * ~

Sally was already in bed with the covers up to her neck when John returned after swallowing the little blue pill in the bathroom. He brushed his teeth and dabbed a trace of Santa Fe cologne on each side of his neck for good measure.

"This may take a few minutes," John said as he stepped out of his boxers and slipped under the sheet. Discovering she was naked, he added, "Or not."

She nuzzled his neck, sending shivers throughout his sensitized body.

"You smell nice," she murmured. Maybe that was his special power, he thought with a faint smile.

Their legs entangled, and hands explored each other. They kissed passionately like they had years before, when their lives weren't as complicated. Free and unconstrained. Instead of minutes, it was mere seconds before he rolled over and entered her. They moved in quiet rhythm, with deep and ravenous kisses. Every motion electric with purpose and meaning. They were lost in each other.

Then the phone rang.

John thrust one more time, raising his head. "Damn!"

Sally slid out from under him and picked up the phone on the third ring.

"Oh, hi Brody." She attempted to gain a degree of composure, sitting on the side of the bed with the sheet wrapped around her and speaking in a deliberate tone.

"What are you guys doing?"

"What?" She blushed.

"How's everything going?"

"Oh, we're having a lovely time. Stayed very busy today. Went to the Parliament and to the spa. What's up with you?"

"Nothing much," he said. "Been going to rehab. That's about it."

"How's grandmother?"

"She's napping in front of the TV right now," Brody said. "But to be honest, I can't wait for her to return to Arizona. That's all she talks about...getting back with her friends. Going to movies and shopping. Playing cards. Even swimming. Can you imagine her in a bathing suit? Anyway, it gets on my nerves after a while."

"I'm sure she's homesick. She misses her friends. You should be more sympathetic."

"Whatever."

"Why don't you do something with her, like go to a movie or take her out to lunch? That would thrill her to no end."

"Get real."

"One of these days you're going to be old. You might want to give some thought to how you would like to be treated."

"Maybe."

"You should be thankful you even have a grandparent. You should show her more respect for all she's done for you. One of these days she won't be around."

"Yeah, like back in Arizona."

"Brody, I don't mean Arizona. She's not going to be with us forever. Treasure these moments."

"But she's always bugging me about something. Follows me all over the house. I don't know if she's spying on me or what."

"Why would she do that?"

"I dunno. Who knows? Maybe she thinks I'll start taking drugs again? I just wish she'd give me some space when I'm here. I even look forward to attending those absurd rehab classes to get away from her for a few hours."

"They're not absurd," Sally said. "You need them to help you from going back to using drugs."

"Mom, I'm past that. I'm clean. Trust me."

"I've heard that line before. Furthermore, I hate that phrase."

"Thanks a lot. I'm doing my best."

"I know you are, so stay that way." Sally rolled her eyes at John. "How's Whiskers?"

"Don't tell Dad but he got away from me today. Scared the crap out of me."

"What?"

"I was getting ready to take him for a walk this morning when he ran out the front door without the leash. I finally caught up with him halfway down the street. He was going toward the park. I thought he was going to get run over a couple times. I don't know why he did it, unless he was looking for Dad."

"I'm glad there was a happy ending." Sally glanced at John. "Anything else?"

"Oh, yeah," he said. "Is there any cash around here? I'm running a little low on funds."

"Honey, we've only been away for a few days. How can you be out of money?"

John looked at her with pressed lips.

"I've gone out with a gal a few times."

"I don't know what to tell you. Have you asked your grandmother?"

"I don't want to bother her about it," Brody said. "You know how she is. I'd never hear the end of it."

"I'll talk to your dad and see what we can do," Sally said. "I'll let you know."

"You can't talk to him now?"

"Uh, he's down in the lobby, buying snacks in the gift shop."

John crinkled his nose.

"Then call me back as soon as you hear something. Or send a text."

"It won't be tonight," Sally said. "It's getting late here."

"So why is Dad buying snacks?"

Sally held her breath for a couple seconds and exhaled. "Brody, I'll get back with you. Tell Mother I asked about her."

After putting down the handset, Sally crossed her arms over the sheet. "Can you believe our son?"

"He needs money?" John shrugged. "So what's new?"

"Are you going to call him back?"

"What's the hurry? Can't he ask your mother for money? It hasn't stopped him in the past."

Sally rolled back into bed and slipped under the sheet. "What are we going to do?"

"I'm not going to do a damn thing right now."

"Now don't you go and get your blood pressure up."

"There's some triggers that I can't control. Brody is one of them. You know that."

Sally patted the bed, a weary smile on her face. "Come here. Lie back down and try to relax."

John still had the effects of the ED pill, and would for the next few hours or longer, but he wasn't in the mood for lovemaking. He felt foolish and pulled the sheet over his mid-section. After a few seconds, he scooted back under the covers, his head on the pillow, and stared at the white ceiling. Sally rested her head on his shoulder and stretched an arm across his chest.

"It's always something with him," John said. "He never ceases to amaze me. Or I should say, annoy me."

"Let's not let him, or anything, spoil our vacation," Sally said. "Okay?"

"Honey, it's not the money that concerns me. There's always something going on behind the façade that's bothersome. I hope it's a girl problem rather than drugs, but I wouldn't count on it."

"But he said the girl was from his rehab group. Did he tell you that she worked at Crossroads?"

"What he says and what's going on can be two different things. You know that. For all we know, she could be a user like him. Or a dealer."

"Don't say that."

"Well, it's true."

"There's nothing we can do about it here," Sally said. "Let's try to take him at his word."

John turned toward her. "I agree there's nothing we can do, especially right now. But I'm not going to take his word. He's burned me too many times doing that. He hasn't earned my trust. Maybe yours, but not mine."

"But John, he's been clean since he's gotten out of rehab. And he's been going to classes on a regular basis. There comes a time when you must start showing some trust in him. He's not a child."

John turned his head again, staring at the ceiling. "We'll see."

"Besides, Mother's there so things can't be too bad."

John belted a single laugh. "And that's supposed to be reassuring?"

Sally turned away from him. "Let's go to sleep."

John tapped her shoulder. "Did he mention something about Whiskers?"

"It was nothing," she said. "Now go to sleep."

Ten

John tossed and turned in his sleep, groaning several times during the night. Sally tapped his shoulder to get him settled so she could sleep. If they'd been back in Kentucky, she would have escaped to the couch in the den.

He awoke shortly after daybreak, surprised to hear Sally in the shower. He was usually the first one up and about in the morning, preparing coffee, letting Whiskers outside for a few minutes, and reading the newspaper. He moseyed to the bathroom, splashing cold water on his face at the sink. "You're up early. Mind if I join you?"

"The water's still warm so you'd best hurry," she said. "And my back could use a little scrubbing."

John slipped out of his boxers and stepped into the shower stall. As Sally shampooed her hair, he took a wet washcloth, lathered it with bar soap, and massaged her back.

"Ah, that feels good," she cooed.

"My pleasure."

She turned and faced him, smoothing lather away from her blue eyes. "You had a rough night sleeping."

"I can't imagine why."

"Are you feeling better this morning?"

"A bit." John began rubbing the cloth over her neck and shoulders. "We'll see after I talk to Brody."

"When do you plan to call?"

"Since there's the time difference, and he usually gets up around nine or so, I'll try around two this afternoon. I don't want to disturb his beauty sleep."

"I thought his rehab classes were in the mornings?"

"I guess I'll be giving him a wakeup call then."

"Don't be too hard on him."

"You should be telling me the opposite."

"By the way, is there money for him at the house?"

"Believe it or not, I left a contingency fund in case something like this happened. I was hoping I wouldn't have to use it. I should have known better."

"How much?"

"Five hundred dollars."

"You're going to give him that much?" Sally opened the shower door and stepped out.

"I may be getting old but I'm not old and foolish." John poured shampoo in his hand and began washing his thin scalp and beard. "I'm not going to hand over five hundred. You know better than that."

"What do you mean?" Sally asked as she toweled off.

"I left a hundred in the cookie jar, two hundred in my tool box, and two hundred with Bert."

"Bert?"

"I told Bert it was in case of an emergency for Brody and your mom, and if needed, Brody would ask him for it."

"And Bert knows not to tell Brody about it beforehand?"

"Yep." John finished washing and turned off the faucet. "And he swore to do it, even zipping his mouth with his hand. That's as good as it gets with Bert."

"I hope it works."

"Hey, we forgot to go back to the lobby last night to check on the today's itinerary. Any idea what we'll be doing?"

Sally shook her head. "It's still early. You can go down and check after you get dressed."

"How about we both go down after we get dressed and eat some breakfast as well?"

"I guess we can do that."

~ * ~

The message board listed a trip to Memento Park, where stark Soviet statues and plaques from the Communist era were on display.

"Let's think about this one," John said.

"It might be fun," Sally said.

"There's also a trip to the Great Synagogue."

"That might be even better. We can talk about it during breakfast."

They went through the buffet line and found two tables pushed together in the crowded dining room. A man and woman from the South Carolina contingent were at each end.

"Mind if we sit here?" John asked.

"Sorry, but these are saved," the woman said. Her nametag read Doretta.

"Saved?"

"For family," the man said with a slight curl to his mouth that could be interpreted as a smile or a smirk. His nametag read Delbert. "They'll be here any minute."

"Hmm, didn't realize the place had reserved tables," John said, tilting his head. "Learn something new every day."

Delbert looked down and away.

John glanced around and noticed a table being vacated by a couple. He and Sally glided between tables and other diners to claim the spot. They cleared the table before the busy wait staff arrived and hurried to the breakfast line.

"Can you believe those folks have the nerve to do that?" John asked as he watched Doretta, flashing an arrogant grin, wave off several other diners with a flick of her hand.

"They're not friendly to anyone except Paula," Sally said.

"Of course, they think they're special and the tour is all about them."

"At least they keep to themselves."

"I'm almost tempted to go back and sit right in the middle. I wonder what they'd do."

"Probably make a scene. They're not worth the time and effort."

John glanced back at the tables and saw Doretta waving a hand to the others in her family circle. They slithered in single file toward her as Delbert grinned and pulled back the chairs. Moretta, wearing a gray sweatpants and sweatshirt, flexed her shoulders and rolled her neck a few times before leading them to the buffet bar.

Before John and Sally took a bite, a couple from their tour group walked over to their table.

"Mind if we join you?" the man asked, already pulling out a chair.

"Please do," John said. "Busy place this morning."

"Frank Finsterwald," the man said, reaching out to shake John's hand. "And my sweetie, Dorothy."

John smiled and introduced Sally.

Other than a few nods and smiles since arriving in Budapest, John had tried to avoid the Finsterwalds, who were in their 60s. Frank was tall, overweight, and loud, and came across as an affable bully. Dorothy always donned showy, maybe even gaudy, exercise outfits with matching shoes. If attempting to give the appearance of being fit, she came across as someone trying to mask her age as her round belly sent a different message.

"You guys having a good trip?' Frank asked, munching on a bagel. "Ain't seen nothing like it in Jersey."

"I doubt if you'd find it in Kentucky, unless the castle in Versailles," John said.

Dorothy cleared her throat. "Isn't that pronounced 'ver si?'"

"No ma'am," John said. "We call it what it looks like. Ver-sales. But I know what you mean. A common mistake from non-Kentuckians."

"No wonder Kentucky doesn't rank high in education," Dorothy said with a twisted grin.

"You might want to visit Athens as well," Sally said. "We pronounce it 'a-thins.'"

"You've got to be kidding me." Dorothy leaned back with a wide-eyed smirk. "Well. That's strange, too."

"We're smart enough to pronounce Versailles as the French do when in France and as the Greeks when in Greece," John said in an even voice. "And does it really make any difference?"

Frank chuckled. "It adds to the hillbilly stereotype."

"I bet you have some strange pronunciation in New Jersey."

"I don't think so," Dorothy said.

"Don't you say 'Jerzee' rather than 'Jersey?'"

"He's got you on that one, sweetie pie," Frank chuckled.

"How about "Joisey?'" John asked.

"We don't say that," Dorothy's eyes narrowed. "People just think we do."

"I didn't mean to offend you."

"That's okay," Frank said. "We hear it all the time. I don't give it much thought."

"But I do." Dorothy took a bite of toast and jelly.

"Kind of adds to a stereotype, eh?" John said.

"Whatever," Dorothy said, her jaw tightened.

John smiled. "We'll discuss the many ways to pronounce Louisville some other time."

"Suits me."

"Oh well, what have you planned for today?" John said, trying to defuse the situation by diverting the conversation in a new direction.

"We're not sure." Frank slurped some coffee. "Not sure I want to visit that Jewish church. As for the Soviet monuments, it kinda pisses me off a little."

"Why is that, Mr. Finsterwald?" Sally asked.

Frank stuffed a pancake in his mouth, took a couple bites, and swallowed. "Reminds me of what's going back home. Removing history. And hon, call me Frank."

"Removing history...Frank?" Sally cocked her head. "What do you mean?"

"You know, taking down Confederate statues in some of those Southern cities. Part of our country's heritage. I always liked seeing those monuments when we visit the South. Gave those cities some class."

"But they represent slavery and bondage of black people," Sally said.

"Now don't get me wrong, because I have a few friends who are black." Frank ran his tongue over his tiny front teeth. "But the Civil War was more than one hundred and fifty years ago. That's history. People need to get over it."

"You might have different thoughts about it if you were black," John said.

"Well, I'm not, thank god." Frank let out a hearty chuckle. "I'm thankful for that."

"The people in Budapest removed the statues because they represented oppression. They didn't want to celebrate that, especially in public places. They were grim reminders of harsh times."

"Not me. I'm not offended." Frank's boisterous voice drew attention from several people at nearby tables.

"If you had lived here under communist rule you might have a different opinion."

Frank shrugged. "Hard to say. Depends on the circumstances. I bet some of them lived high on the hog. Ain't that a Southern saying?"

Sally eased her chair back, unsmiling. "I hate to leave good company, but I need to go back to the room and freshen up. Ya'll have a lovely day now. Hear?"

John covered a hand over his mouth so the Finsterwalds couldn't detect the smile on his face over Sally spouting some Southern charm. "Wait for me, darlin'. I need to make a few calls." He rose from his chair. "See ya'll later."

Frank and Dorothy sat clueless and confused as John trailed Sally out of the dining room.

"Get your feathers ruffled a bit?" John asked as they stood waiting for the elevator.

"What do you think?" Sally tapped her foot like a drummer. "What an ignoramus."

"Which one?"

"Both!"

The elevator door opened and out stepped the Graybars. They waved and headed toward the breakfast buffet. John and Sally got inside and pushed the button to their floor.

"What do you want to do today?" John asked.

"Anything that doesn't involve those Finsterwalds."

"I'd like to explore the city," he said. "Would you like to walk across the Chain Bridge and go back to the castle? The weather's supposed to be nice. I thought the rain kinda spoiled it last time."

"I'm up for it."

"Even go to the communist statues?"

"Let me think about that one. That's a place that would attract the Finsterwalds, and for all the wrong reasons. Do you think they went to the House of Terror?"

"I'm sure they did since it was part of the guided tour."

"I don't recall seeing them."

"You're probably right. He'd be hard to miss. Maybe he sleepwalked through it. Or stayed on the bus."

When they returned to their room, Sally sat on the chair and put on walking shoes. "You'd better go to the bathroom. You know you always have to go when we're out."

"I'll be okay," John said, sitting on the corner of the unmade bed.

"Honey, you had water and coffee at breakfast this morning. Don't take any chances. We don't know where we'll find a public restroom or restaurant. You know how you get. Please?"

"I could take a leak in the Danube, right off the Chain Bridge. Isn't that what a hillbilly would do?"

"And cause an international incident."

"Only kidding, sweetie. I'll do as you command. You finish getting ready, so we can get an early start on the day."

Minutes later, they strolled down Terec Boulevard until John stopped in his tracks. "Damnit!"

"What's the matter, honey?" Sally asked

"Forgot my camera."

Sally reached into her oversized purse and pulled out the camera. "Does it look like this?"

"You're a lifesaver."

She grinned. "I know."

"What made you decide to pack it?"

"It was on the desk. When you went to the bathroom, I picked it up and put it in my purse. I figured you might need it."

"You think?"

John took the camera from her as they proceeded unhurried toward Chain Bridge, stopping at various points along the way to take photos of buildings, flower gardens, and statues. They even managed a few selfies when there was a break in the pedestrian traffic.

As they walked up the stone steps at the base of the suspension bridge, Sally turned and posed for a photo. When they reached the top, John took another, with Buda Castle in the background. He stared at the viewfinder and discovered she had been photo bombed. He lowered the camera, grabbed Sally's elbow, and froze.

She squinched her nose, bewildered by his action. He motioned with his head to look behind her. Fifteen feet away stood the Finsterwalds.

"Shit," John mumbled to himself as they turned their backs and took several soft steps in the opposite direction as if it would make any difference if the Finsterwalds could hear them or not. And it didn't.

"Hey!" Frank bellowed, waving a hand back and forth that attracted everyone's attention in the compact passage.

John and Sally stopped in their tracks, turned around and faced them. Dorothy smiled and waved with both hands fluttering like a bird.

"Well, hi there," John said with a strained smile. "What a surprise to see you here. We thought you'd be going to Memento Park to see the statues."

"Got out of the mood after breakfast." Frank gawped at Sally as if it were her fault for the change in plans.

"It's probably still worth a visit," John said.

"Maybe later." Frank and Dorothy inched toward them. "We thought we'd get some exercise on this magnificent day." He spread his sagging arms and looked up to the vibrant blue sky as a long-legged buzzard soared in the distance.

"Same here," John said, less enthusiastically.

"Why don't we discover the city together?" Dorothy tilted her head, grinning from ear to ear.

John glanced at Sally, wanting her to respond or at least offer an opinion. Especially an excuse to decline. But she seemed equally stunned, perhaps even shocked at this unexpected engagement with the Finsterwalds. She stared back at him, voiceless.

John cleared his throat several times, leading to a brief coughing spell as the Finsterwalds scrutinized him, waiting for an answer. Since it was apparent Sally wasn't going to respond, he blurted, "Uh, sure. Why not?"

"Then follow us, guys." Frank took Dorothy's hand. "We thought we'd cross the bridge and visit the castle again. We didn't get to see as much as we wanted to last time because of the fuckin' rain. Pardon my French."

"Watch your tongue, Frankie." Dorothy narrowed her eyes. "We're not back in Jersey, you know."

John and Sally followed like obedient sheep, stopping twice as John took photos of Frank and Dorothy with their smartphone. Three quarters of the way across the bridge, Frank lumbered a couple feet behind Dorothy, decked out in a pink-and-black jogging outfit as she waddled in front.

"Are you sure you folks want to continue walking?" John asked as they mounted steps to the castle. "We can take the funicular."

"Nah, I need the exercise." Frank leaned against a stone wall. "Burn some calories."

"We should take the funicular, Frankie," Dorothy said. "My hip is aching. And I know your knees must hurt."

"I'm fine," he said, huffing and puffing up a few more steps. "You take that damn tram, funicular, or whatever in hell they call it."

"I'm told it offers some beautiful views of the Pest side of the Danube," Sally said.

"The Pest? What in the hell are you talking about? That sounds like rats or roaches or something."

Sally turned to John, surprised by Frank's gruff response.

"The river divides the city," John said. "This side is called Buda and the other side is Pest. When the city merged in the 1870s, it took the name Budapest."

"I'll be damned." Frank stopped and slapped his thigh. "You learn something new every day. You should have been a guide, John."

"I beg your pardon?" John said.

"You seem to know a lot about the place. I'm impressed."

"Don't read too much into that, John," Dorothy said. "It doesn't take much to impress Frankie."

John chuckled. "I try to do a little homework before I go somewhere for a visit. I guess it's the newspaperman in me."

"Newspaper? Did you work in circulation, advertising or something?"

"Editorial."

"Uh, okay. I had a few friends who worked for a newspaper. One was in circulation and one was an old fart who was a press operator."

"Several departments in newspapers."

"Can we start moving again, Frankie? My butt's getting stiff," Dorothy asked. "We didn't come here to talk about newspapers. And let's take the funicular. It might be fun. We've never been on one before."

"If that's what you want to do, honey bun, then you go right ahead. I'm going to keep going this way."

"Now Frankie, quit trying to be macho."

"I've come this far, so I'm going to finish. Anyone care to join me?"

"I will," John said. "Why don't the women take the funicular and we'll meet them at the top?"

"Sounds like a great idea," Frank said. "This is too much for a woman."

Sally looked at him, pokerfaced. "Really?"

Sally and Dorothy turned around and walked down the steps toward the funicular.

"Take your time, girls," Frank said. "We'll see you in a bit."

"Ready?" John said to Frank, who hadn't budged from his position against the wall. "The funicular only takes three or four minutes to get to the top, so we'd better get moving."

Frank took a deep breath. "If you say so."

It took two more stops for Frank to catch his breath before they made it to the top landing. Sally and Dorothy sat on a bench about fifty yards away, chatting.

"How are you doing, macho man?" Dorothy shouted. "We've been here at least ten minutes. Did you prove anything other than being out of shape?"

Frank placed his hands on his knees and ignored her chides. His face was ashen.

"Everything okay?" John asked. "You don't look like you feel well."

Frank didn't reply. He took a rumbling breath, then puked as passersby scattered away from the yellow-tinged vomit on the walkway. John placed his hands on Frank's shoulders to steady him as he heaved more bile. Dorothy hesitated for a moment, as if in a daze, before rushing to his side.

"What did I tell you, Frankie?" she said. "I knew you'd get sick. But you never listen. Trying to be a macho man for everyone."

"Honey bun—"

"Don't honey bun me. "You should—"

"Shouldn't we take him to a bench?" John said, glancing at Dorothy. She tightened her lips.

Within a minute, security personnel arrived as John tried to guide the weak and wavering hulk to the side. They summoned medical help, who appeared within seconds on a mobile cart. They checked Frank's vitals before leading him to the cart. Dorothy sat next to him as they whisked off to the first-aid treatment center on the grounds.

John and Sally watched the direction of the cart, then hurried through the throng of tourists to keep it in sight.

"I hope it's nothing more than an upset stomach," Sally said as they jogged in step past Matthias fountain.

"He had difficulty breathing all the way up," John said. "He was determined to make it to the top, even if it killed him."

"I think it almost did."

Frank rested on a small bed for thirty minutes, and his stomach seemed settled from his overexertion. He regained some color in his face. He took several steps toward the door and stopped. He took a deep breath.

"Are you up to it, macho man?" Dorothy asked, standing next to him.

"Yes, dear, I'm okay. It must have been something I ate."

"We all had breakfast at the same place and we're fine. Maybe it was the ten pancakes you inhaled."

"So?" Frank massaged his bulging belly. "Can we drop it?"

"Are you guys heading back to the hotel?" John asked when they stepped outside.

"Yeah," Frank said. "I still feel a little puny."

"You look puny," Dorothy said.

"Can you make it back? We'd like to check out the museums here before returning to the hotel."

"Yeah, we're good," Frank hobbled out of the first-aid station. "You go on."

"Way to go, Frankie," Dorothy said. "I wanted to see those places too."

"Then go with them. I can make it back by myself."

"Sure." Dorothy laughed. "You couldn't find your way out of a paper bag. I'm going with you."

"Okay." Frank apparently didn't want to journey back to the hotel by himself.

"Do you want to take the funicular or are you going to walk down, macho man?"

"We'll take the funicular," Frank said. "Only because you might have trouble going down the steps."

Dorothy snickered. "Sure, big guy."

"See you guys later." Frank's head slumped as they tottered, arms locked, toward the funicular.

"Hope you feel better soon," John said as he and Sally dashed off in the opposite direction into a throng of people as if they were afraid the Finsterwalds would change their minds and want to join them. They didn't want to take any chance of that happening.

"They made this day eventful," John said, not daring to look behind him for fear of who could be there. "I still don't think he's doing well. His coloring seemed off."

"He should seek more medical attention," Sally said. "But he's so headstrong."

"He wouldn't do it to spite his loving, soft-hearted wife."

"They sure show a different side when away from the group."

"All smooching and holding hands when around others," John said. "And digging at each other when away from the group."

"Just like other married couples."

"Huh?"

"We've had our spats," Sally said. "Remember Heroes Square?"

John sighed. "Point taken."

"At least we don't put each other down in public," Sally said. "At least I don't think so. Do we?"

"I try not to."

"Me too."

"We may not be all over each other, you know, lovey-dovey when we're around others, but we know where our hearts are."

"That's sweet, John." Sally nuzzled his arm for a couple seconds.

"Just don't call me macho man."

They laughed.

They spent three hours in the Museum of Music History and National Gallery. It was still daylight when they left, taking the funicular without discussion, and crossing Chain Bridge. They discovered a Hard Rock Café along the way and stopped for dinner.

"So much for the Hungarian experience," Sally said inside the music-inspired restaurant with framed signed guitars and various memorabilia on the walls, like the ones in America.

"Rock 'n' roll is a universal language," John said before taking a swallow of Dreher draft beer.

"It's certainly been the soundtrack of our lives," Sally said. "But I still like Sinatra, Martin, and Como once in a while."

"We should have gone to a Holiday Inn lounge. I wonder if they're still around, with the piano bar and all?"

"Probably so. In Jersey?"

"You better watch where you say that. You'll get us in trouble."

"I know better," Sally said, smiling. "I suppose it's just the hillbilly in me."

"You've always been my Southern belle."

"And you, my Southern gent."

They clanged their mugs together in a mock toast. "Here's to being a hillbilly," John said.

They paused for a few seconds as The Moody Blues' "Question" played through the multiple speakers.

"Remember when we saw them at Rupp Arena, with a full orchestra?" Sally asked.

"How could I forget? A great concert. And different."

"I miss those days."

"Me, too." John appeared lost in memories, staring off into the distance.

"I'm surprised we still have our hearing after all those loud concerts we attended."

John blinked, snapping back to the present. "Hard rock practically gives me a headache now, especially when I'm not in the mood for it. And I'm not sure if I ever am anymore, except occasionally on the radio. I never thought I'd say that."

"Because of the memories?"

"Yep. My youth. Our youth. Good times."

"What about today's music?' she asked. "Rap and hip-hop?"

"No comment. It's another generation's music so I respect that. Remember how the older folks used to rail against the Beatles and Stones back in the sixties? I'm not going to be that way. I may not listen to much of the new music, but I'm not going to trash it either. And that includes all kinds of music...country, jazz, classical, you name it. As they used to say, different strokes for different folks."

"Remember those concerts we went to back in college?"

"Those were the days," John said as if lost in thought again as an Elton John song played in the background. "Moody Blues, Billy Joel, Rare Earth, Yardbirds, and so many more."

He chuckled.

"What's funny?"

"Remember Marianne Faithfull's 'Those Were the Days?'"

"That was Mary Hopkin," Sally said. "That's one of the first records I ever bought."

"Wow, lady, you know your rock 'n' roll."

"We should go to concerts again," Sally said as she picked through her garden salad. "We had such a wonderful time."

"I don't think I could handle the crowds, the noise and the traffic," he said, lifting his hands. "Another sign of getting older. As Jethro Tull sang, 'Too old to rock 'n' roll, too young to die.'"

"We can go to smaller venues," she said. "That wouldn't be bad, old man."

"That we can do," John said as he took hold of his veggie burger. "And we will, rock 'n' roll woman."

"Buffalo Springfield."

"Now I'm really impressed. Did you buy that as well?"

"Honestly, it was part of your collection when we started dating," she said. "I always liked them."

"So that's where you got your great taste in music."

"Let's not get carried away," she said.

~ * ~

When they returned to the hotel at dusk, several travelers were gathered around the itinerary board in the lobby as Pauline pinned the next day's agenda and time schedule.

"You must have had an exciting day," Pauline said to John as she squeezed from the group.

"Not sure it was exciting," John said. "It was educational, and the museums at Buda Castle were fascinating. And we did a lot of walking."

"You do know Mr. Finsterwald may have suffered a heart attack?"

"What?" John stepped backward.

"Oh, I thought you knew. Didn't you go with them to the castle?"

"He got sick walking up to the castle and had to rest, then we went our separate ways."

"This is the first we've heard about it," Sally said. "We thought he was okay."

"He started having chest pains when they went down the funicular," Pauline said. "They were able to get an ambulance and transport him to the hospital."

"Where's Dorothy?" John asked.

"She's at the hospital. I spoke with her about ten minutes ago and he's stabilized."

"He didn't look good," Sally said. "Kind of pale."

"I doubt if they'll be with us the rest of the trip." Pauline said. "I do hope to hear from Mrs. Finsterwald soon about their plans."

"I'm so sorry to hear that." Sally gave a deadpanned look at John.

"It's sad because they seem so crazy about each other." Pauline pressed her lips as if holding back tears. "Dorothy said it was a second honeymoon for them."

"How sweet," Sally said. "And how sad, too."

"They're definitely lovebirds." John bit his tongue, avoiding eye contact with Sally.

~ * ~

The flashing light on the phone greeted them when they returned to their room.

"I wonder who that could be," John said.

"I'll give you one guess."

John chuckled. "See how much he needs."

After checking the message, Sally made the call. Geraldine answered.

"Hi, Mother," she said. "I didn't expect you to pick up the phone."

"What's that supposed to mean? I live here, don't I? Or have you forgotten?"

Sally closed her eyes and took a short breath. "Brody called, and I thought he'd answer."

"I hope you're not disappointed. Do you want to call back?"

"Now, Mother, you know what I mean."

"Brody isn't here," she said. "He said he had something to do at that drug place."

"When do you expect him home?"

"How would I know? He's a grown man. He comes and goes as he pleases. He doesn't consult with me."

Sally placed a hand on her temple and took a deep breath. "Mother, do you have any idea what he wanted when he called?"

"He doesn't tell me anything. He only does as he pleases."

"Is everything okay?"

"Let's say I can't wait until you and John return from your fancy vacation. I want to go back home."

"Only a few more days."

John mouthed to Sally to ask about Whiskers.

"How's Whiskers?" she asked.

"How's Whiskers? Are you serious? You make a call from across the ocean and wonder how that mutt is. Don't you care about me?"

"Mother, of course I do," Sally said. "You know better than to say that."

Geraldine's voice cracked. "I don't know anymore."

Sally heard Whiskers barking in the distance.

"Everything's fine with you?" she said.

"I'm doing well for an old woman who had a fractured hip," Geraldine said. "I don't know if I ever felt so neglected in my life. I may have to call Wendell."

"You should," Sally said. "And tell him we said hi."

"I'll think about it."

"Anything else we should know?"

"I talked to Chloe yesterday. She was sweet enough to check in on me. At least someone cares about me."

"Did she have anything else to say?"

"She told me she loved me but hates that I have to be left alone. I bet Wendell wouldn't have done this to me."

"I need to be getting off here. Please tell Brody I called."

"When I see him again."

Sally placed the phone back on the handset, then sat on the side of the bed, weeping. "I don't believe I'll understand or please Mother for as long as I live. If it's not one thing, it's another. She's never happy about anything. She even had the nerve to say my brother would have shown her more attention."

John went to the bathroom and returned with a handful of facial tissues. "Now settle down. There's no reason to get upset."

Sally wiped her eyes, then dabbed a tissue over her nose. "She thinks everything's about her."

John lifted his hands. "What's new?"

"You'd think that while we're on vacation, one we haven't taken in several years, she'd have something nice to say. Like how *we* are doing?"

"Consider the source."

"That's easy for you to say. She's not your mother."

"Thank goodness."

Sally gave him an icy stare, then burst out laughing. "You're right. Nothing changes with her. And I don't know if I'd wish her on anyone."

John kissed her cheek. "What's up with Brody?"

"He wasn't there, of course. She said he was at Crossroads and didn't know when he'd return."

"We don't know what he wanted?"

"We know. He didn't tell her."

"What about Whiskers?"

"Are you telling me you wanted to make an expensive call back home to know how your little mutt is doing?"

John's reared back his head and blinked several times. "Huh?"

"Honey," Sally said as she tapped his knee. "Don't get upset. I'm paraphrasing Mother. But I did hear our little guy barking so he's alive and well."

"This may sound crazy, but I have kind of mixed feelings about our vacation. I love it here but I'm getting kinda anxious about getting back home."

"I know what you mean. You can't help but feel a little helpless about everything"

"And vacations are for a people to relax and get their minds off things. It's not working on this trip."

"At least we have something to look forward to, like sending Mother back to Arizona," Sally said. "And keeping a closer eye on Brody. It can't get any worse."

John pointed a forefinger at her. "Don't say that, Sally. Things can get worse. And knowing our luck, they will."

"Let's not go there. Let's enjoy the present."

"What do you have in mind?"

She gave him a naughty smile. "Do you have any more of your magic pills?"

He raised his brows and grinned. "I do, sweet lady."

"Well?" She pulled back the covers.

John pecked her on the mouth and fetched his travel bag. He swallowed a pill with a glass of water in the bathroom and returned to the foot of the bed. "Give me a few minutes."

He noticed her tossed clothes on the easy chair. He let his clothes drop to the floor at the foot of the bed, his desire growing as he crawled toward her.

"I can't wait." Sally's mouth puckered.

"Ready to rock 'n' roll?"

"Just like in the good ol' days."

Eleven

Though they'd been away for only six days, John lay awake in bed, his thoughts swirling about being back home in Kentucky. It was his comfort zone, even with Brody, Geraldine, and dealing with life's everyday challenges and rewards. Worrying about Chloe only intensified his feelings. The old saying by legendary politician Happy Chandler came to mind about never meeting a Kentuckian "who wasn't either thinking about going home or actually going home."

While there was some travel early in his career as a sportswriter, usually quick stops to cover college games and back home the next day, his later years as sports editor kept him in the office. He figured that turned him into a homebody, something he'd never predicted in his younger days, especially after two years in the military. There'd be no boundaries as he traveled the seven corners of the Earth.

But real life got in the way. Marriage. Children. Career. And the countless responsibilities that came with growing older. Those dreams to see the world ended up as trips to Disney World,

Dollywood, Myrtle Beach, municipal zoos, and various national and state parks.

But here in Budapest, as an aging baby boomer came the realization that many of his goals as a young man been pipe dreams. Maybe he had a few regrets but they were decisions he made along life's highway. He learned to live with them—and move on in other directions.

He enjoyed travel but not living out of suitcases. Most of their recent vacations involved loading several suitcases in the car trunk and hitting the road with Sally to drivable destinations. They'd journey home when they ran out of clean clothes. Or if prior commitments brought them back. And there would be long weekend trips to visit Brody in Chicago or Chloe in New York but those had become fewer and far between in recent years.

For this trip, they had learned from travel sites on the Internet to bring interchangeable clothes for half the trip to cut back on packing. Roughing it involved handwashing socks, underwear, and shirts in the sink and hanging them up to dry. He wondered if it was sage advice from those who dared to hitchhike across the continent decades ago, carrying their meager belongings in a backpack and sleeping in hostels. It was still part of the adventure.

Sally stirred in John's warm embrace as sunlight seeped through the dark blue curtain panels. If he were back home, he would have slipped out of bed and tiptoed to the kitchen and prepared a pot of coffee, reading the newspaper at the counter while waiting for her to make her presence known. Not this morning. Having his soul-mate nestled under his chin, even if only for a short while, brought contentment. Maybe he should stay in bed a bit longer after they return home. Nah. There's Whiskers to take care of and the early morning routine that has been part of his life since, well, forever it seemed.

Sally straightened her arms, then covered her mouth, and let out a wispy yawn. She kissed his neck. "Have you been awake long?"

"Not too long," John said. "Thinking about things."

"About going back home?"

"Were you reading my mind?"

"I'm a little antsy about leaving. I don't know why because I'm not sure what we'll be going home to."

John sighed. "I know what you mean."

"Do you think we'll hear from Brody today?"

"The ball's in his court."

"I hope there's nothing bad going on back there."

"My worst nightmare," John said.

"I guess Chloe's all right."

"I'm not sure she'd call and complain about anything unless it was urgent. We're safe in that department. For now."

"We should be thankful we haven't heard from Mother. I don't know if she'd be able to make a call. I think she'd make it more difficult than it is... simply dialing the country code and number."

"I'd give her more credit than that. She's a sharp old cookie. She just thinks people should call her rather than the other way around. And that's what we've done."

"I think you might be right."

"I know I am."

"I enjoyed dinner last night," she said.

"Being at the Hard Rock?"

"That was nice but it was being able to sit there and reminisce about things in our past, even if it was just music. We don't do that much anymore."

"I know what you mean. We're always so busy with other things going on."

"We used to have good conversations about books, movies, TV programs, and plays."

"Maybe because we used to do those things on a regular basis."

"Let's start doing them again."

"Fine by me," John said. "It'd sure beat talking about your mother, Brody's problems, and other downers."

Sally sat up, pulling the white sheet to her bare shoulders. "I've been worried about Frank Finsterwald and how he's doing."

"I'm sure we'll find out when we go to breakfast."

"Speaking of breakfast and today, what's on the travel agenda?"

"We got so caught up in the Finsterwalds I didn't even look at the board last night," John said. "I'll run down there and see what's up."

"I'll take a quick shower while you're gone."

"You can't wait and take one with me?"

"You sound like we're newlyweds."

John wrapped his arms around her and nibbled her earlobe. "I can't help it, with a ravishing lady like you."

"Those magic pills of yours are giving you delusions."

"It's not the pills, sweetheart," he said. "You've always turned me on."

"You silver-tongued devil."

John could feel his desire for her growing, even without the aid of the blue pill. He pulled her back on the bed, and they kissed and touched each other before she straddled him, and they became one. The pulsing harmony continued until they reached climax together. She collapsed on top of him, resting her head on his shoulder. They didn't utter a word, relishing the special moment neither wanted to end anytime soon.

But three hard knocks on the door jarred them out of their passionate embrace.

Thinking it could be room service or some other hotel staff, John shot out of bed, slipped on his pants, Henley shirt, and went barefoot to the door. He opened it a crack, only to see Dorothy Finsterwald staring up at him with heavy-lidded brown eyes.

Before John opened his mouth, Dorothy shoved the door open and stepped inside the room. Sally, startled by the intrusion, pushed her body toward the headboard, clasping the sheet to her neck.

"I didn't know who to ask." Dorothy's lower lip trembled. "Frankie's being discharged from the hospital this morning and I was wanting someone to go with me. Would you mind, John?"

"Uh, sure," John crinkled his nose. He glanced at Sally, bundled under the sheet, prompting Dorothy to do the same.

"Oh, I'm sorry," Dorothy said without blinking an eye. "I didn't know you were in bed. Did I disturb you?"

"No," Sally said in a rare raspy voice as she could barely speak. "I was getting ready to shower and John was going downstairs to check today's travel itinerary."

"What time do you want to go to the hospital?" John stuffed his hands in his pockets. "Soon?"

"He'll be discharged around nine, so you have time to eat breakfast or whatever else you want to do. The hospital isn't that far away. The concierge said we could take a taxi or the metro."

"I'll meet you in the dining room in about thirty minutes. We can eat and then go after Frank," John said. "It shouldn't be a problem."

"Didn't he have a heart attack?" Sally asked. "That's what we heard last night."

"They thought he did but it was gastroesophageal reflux." Dorothy pressed her lips. "Frankie's had those before but never as serious as the one yesterday. It scared the daylights out of both of us. He needs to take it easy instead of being a foolish old macho man."

"Doesn't he take acid reflux pills?"

"Are you serious?" Dorothy said, eyes widened. "He just doesn't take them until it's too late. And he didn't take any with us yesterday. I tried to tell the doctor but they wanted to run tests to make sure he didn't have a heart attack. What a waste of time."

"Better safe than sorry," John said.

Dorothy exited as quickly as she entered, without even a goodbye.

"Do you think it's safe for me to get up?" Sally shifted her bare legs out of the bed.

John turned the deadbolt on the door. "Now it is."

"Would you mind if I stayed back here? I don't want to spend much more time with them."

"Thanks a lot," John said. "But I understand. I shouldn't be gone that long if he's discharged at nine."

"Watch what you say." Sally tossed the sheet on the bed and dashed to the bathroom.

"Yep. Famous last words. Let's hope I won't be gone too long. If I'm not back by noon, send out an emergency squad for me."

"Just don't try to be a macho man."

"Ha, ha. Don't you worry about that."

John brushed his teeth, trimmed his beard, and changed clothes while Sally showered. He lingered in the room, flipping through the TV channels, checking his smartphone, and ended up trimming his fingernails before going downstairs at the appointed time.

Dorothy stood and waved when he arrived in the dining room. She wasn't difficult to spot, wearing another exercise outfit, this time decked out in black with red piping on the arms and legs. John acknowledged her by lifting a hand, then poured a cup of coffee at the beverage counter before joining her.

"I hope I'm not being too pushy by asking you to come with me," Dorothy said. "I don't know that many people on the tour. Pauline has to be with the others."

"That's understandable," John said. "And it's no problem. I'm glad it's not any more serious with Frank."

"Frankie has become something of a slob in recent years. I bet he's seventy-five pounds or more overweight. You'd never guess he used to be so careful about how he appeared in public. He played football in high school and could have gone to college on an athletic scholarship, but he wasn't studious. We used to belong to a fitness center. Now it's only me, as you can tell." Dorothy beamed as she glanced down at her body.

John took a sip of his coffee.

"Nowadays Frankie doesn't give a damn about how he looks, one way or the other. It's embarrassing at times."

"I can be that way, too, especially since I retired. I don't have to dress for work and I seldom go to social functions. The life of Riley, so to speak."

"But you're in good shape."

"I try to walk every day with my dog and keep active like that. But nothing too strenuous anymore. I threw my back out last year at the Y trying to do too much. I learned you gotta be more careful as you grow older. Even had an angina attack around Christmas. Can't take too many chances."

"I'd never worry about Frankie doing too much unless it was something stupid like yesterday. I think he was just trying to impress you guys. That macho man stuff."

"He should take it easy then. I've had several friends my age hospitalized for overdoing it. A few even passed away."

"I should be so lucky."

"Huh?"

"Oh, nothing." She pinched her chin. "I was thinking out loud. Frankie gets me so angry at times. He can be so dumb. Ready to go?"

As they left the dining room, Sally stepped off the elevator with the Graybars. She wiggled her brows and followed the couple to the restaurant. John responded with a crooked smile.

John and Dorothy got a taxi and arrived at the hospital at eight-fifteen. She exited the vehicle and waited for John at the front entrance while he got stuck with the fare.

"Maybe Frank will get an early discharge," John said as they walked through the revolving door into the lobby.

Dorothy raised her thin eyebrows and strutted a few steps ahead of John to the front desk. A young receptionist, speaking fluent English, directed them to the second floor. They located Frank, reclined in bed, wearing a loose gown and staring at silent images on a TV like he was either mesmerized or hypnotized.

Dorothy rushed to him, smooching his cheek. "How are you, sweetie pie?"

"I could be better but I'm not complaining," he grumbled. "I'm waiting for someone to come here so I can get bust out of this joint."

"It's not even eight-thirty."

Frank looked at John with a twisted mouth. "I sure as hell didn't expect to see you this morning."

"Dorothy asked me to come along."

Frank squinted at Dorothy. "You didn't need to bring anyone."

"Honey, I don't know my way around this big, strange city," she said with a puckered mouth. "You didn't want me to get lost, did you?"

"Of course not, baby."

"Mr. Ross was kind enough to ride along with me. I hope that's okay?"

"Yeah, I guess." Frank shrugged before grabbing a tissue and blowing his hawk-beak nose, sounding more like a blaring bugle that resonated through the room.

John stood in the doorway, shifting from one leg to the other. "I'll go down to the visitors lounge. Let me know when you're ready to go back to the hotel."

When they didn't reply, John slipped away to the hallway, and made a side trip to the restroom. He wondered why he had volunteered to go with Dorothy? Or been recruited? Did she just want company? He would have preferred being back at the hotel, making plans with Sally. Maybe even making love with Sally. Instead, he found himself helping someone capable of taking care of things herself. At least it seemed that way.

An hour later, Dorothy showed up in the sparse lounge, showing a long face that John wasn't sure was real or fake. "Frankie's still in his room. I'm *soooo* sorry, John. I don't know how much longer it'll be until he's discharged. I didn't think it would be this long. And he's getting upset about it. Really agitated."

"Those things happen." John put down a magazine and rose from the padded chair. "Sounds like a typical hospital. We'll just have to wait."

"I hope you don't mind." She pressed her lips together.

"Hey, no problem." He opened his hands. "Let me know when you folks are ready to leave. I'll be here."

Without warning, Dorothy wrapped her arms around John and squeezed, nearly knocking him off his feet. "You're so sweet, John. I knew you'd understand."

When she released her hold, John stepped back. "Just being helpful."

John's expected short wait turned into three long hours as he was confined to the room except for one trip to the restroom and another to a snack area. He catnapped, tried to watch TV, and stepped out into the hallway, anything to kill time until Frank's release. He once meandered toward Frank's room but turned around when he heard Frank's robust laughter. So much for being upset and agitated.

The unlikely threesome finally returned to the hotel shortly after noon. And again, John paid the taxi fare as Dorothy assisted Frank as he hobbled into the lobby. Several in the group came over and inquired about his condition, patting him on the back and wishing him a speedy recovery.

John followed less than a minute later, with no fanfare. Frank, droopy eyed and hunkered over more than usual, shook his hand and shuffled toward the elevator like a person in need of a walker. Dorothy hesitated a few seconds before giving John another bear hug, one for which he was semi-prepared as he stood rigid as a signpost. But there was another surprise as she planted a prolonged kiss on his cheekbone, right above his beard line.

John rubbed the back of his head, his face flushed, after the unexpected display of affection. "I hope he feels better and takes it easy. Let me know if you need anything."

"Oh, we will," Dorothy said, beaming.

John sauntered to the poster board after the elevator door closed. He noticed the group had left more than two hours earlier to tour historic Gellért Hill. After they returned around one, it was another free afternoon to explore the city.

Sally was dressed and dozing under the bedspread when he returned to the room. He tapped her leg, waking her from the catnap.

"That sure took long enough." She blinked her eyes several times. "I thought you'd be back a lot sooner."

"Me, too," John said as he sat next to her. "Only about five hours but seems like ten. Lots of paperwork."

"At least you're back."

"And our brand new friends from New Jersey are back in their room and doing well. At least I hope so." A smile brightened his face. "For the remainder of the day."

"Nothing serious with Frank?"

"Just that acid reflux stuff. He's going to survive."

"I'm sure they're relieved it was only that."

"No doubt Frank is, but not so sure about Dorothy."

"What do you mean?"

"A feeling I got that they're not what they appear to be." John leaned back in the easy chair. "A continuation from our time with them yesterday, if you know what I mean. They're difficult to read."

"That doesn't surprise me."

"Another thing."

"What?"

"I don't know if it's my imagination but she's kind of a flirt."

Sally laughed. "I kinda picked up on that yesterday. She is rather outgoing."

John wrinkled his nose. "You did?"

"She kinda gave you the eye. Gals can pick up on those things."

"More of that intuition thing?"

"You know it."

"Well, I didn't notice it. But today she gave me a couple hugs and even a kiss on the cheek."

"I wondered how you got that big red smear on your face."

"Are you serious?"

He dashed to the bathroom mirror, noticed the ruby-red smudge, and wiped it off with a damp washcloth. "Damn."

"I guess I'd better keep an eye on you two!"

John sat back down on the easy chair. "Funny. Please keep me away from them. Or them away from me. Or whatever."

Sally walked over and kissed the top of his head. "I'll do my best."

"Enjoy breakfast with the Graybars?"

"They're a nice couple," Sally said. "I'd like to get to know them better."

"And less of the Finsterwalds?"

"I doubt if we'll see much of them from now on."

John crossed his fingers. "We can only hope."

Sally's eyes twinkled. "That's not a nice thing to say...but it would be nice."

"We missed the morning trip to Gellért Hill. I would have liked to see that Liberty statue and the church in a cave. Now we have a free afternoon. Anything you'd like to do?"

"I wouldn't mind walking down Andrássy Avenue and buying a few souvenirs to take back home." She eased down on his lap. "And I am getting a bit hungry since I only had a light breakfast."

"We'll find a place to eat, then go souvenir shopping," John said. "I need to get out and stretch my legs after being cooped up in a hospital for more than four hours."

"I'll be ready to go in twenty minutes. I just need to freshen my makeup."

"I've been gone this long and you still need another twenty minutes?" John asked.

"A gal has to look her best when there's competition."

"There's no competition," John said. "There's no reason to worry, sweetheart. I only have eyes for you."

"I know that," she said. "But it's still nice to hear from my macho man."

"You better watch it." John, grinning, tapped her butt as she escaped from his lap to the bathroom. "Unless you want to be called macho woman."

She peeked out the bathroom door. "Let me give that some thought. That sounds a little sexy."

"Really?"

"I changed my mind."

"I think I know why. It reminds you of someone."

"You've got that right."

"See, I have some of that intuition as well."

When they stepped off the elevator, their fellow travelers streamed into the lobby. At the same time, Frank and Dorothy emerged from the other elevator. John wanted to turn around and go back to the room, but it was too late since he had already made eye contact with them.

"What in the hell are they doing here?" John grimaced. Sally shrugged as they stepped to the side.

Pauline strolled over to the Finsterwalds. "I'm glad to see that you're up and about, Mr. Finsterwald. I assume it wasn't that serious."

"Gastro something or other," he groused. "Had it before. Nothin' serious."

"Better than having a heart attack."

"I'll take it easy today," Frank said. "I'm okay, just a little scare. And they gave me some pills to take care of it."

Pauline looked at Dorothy. "Why didn't you ask me to go to the hospital with you today?"

"I didn't want you to go to the trouble because I knew you'd be busy with the tour."

"It wouldn't have been any problem. That's part of my job. Andras takes care of things when I'm unavailable."

Dorothy nodded toward John. "John Ross volunteered to go with me, so it wasn't a problem at all. He's such a sweetie."

John gave Sally a disbelieving glance. When Dorothy turned her attention back to Pauline, Sally clutched John's hand and practically dragged him out of the hotel. They scampered down the street and turned the corner at the first intersection. And waited.

"What's this all about?" John asked, still in her tight grip. "Are you trying to give me a heart attack?"

"Do you want to spend your afternoon with the Finsterwalds?"

"Thanks for the heads up, dear. That never occurred to me."

Sally peered around the corner as the Finsterwalds walked out to the street and looked both ways. Sally's hold on John's hand eased when they proceeded in the opposite direction.

"That was a close call." Sally puffed her cheeks.

"You've got to be careful because you never know when you're going to run into a couple from New Jersey." John chuckled as they headed toward Andrássy Avenue.

After several blocks they found temporary refuge in a small café. The waiter suggested several Hungarian dishes for lunch. They placed their order for cold cherry soup, a *finomőzeléks* dish of mixed vegetables in a white sauce, and cappuccinos to sip before their food arrived.

"Could you believe she told Pauline that you volunteered to go with her to the hospital?" Sally asked. "That woman is unreal."

"And she didn't even ask Pauline if she would go with her. I don't mind helping someone in need, but I like for them to be straight with me. I'm not happy about it."

"Let's hope we won't run into them today. I mean, what are the odds? This is a big city. They went in one direction, we went in another."

"I'm totally surprised that he's even out today. He's the last person I expected to see. His ass should be in bed."

Sally snickered. "Must be the macho man in him."

"Whatever." John shook his head. "I hope he doesn't overdo it even if he is a goof. That guy's asking for trouble."

"He didn't even look like there had been a problem."

"When we came back from the hospital, he was haggard, moving around like an, er, old man," John said. "I didn't think he'd make it to the elevator. Now he's up and about like nothing happened. They must have given him some joy juice."

"Surprised me. Maybe Dorothy worked wonders in the room? She could have the magic touch."

"Let's not go there. I don't want to lose my appetite."

The waiter returned with their lunch. They glanced out the large window as they ate and people-watched—especially on the lookout for Frank and Dorothy. They finished their meal with *Dobos*, a sponge cake with chocolate buttercream.

Stopping at several souvenir shops after lunch, they purchased a handmade doll for Whitney, earrings for Chloe, a necklace for Sam, and a money clip for Brody. Sally wasn't sure what to buy Geraldine since she was sure her mother wouldn't like anything she picked out for her. Either that or make a big fuss about buying her a gift. Her mother was never satisfied.

"You didn't need to get anything for Brody," John said as they walked toward the Danube River.

"Why's that?"

"He would have preferred money." John grinned.

"You're right," Sally said. "He'll be disappointed getting a money clip without money."

"Maybe we should put a few forints in it and make him think it's a lot."

"That'd be funny."

"Hey, I've got a suggestion for us if you're not too tired."

"I'm game for anything."

"Follow me." Ten minutes later they stood near a boat ramp. "Up for a river cruise? I read about it in one of the magazines in the room."

"That'd be nice and relaxing," Sally said. "You know how much I enjoy being on the water."

Sally sat on a bench while John walked over to a booth to purchase tickets. He returned with two held high and a bright smile. But that joy dissipated like smoke from a dying ember. Sally twisted her head.

"Oh my, goodness. Look who's here."

Sally recognized the voice behind her, closing her eyes before turning around. Dorothy Finsterwald.

John forced a smile as he approached them. "We sure didn't expect to see you this afternoon."

"You folks hightailed it from the hotel," Frank said as he lumbered toward John. "We tried to find you but gave up. But I suppose we must think alike. Looks like you're going on the boat ride, too."

"We thought it'd be a nice way to see some of the city and get off our feet for a while," John said.

"This is so great," Dorothy gushed. "We can spend the rest of the day together."

"Oh, how nice," Sally said with a frosty smile. "And what a surprise."

John was about to sit next to Sally at the end of the bench, but Dorothy plopped down beside her.

Dorothy thumped the empty space next to her. "Come on, John, you can sit here. There's plenty of room."

"I'm good," he said. "I need to stretch my legs after being at the hospital all morning."

"Don't think I don't understand. It was a long morning for all of us. Well, maybe not for Sally. She got to rest and relax in the hotel."

"Pure enjoyment," Sally said, stoned-faced.

Frank took the opportunity to sit next to Dorothy, squeezing her pink spandex-covered thigh with his puffy fingers.

"The boat should arrive in about twenty minutes," John said. "I'm glad we've got nice weather."

"Oh, who cares about the weather when you're with friends," Dorothy said. "Right, guys?"

"Unless you don't mind getting soaked," Sally said, triggering a scowl from Dorothy. "Only kidding. Remember that first trip to the castle?"

"I almost forgot. You're so right, Sally. That day was so miserable. But we really weren't friends then like we are now. We can brave any kind of weather, so to speak."

Sally looked straight ahead. "So true."

"And yesterday was a nightmare, for all of us."

"Especially for Frank."

"You can say that again," Frank said, leaning around Dorothy.

"Especially for Frank," Sally repeated.

Dorothy giggled. "You're so funny, Sally. You must get that from John."

John covered his mouth and looked off into the distance.

By the time they boarded the boat, about twenty others had joined them for the river tour. John managed to sit with Sally between him and Dorothy, and Frank at the other end. Dorothy made nonstop observations about the trip, pointing in all directions.

John dozed off within twenty minutes...his head drooped forward as the boat bounced against the river's gentle ripples. The boat bumped against the dock on its return an hour later, jolting him from his unplanned siesta.

"You missed a lovely cruise," Dorothy said.

"I was more tired than I realized." John stifled a yawn.

"I took the opportunity to take a few photographs," Sally said. "I hope you don't mind."

"I didn't even realize we had the camera with us. I hope you got some good ones so I can relive it."

Dorothy asked a crewmember to snap a photograph of them, with Castle Hill in the background. She managed to stand next to John in the middle. John, Sally and Frank gave weary smiles while Dorothy beamed wide at the camera. John handed the pilot a tip as they stepped off the boat.

"What are we going to do now?" Dorothy asked.

"Aren't you afraid you're going to overexert yourself, Frank?" John asked. "You shouldn't push your limits."

"Oh, macho man is just getting started," Dorothy said, giving him a hug around his waist. "Right, hon?"

Frank rubbed his eyes. "Sure, sweetie. I took my pill so I'm up for anything."

"I don't want to spoil the party but I'm exhausted," Sally said. "I'd like to return to the hotel. But don't mind me, you guys go ahead and do what you want to do."

"Can you get back to the hotel okay?' Dorothy asked. "I don't see any taxis around here."

"I'm pretty good with directions."

"We'll see you in a few hours then," Dorothy said, taking a hold of Frank's hand. "We can make plans for this evening. Come on, John."

John's brows creased. "What?"

"Aren't you coming with us?" Dorothy's brows furrowed.

John placed an arm around Sally's shoulder. "I'm going back to the hotel, folks. It's been a long day for me too."

"Sweetie, don't you think we should go back as well?" Frank frowned. "I am getting a little bushed."

"You fuddy duddies." Dorothy placed her hands on her hips. "I'm with some old people."

John chuckled. "You got that right."

Dorothy didn't crack a smile, instead took Frank's hand. "Let's go."

John hailed a taxi to return them to the hotel. They sat without saying a word, the only sound being soft Hungarian music on the radio. John paid the fare while Frank and Dorothy disappeared through the entrance. Sally stayed with John on the sidewalk for a couple minutes, hoping their companions were out of sight and sound for the remainder of the day.

"Do you think it's safe to go inside?" John asked, wringing his hands.

"We can't stay out here forever." Sally held the bag of souvenirs and led the way into the lobby.

Next to the elevator stood Frank, holding the door open as they turned the corner. Dorothy stood inside, her eyes squinted and mouth clamped like a spoiled child.

"You guys coming or not?" Frank asked, lifting his arm as if to guide them inside the small enclosure. "We don't have all day."

"You shouldn't have waited," John said as they scurried inside the elevator. "But thanks anyway."

"Any plans for the evening?" Dorothy asked as the door closed.

"We're going to relax," Sally said. "It's been a long day."

"Speaking of a long day, I wonder what's on the itinerary for tomorrow," John said. "We should have looked."

"They're going to the city park and nearby museums," Dorothy said, breaking her silence. "Doesn't sound too exciting to me."

"That should be interesting," John said.

"Okay, we'll go too." Dorothy flashed her pearly whites.

When the elevator stopped at the Finsterwalds' floor, Frank stepped off first as John reached to hold the door open for Dorothy. "Ain't Frankie the gentleman," she said to no one in particular.

"See you tomorrow," Sally said. "Get a good night's sleep."

"Same to you, guys," Frank's hand quivered as the door closed.

"He doesn't look well," John said. "He should have rested today."

"Maybe we should have rested."

"I wonder if it was Dorothy's idea."

"You can bet on that."

"A sure bet."

"I hate to say this, but I can't wait to get back to Kentucky," Sally said, a tone of resignation in her voice.

The elevator remained motionless. "I guess I should push the button if we want to go to our floor." John laughed.

The elevator door then reopened. "We'll save a place for you at breakfast," Dorothy said, brows arched high. "Around eight?"

"Uh, sure," John said.

"Don't be late. *Ciao!*"

The door eased shut again. John and Sally looked at each other for a few seconds, waiting to see if the door would reopen. John pressed the button. They held their breaths until the elevator began to move.

"When do we leave for home?" John asked.

"Three more days."

"It won't be soon enough."

As John opened the door to their room, the phone rang. Sally rushed over and answered it.

"Hello Brody," she said. "You caught us just as we got back."

John sat on the side of the bed, and Sally edged next to him, holding the receiver so both could listen to Brody.

"I could use a little cash," Brody said in a dull monotone. "Getting short on funds here. Did you forget about me?"

"Thanks for asking about how we're doing," Sally said.

"Come on, Mom." They heard Brody blow out a long breath. "Okay, how're you doing?"

"We're having a wonderful time," Sally said in mock chirpy tone. "Thank you for asking. Miss us?"

"Please."

"Now Brody, is that any way to be?"

"Okay, Mom, I miss you and Dad."

"We miss you, too."

"About the money?"

"How much do you need?"

"Whatever you can spare."

"What do you need it for?"

"Mom, is Dad listening in? Are you talking to him?"

"Yes, Brody. He's listening."

"Hello, Dad," Brody said in a somber monotone. "I sure could use a few dollars."

John took the receiver from Sally. "What do you need it for?"

"Shit," Brody said. "Do we have to go through this routine every time I need a buck or two?"

"Sometimes beggars have to do that."

"I'm a beggar now?"

"Forget it," John said, pressing his lips together for a second. "How much do you need?"

"Couple hundred?"

"Go to the tool box in the garage and you'll find it there," John said. "We'll be home in a few days so I hope that'll tide you over until then. Keep that in mind."

Brody laughed. "I should have asked for more."

John remained quiet.

"I've got a date this evening," Brody said. "That's one reason. And I need to buy some gas and some stuff for grandmother. She's been asking for some sweets."

"No eggnog," Sally said.

"Sure thing."

"How's everything else?" John asked. "Grandmother? Whiskers? Rehab?"

"Everything's about the same," Brody said. "Grandmother never stops jabbering about returning to Arizona. Whiskers hangs around the front door. The rehab's going okay. I'm still clean so I guess it's working. Nothing much changes around here."

"That's great to hear. As the coaches used to say, 'stay focused.'"

"Talked to Chloe again and she seemed a little depressed but wouldn't tell me what's up. Told me not to tell you or Mom so don't breathe a word to her that I said something."

"Thanks for letting me know. Anything else?"

"Maybe after you get home."

"What does that mean?"

"You'll see."

"I hope it's something positive," John said.

"It's hard to say. That's another reason I needed some cash."

"You know I don't like surprises, son."

"Speaking of surprises, wasn't Breck Rogers a friend of yours?"

"Yes he is. I've known him for quite a few years. He was chief photographer at the paper. Great guy."

"He kicked the bucket."

"What?"

"I read in the paper this morning that he suffered a major heart attack."

John fell silent for a few seconds, pressing his lips together to hold back his emotions.

"You still there, Dad?"

"I'm here. Let me hand you over to your mom. See you in a few days, son. Stay clean."

John passed the phone to Sally, who gave him a puzzled look. "Are you okay?" she asked.

"Breck Rogers passed away." John stared out the window. "Heart attack."

Sally watched him, then spoke to Brody. "I need to get off here now. We'll be back in a few days."

"Safe travels." Click. No doubt Brody was on his way to the tool box.

Sally walked over to John, resting her head against his back and placing her arms around his waist. "I'm so sorry, John."

John wiped tears from his cheeks. "It's hard to believe. He always seemed so healthy and full of life. Simply a nice person. It makes you realize how fragile life is, as if we didn't already know that. It's never easy losing a friend."

"I know it hurts."

"I feel awful that I can't attend his funeral. He was always trying to get me to join the paper's retirement group. Never any pressure about it. He loved being around and helping others. Never an unkind word about anyone. I still can't believe it."

John turned around with puckered mouth and tear-filled eyes. Sally hugged and kissed him on the cheek. "I love you."

John sank in the easy chair, momentarily lost in thought over his friend's unexpected passing.

"Anything else from Brody?"

"He had other news, but wouldn't tell me what it was," John said. "Mentioned it was part of the reason he needed money."

"Wonder what that could be?"

"Knowing Brody, it could be anything. I almost don't want to know."

"I suppose we'll find out sooner or later."

"And it appears nothing much else has changed since we've been gone. Your mother still talks about returning to Arizona. I hope we can oblige her very soon."

"I know," Sally said. "And to be honest, I don't blame her. That's her home."

"I hear ya," John said with a half-hearted grin. "If she hadn't fallen back in January, she would have already been there. Let's hope that doesn't happen again."

"I know."

"What's funny is that if she were back in Arizona, she'd probably be complaining about wanting to be in Kentucky."

"Or wanting us to move out there."

"I couldn't stand the heat, in more ways than one."

"Maybe Brody will find a job when we get back."

John let out a vigorous laugh. "Let's not push our luck. One thing at a time, sweetheart."

"With us being there it might motivate him to be more active about it."

"Honey, I agree. He needs to be carrying his weight. He's not a child."

"But he is going through the rehab program, so we have to give him some space."

John shook his head. "There you go again."

"What?"

"Being the enabler."

"I want the best for him."

"Me, too."

"Please, John, let's not argue."

"Mind if I go down to the bar?" John asked. "I feel like a beer."

"That's fine. I'll read."

He walked to the door and turned around. "You're welcome to come along."

"Go on."

"I'm not angry," he said. "Just need to clear my head."

"I understand. Take your time."

John sat on a stool in the middle of the bar and ordered a Soproni Fekete Démon. The bartender stood a few feet away, wiping glasses with a white cloth, gazing at a muted-Hungarian variety show on the TV. Several couples sat at candle-lit tables, chatting in barely audible tones as not to disturb others in the room.

John stared at the large mirror that ran from one end of the bar to the other, took a sip from his glass, when he someone tapped his shoulder. He turned as Ty Lewis sat next to him.

"I hope you don't mind a little company," Ty said with a thin smile.

"Please do," John said. "Can I buy you a beer?"

"Sure. I'll have what you're drinking."

John raised his hand, got the attention of the bartender and ordered another Soproni.

"How do you like Budapest?" John asked.

"It's been great so far," Ty said before taking a swallow of beer. "We have a nice group."

"Quite a variety."

"Didn't you tell me you're from Kentucky?"

"Retired from the newspaper in Lexington last year. This trip is a gift from my son and daughter."

"It's special then."

"I know you're too young to be retired," John said. "Unless you won a lottery."

"I'm close to retirement. I've worked in state government as a computer programmer for nearly twenty-five years and can retire at fifty-five. I've got about eight more years."

"Must be nice."

"I hope to do a lot of traveling when that times comes. I also have other plans that I've put off because of my career."

"Married? Kids?"

Ty laughed. "Neither. I was married for a brief time, but we didn't see things eye-to-eye on a few things. I think I enjoy my freedom to come and go as I please too much to get saddled down with family."

"Wise decision."

"Really?"

"I didn't mean for it to sound like that," John said. "What I'm saying is that a person shouldn't do something they aren't committed to doing. There's pluses and minuses to being married."

"I was raised by a single parent, so I know how difficult that can be."

"Parents divorced?"

"My dad was killed in Vietnam. I wasn't even a year old. My mother had me and my older brother and sister at the time. She worked two jobs to support us. It wasn't easy."

"I can't imagine. My parents were killed in a car accident, but they were in their early sixties."

"Your children married?"

"My son is single, living at home, and my daughter, who lives in New York, has a partner. She's had a health issue, so we've been a bit concerned about her on this trip."

"Sorry to hear that," Ty said. "Time for another beer?"

"Why not," John said as he lifted his glass. "It's probably around five o'clock back home."

After the bartender brought their beers, John told Ty about Breck Rogers' passing.

"If you don't mind me saying, you looked a little down when I came in," Ty said.

"The deaths of friends and close relatives are one of the perils of growing older."

"Makes you think of your own mortality?"

John shrugged. "Not really. I know I'm gonna die one of these days. I won't be around to lament my passing."

"Never thought of it that way."

"Sorry if I'm depressing you."

"No problem," Ty said.

"What are your plans after you return home?"

"I'm a baseball fan so I'll probably be going to Milwaukee a few times to see the Brewers. And maybe Chicago to watch the Cubs or White Sox. I try to make it to Wrigley Field at least once a year."

"Maybe we can meet up there sometime," John said. "My son used to live in Chicago before he ran into to some personal problems. Sally and I love the museums."

"I'd like that." Ty said, grinning. He pulled out his wallet and removed a business card and handed it to John. "Email or call me whenever it's good for you. I'm pretty flexible. One of the advantages of being single."

"I'll do that. Although I'm retired, I wouldn't be surprised if you're more free time than I do."

"I'm looking forward to it."

John finished his beer with one quick swallow. "I guess I should be getting back to the room. Sally's probably wondering what's happened to me."

"Glad we got to chat for a bit."

"Same here, Ty. Enjoyed the company."

John slid off the stool, shook Ty's hand, and left the bar. As he waited next to the elevator, a smile came to his face. A trip to Chicago would be nice summer trip, perhaps an escape, if things weren't rosy on the home front.

When John returned to the room, Sally was snuggled against a pillow with her eyes closed. He tiptoed around the bed to the easy chair, took off his clothes, and slipped into the bed next to her, placing his arm around her waist.

"I thought you'd be back sooner," she murmured.

"Ty came in and we talked for a while. Ended up drinking a couple beers. Interesting guy."

"Feel better?"

"I think so."

Sally snuggled closer. "Love you."

John kissed the back of her neck. "Love you, too."

Twelve

As the elevator descended to the first floor the next morning, John stared expressionless at Sally. He was tired after another restless night as they entered another day in their European adventure. His thoughts scattered in all directions; his body out of sync.

Maybe it was the hotel bed. He missed his bed back in Kentucky. It creased in the right places for his body. This one yielded in the wrong places. Besides, the pillow was too hard for his liking. Maybe it was something else, like the change in diet or the time difference. Or perhaps when he nearly slipped in the bathroom a few days earlier and it was now just catching up with him.

He shook his head.

"Are you okay?" Sally asked.

"I'm good," he mumbled. "Just clearing my head from some stupid thoughts."

"You had another hard night's sleep."

"No shit."

"Do you want to go back to the room?"

"No, but I'm not sure I'm up for breakfast," he grumbled as the door opened to a busy and noisy lobby.

"Me either." She squeezed his hand. "Maybe we should skip it."

"Tempting but I'm hungry."

Entering the dining area, they noticed Moretta and Doretta standing sentry over six seats propped up against tables like it was the ark of the tabernacle. Several couples walked up to them carrying full plates only to be waved off with snobby smiles.

John swore he heard a young man say, "Bite me" to them, provoking a nasty scowl from Doretta. He was fortunate Moretta didn't respond with a head lock.

They spotted Frank near the middle of the room, waving both arms back and forth to get their attention. He got the notice of other diners as well. John and Sally nodded and reluctantly made their way to the table.

"Good morning, friends!" Frank said. "We weren't sure if you'd make it."

"Why would you say that?" John said as he pulled out a chair for Sally. "We're breakfast eaters."

"You guys seemed a bit preoccupied when we last saw you," said Dorothy, wearing a lime green and yellow exercise outfit that wouldn't go unnoticed for the wrong reasons. "Like something was on your mind."

"A bit tired." Sally took a sip of water. "Sleep well?"

"Like a baby," Frank said, a napkin tucked under his shirt collar.

"Yeah, like a baby that roars like a lion." Dorothy shook her head. "As for me, I made it through the night."

"Excuse us while we go through the breakfast line," John said.

"We'll save your seats unless we get better offers from someone else." Frank's blaring voice brought a few more glances in their direction. Dorothy's mouth opened in disbelief.

Sally followed John to the long U-shaped table. She scooped runny scrambled eggs, beans, and pieces of fruits onto her white plate.

"I don't know if I can make it through the day," Sally murmured. "We're already off on the wrong foot."

"We've made it this far," John said as glanced over the rich pastries before deciding on a *kakaós csiga*, a chocolate roll. "What's another day?"

"I thought you were hungry," Sally asked. "No fruits, eggs, omelets, yogurt or something more substantial?"

"I may go back through the line. For some reason I have a sweets craving. Don't ask me why."

John looked at her choices for a moment then went back and got a bowl of oatmeal with blueberries, scrambled eggs, two slices of wheat toast and a glass of apple juice before putting the chocolate roll back in the plastic-covered bin.

"You're right," he said. "I don't need that. But that doesn't mean I don't have the right to go back and get another one."

Sally laughed. "Go on and take it. It's not going to hurt you. Indulge a little."

John reached back in and took the roll. "If you say so."

When they returned to the table, Frank had stepped away to the restroom.

"If you're following Frankie's breakfast, you need to go back and get some pancakes as well," Dorothy said, looking at John's plate.

"I may do that," John said before taking a sip of juice. "May as well go all out while we're here."

Dorothy's selections were a colorful variety of fruits—blueberries, strawberries, apple slices, mandarin oranges, and plums—along with a scoop of vanilla yogurt for dipping. She barely touched the food, taking a few small bites as if she were trying to preserve her creation. As for Frank's breakfast, it appeared to be a sampling of everything at the buffet, with an emphasis on sweets.

"We're sure going to miss you guys when this is over," Dorothy said as she touched both their forearms. "That's one of the nice things about traveling; you get to meet some of the nicest people."

"It's mutual, Dorothy," Sally said with a faint smile.

"And a few odd balls," John said.

"I hope you're not talking about us." Dorothy pushed out her lower lip.

"You should know better than that." John felt Sally's foot tap his ankle.

"I'm just fooling with you," Dorothy said. "I know what you mean. Like Phil and Edna, that couple from Indiana. They sorta keep to themselves. They haven't said a word to us."

"That's because they're deaf," Sally said.

"I didn't know that. I feel so ashamed now. I thought they were just being snobs."

"They're a nice couple," John said. "You should get to know them."

"I don't know that sign-language stuff," Dorothy said, the corners of her mouth turned down.

"They're lip readers, so you can communicate with them to some extent," Sally said. "A smile goes a long way."

"I'll try to remember that," Dorothy said. "Anyways, I hope we can meet you guys again after we get back home. Let's not forget to exchange addresses before we leave."

"We'll do that," Sally said. "Absolutely."

John kept his head down, picking at his food. He avoided eye contact with Sally, fearing she would look cross-eyed at him.

"So, do you have any future travel plans?" Dorothy asked. "Frankie and I try to make two or three trips a year."

"Nothing at the present," John said. "We're not much on planning. More spontaneous."

"You guys need to come up and spend a week with us on the Jersey shore. We have a small cottage a couple hundred yards from the ocean."

"We'll keep that in mind." John took a sip of coffee. "That'd be nice, wouldn't it, Sally?"

Sally nearly choked on a peach slice before uttering, "Yes, dear. It would," while covering her mouth.

"Are you okay, sweetie?" Dorothy asked, touching Sally's hand.

"A piece of fruit went down the wrong way." Sally palmed her chest. "Yes, that'd be a nice trip. John has always talked about going to the Jersey shore."

John lowered his head and coughed several times before taking a swallow from his glass of water. He glared at Sally as if she'd lost her mind.

"Really, John?" Dorothy asked.

John continued to stare at Sally, who wouldn't make eye contact. "Near the top of our bucket list."

Dorothy's eyes sparkled from the unexpected announcement. "That's wonderful."

"What can I say? I just try to make Sally happy." John tipped his coffee cup toward Sally and grinned.

"You've made me happy too."

"I guess that makes us happy campers," Sally said, the smile lines around her eyes growing deeper.

"Now, you check your calendars a little later and we'll set a date," Dorothy said as Frank waddled to the table.

"That's so sweet of you," Sally said.

"What's so sweet?" Frank said as he returned to his seat. "You guys talking about me?"

"Get real, Frankie," Dorothy said. "We're making plans for John and Sally to come visit us this year."

"That'd be cool," he said. "We got this place near the ocean. It's not much..."

"I've already told them that, Frankie," Dorothy said, raising her voice.

"Okay, okay. We could drive over to Atlantic City or even to the city and have some fun."

"Frankie, I was going to tell them that." Dorothy scrunched up her face. "Do you mind?"

"We'll think about it," John said, trying to defuse a potential powder keg.

"There's no thinking about it." Dorothy thumped John's shoulder with her fist, harder than he expected. "You guys are going to come and visit us and that's it. No ifs, ands, or buts about it. It's on your bucket list. Understand?"

John rubbed his shoulder for a few seconds. "Sure."

"I'll get back with you," Sally said. "We've got a few pressing things going on at home that we need to take care of right now. But we'll let you know when it's a good time for us."

"We don't want any goddamn excuses," Frank said, dropping his chin. "Comprehendo?"

"We do," John said. "Give us a little time."

"What are your plans, Frank?" Sally asked.

"For today?"

"Of course, today, Frankie!" Dorothy said. "What do you think she's talking about? Next week? Next month?"

"I thought she might be referring to their trip to see us."

Dorothy shook her head. "You amaze me, Frankie. You can be so dense at times."

"That's okay, Frank," Sally said. "My fault for confusing you. I was vague."

Frank's face turned a light red.

"It doesn't take much to confuse him," Dorothy said. "You should know that by now."

Frank wiped a napkin over his mouth. "There's a trip to a cathedral in Vishegrad, wherever in the hell that is. Pauline says it'll take about an hour or so to get there. I'm not sure I want to sit on the bus that long."

Dorothy frowned. "Doesn't sound too exciting to me either."

"You folks should stay here and hike around the town," John said. "There's still a lot to see."

"Only if you join us, old buddy," Frank said.

"Uh, the bus trip sounds interesting to me," Sally said.

"Yeah, don't let us keep you from doing your thing," John said. "I'd like to take it a little easy on my feet today. We did lots of walking yesterday."

"You know, John, that makes a helluva lot of sense," Frank said. "I never thought about that. My feet hurt, too. My knees ache as well. Even my ass. Hell, I'm sore all over. We'll go with you guys on the bus."

"Let's all try to sit in the same row," Dorothy said with a perky grin. "It's more fun that way."

"Uh, sure." John looked at Sally with woeful eyes. "A great way to spend the day."

Dorothy looked first at John and then Sally, flicking her brows with a bouncy smile. "I can't wait."

John glanced at the pastry on his plate. He knew it wasn't something he needed to eat but didn't want to be wasteful. "Do you want it, hon?" he asked Sally.

"I'll pass," she said.

"I'll take it," Frank said, reaching over before John had a chance to reply.

"It's yours." John held out the plate for Frank to take the pastry.

Dorothy shook her head. "Do you really need that?"

"He was going to throw it away."

"That doesn't mean you have to eat everything in sight. You're not a garbage disposal."

Frank stared at her for a moment, then gobbled the pastry in two big swallows as if an act of defiance. A puckish grin spread over his face as he got up from the table. And belched.

~ * ~

John sat by the window and took in the countryside, nudging Sally when they drove by Elvis Presley Park and excavations of Roman ruins that were recently discovered on the outskirts of the city. He found it amusing to see a billboard with actor Morgan

Freeman's face. American influence on the old world was more than he realized, even among ancient ruins.

Sally sat across the narrow aisle from Dorothy and listened to endless babble about celebrities, grandbabies, nosy neighbors, and physical problems. Frank dozed after leaving the hotel, head slumped against the tinted window and taking in deep breaths on occasion that momentarily stirred him from his heavy snooze.

Pauline pointed out places of interest as the bus wound along the narrow two-lane road. Sally used those interruptions to turn toward John and gaze out the window. A few times she looked at him with wild eyes as if to say she'd had enough of Dorothy's ramblings. But it lasted less than a minute as Dorothy would tap her hand and chatter on about something of little or no interest to Sally.

The bus stopped at Szentendre, a picturesque village north of Budapest targeted for tourists, with small shops and cafés on cobblestoned streets. Pauline told them they had an hour to explore the quaint town.

Frank and Dorothy had to pick up items off the floorboard that had spilled from Dorothy's purse after he inadvertently knocked it off her lap when the bus pulled into the parking lot. It was partially her fault because she had nudged him in the side to wake up. It was more of a startling wake-up call for Frank, whose arms flew outward at the sudden intrusion. She gave him an amplified earful of vitriol as others hurried off the bus and dispersed up the cobblestone walk toward the shops.

"You bumbling fool!"

"I didn't mean to," Frank said, bending down to pick up the various odds and ends scattered on the floorboard.

"If you hadn't been in such a damn hurry," she yelled. "It's all your fault."

John took the opportunity to grab Sally's hand and dart up the street behind the others toward the quiet hamlet. After taking several photos in quick succession, and with Frank and Dorothy nowhere in sight, they slipped inside a small café for coffee.

"This place kinda reminds me of Gatlinburg, with all the handicraft and artisan shops," John said. "Maybe Berea."

"That's what I was thinking," Sally said. "I should see if I can find something for Mother."

"We'll do that before we board the bus. I wonder where the Finsterwalds are."

"Do you think it was rude of us to leave them behind?" Sally said. "I feel a little bad about it."

"Not really. She's on the warpath. If anything, I feel sorry for poor old Frank. He's probably still feeling her wrath. That gal's got a hot temper."

"Doesn't it make you happy you're married to someone like me?"

"Now, have I ever complained about being married to you? You should know better than to ask that. Besides, when you get mad, it's more the dreaded silent treatment."

"Oh, really?"

"Now, you know it's the truth."

"I guess you're right." Sally grinned. "I got that from Mother."

"Silence isn't golden when you're angry."

"Are you trying to make me mad, buster?" Sally narrowed her bright eyes.

"Now that's scary."

After finishing their drinks, they ventured into a shop and purchased a brooch for Sally's demanding mother. "I hope she likes it," Sally said as they walked to the bus.

"Too bad if she doesn't. It's the thought that counts."

"If she doesn't, I'll give it to someone else, like Wilma."

"Maybe I should buy something for Bert since he's sorta watching over things while we're away."

"Doesn't he like sweets?"

"Good idea," John said. "We'll buy a box of Hungarian chocolates to take back with us."

The passengers waited on the bus for nearly twenty minutes as the four sisters and their dutiful husbands hadn't returned by the departure time.

"Where in the world could they be?" Pauline said, staring out the front window of the bus. Andras groaned.

"Hell, let's leave without them," Frank bellowed from the rear. Several passengers clapped their hands.

"We can't do that," Pauline said, a tiny smile creasing her lips. "That wouldn't be proper."

"I'll go look for them," John said as he walked toward the front. "They can't be too far away."

"You're too nice," Frank said. "You know they wouldn't do it for you."

"Is that a reason not to?" John said before stepping off the bus.

"I sure as hell wouldn't."

"Me either," another passenger groused.

John jogged up the street, peeking into store windows along the way. He finally located them at the far end of another street, sitting under a patio umbrella at a café. All but Noretta, who puffed on a cigarette while looking into a shop window.

John waved but they didn't notice or were intentionally ignoring him. He figured the latter. When he was fifty feet away, he shouted, "Hey folks, the bus is ready to leave."

Delbert looked at his watch. "What are you talking about? We have another fifteen minutes. Ain't that right, Henry?"

John reached the table, nearly out of breath. "It's been almost an hour and a half. We only had an hour here."

"I told you so, Doretta," said Loretta, wrinkling her pug nose. "But you and Delbert said ninety minutes."

"I thought she said an hour and a half," said Henry, Moretta's husband.

"The bus is where you left it," John said. "I'll let Pauline and the driver know you're on your way."

"We'll go after we finish our drinks," Noretta said with a curt smile. "There's no hurry."

John stopped in his tracks and turned around. "I beg your pardon?"

"We're trying to enjoy our vacation," she said.

"There's about thirty others on the bus trying to do the same. Give that some thought."

"I think we should be going," said Loretta's husband, Ewell. "He's right. They shouldn't have to wait on us."

"We'll go when we're ready to go," Doretta said. "Right, girls?"

Loretta pushed back in her seat. "We'd better go, sis."

Moretta did several leg and arm stretches while Noretta took a deep drag from her cigarette, then stamped it out on the pavement.

John strolled back to the bus, and the wayward couples meandered back fifteen minutes later. When they stepped into the bus, the other passengers began clapping.

"Can we go now?" Andras, their grim-faced bus driver, asked in husky broken English directed at them. The couples lowered their heads and didn't make eye contact with the others as they made their way to their new seats in the rear of the bus.

"We're on a timetable," Pauline said to the group. "We all need to be prompt. People are waiting for us at different destinations."

When the bus arrived at Vishegrad, the passengers marched off in single file to the grassy grounds. Pauline smiled and made it a point to tell Doretta, Noretta, Loretta and Moretta as they each stepped off they needed to return in one hour—even holding up one finger.

A few travelers searched for rest rooms as the trip was about as long as their bladders could handle. The unplanned delay in Szentendre didn't help matters. Sally clutched John's arm to whisk him away from the group. But it was to no avail as Dorothy kept a keen eye on their whereabouts this time. There was no escape from the Finsterwalds.

John and Sally strolled the church grounds, finding some respite when Frank couldn't keep up the pace. Frank sat on benches along the way to catch his breath and rest his sore knees. Dorothy gave up her pursuit as well, despite her orange-and-blue jogging outfit, because of a sore hip.

They hiked to a promenade, where a large statue of St. Stephen stood high above the Danube and provided a panoramic view of Slovakia or the Slovak Republic, a neighboring country that was once part of Czechoslovakia, now the Czech Republic. They sat and gazed across the idyllic tapestry of trees, springs flowers, and peaceful river.

"They're an interesting couple," Sally said.

"Who?"

"Frank and Dorothy."

"Interesting? Odd would be a better description. Or annoying. Or irritating. Or galling. In other words, odd balls."

"Okay, John, you've made your point," Sally said, shaking her head in amusement.

"Must be the journalist in me. Always trying to be descriptive."

"I found out from Dorothy that they have four adult children, but Frank only acknowledges three."

John squeezed his nose. "Why's that?"

"The youngest is gay. She said once Frank found out, he banished the boy from the family."

"Banished?"

"Dorothy said she and the two sisters and brother still have contact with boy, but they've kept it a secret from Frank for about seven or eight years."

"Did you tell her about Chloe?"

"I didn't see any reason to because we don't think it's a big deal. And furthermore, it's none of her business. I wouldn't tell her about Brody's problems either."

"Good idea," John said. "Some things you don't share with strangers. Even if they think of themselves as friends. Anyway, I hope it's a temporary situation."

"Family is another matter."

"Exactly," John said. "What happens in the Ross family stays in the Ross family. Just like Vegas."

"John, be serious!"

"You have to make light of a few things in life."

"Now if you can be serious again, what are we going to do about their invitation to visit them later this year?" Sally asked.

"You're the one who said it was on my bucket list. Why did you do that? That was mean. Cruel. Unnecessary. Nasty."

"I thought it was funny."

"Well, the joke's going to be on you if we end up there," John said, his head bobbing.

Sally shrugged and laughed. "Oops."

"Let's hope Dorothy forgets to exchange addresses, emails, or whatever she wants to do."

Sally cocked her head. "You really believe that's going to happen?"

"Wishful thinking on my part," John stood and gazed into the distance. "We need to get back to the bus. We don't want to get on Andras' and Pauline's shit list. Aren't we going to stop for lunch? I'm getting hungry."

"That's what Pauline said."

"That's she's getting hungry?"

"No, John, you know what I mean, that we'd be stopping soon. But I'd bet she's hungry as well."

They were the last ones on the bus, getting curious glances from some of the travelers, especially the four sisters who reclaimed their seats at the front. John couldn't resist flashing smiles at their haughty faces, knowing he and Sally weren't late and someone didn't have to go looking for them.

"Pauline wanted to leave you here, but I pleaded with her to give you guys five more minutes," Frank bellowed. "You made it with a minute to spare."

"That's mighty kind of you, Frank," John said, sitting on the aisle seat after Sally eased past him to the window. She wriggled her brows at him, knowing he'd be across from a jabbering Dorothy.

John wished Dorothy had run out of things to say from their trip to the religious site. It didn't happen as she started gabbing as soon as the bus pulled out of the parking lot. She wanted to know all about Kentucky and why he chose to live there, of all places. It lasted only twenty minutes, to John's delight, as they stopped at a roadside restaurant.

The manager, holding the door open at the entrance as they paraded inside, greeted them with a stern smile.

"We expected you forty-five minutes ago," he said to Pauline, holding up his watch. "The food is getting cold."

"We had a delay along the way," Pauline said in a contrite tone. "I'm sorry."

Noretta stood a few feet from the door, stealing a quick smoke before entering the establishment. She flicked her cigarette on the parking lot and hurried inside to her sisters, and space reserved at their table. The manager walked over and stomped on the still-burning cigarette, then picked it up and put it in standing ashtray outside the door.

After the light lunch, John told Sally he needed to go to the restroom and would meet her on the bus. Sally visited an adjoining souvenir shop, hoping to find something else for her mother in case she didn't like the brooch. She ended up purchasing a box of chocolates for Bert.

As the others boarded the bus, Sally stood next to the door and waited for John. She heard Frank's booming voice. "Get on board, Sally, your worst half is already seated."

Sally took two steps inside the crowded bus and saw John positioned at a window seat, waving his hand for her come back. He wiggled his brows. She shook her head all the way to the aisle seat, a tiny grin forming from her pursed lips. She plunked down on the aisle seat across from Dorothy, then turned and rapped him on the shoulder with her delicate fist.

"I'm going to get you for this," she said with a scowl. "And I won't forget, buster."

"Are you guys all right?" Dorothy leaned over and squeezed Sally's forearm.

"We're good," Sally said, keeping her eyes focused on John.

"I'm glad you guys changed seats," Dorothy said. "John isn't the most talkative person in the world."

"What do you expect from a journalist?" Frank said. "He communicates by typing words on a computer screen."

John glimpsed at Frank and gave a thumb's up, without saying a word.

As the bus headed back to Budapest, John eased his seat back several inches and closed his eyes. If he had planned on sleeping, it wasn't going to happen. Sally nudged him in the ribs every few miles to make sure he was awake as she listened to Dorothy recall all the plays and musicals she'd seen on Broadway. Tidbits about her children. Her quirky neighbors. Frank napped almost the entire way, jerking and snorting every few minutes, clearly a sufferer of sleep apnea. At least he didn't throw up like he had at the castle.

They arrived at the hotel in late afternoon, enough time for more sightseeing and shopping. Dorothy dropped her sunglasses under the seat, allowing precious seconds for John and Sally to scurry off the bus and flee the Finsterwalds.

John grabbed Sally's hand as they dashed inside the hotel, taking the stairs to the second floor. They stood in the stairwell for five minutes, listening to fading voices come and go in the hallway as people got on and off the two elevators. Then it was quiet.

"Do you think it's safe?" John asked.

Sally cocked her head. "Safe for what?'

"To go back out. Do you think our Yankee sidekicks have disappeared?'

"I don't know," she said. "You'd think so."

"I'm almost afraid to go back down and open the door. I can almost envision them standing there, staring at us in the face, waiting for our return."

"Do you think we should wait a few more minutes?"

"Did Dorothy say what their plans were?"

"If she did, I didn't hear anything. After a while, I kinda tuned her out."

After three more minutes, they ventured back to the hotel lobby. They didn't see any of their fellow travelers. They looked out the swinging front door, and the bus had already departed.

"Let's make a run for it," John said.

"Where to?"

"The marketplace down the street. We can grab a bite to eat."

"Great idea. And I can buy something else for mother as well."

"Huh?"

"Never mind."

~ * ~

After stopping at several stores and deciding they didn't travel nearly five thousand miles to go shopping, they ducked into a small café for something light to eat. The bistro appeared to cater to locals since everything was written or printed in Hungarian, and the soft chatter from the tables were foreign to John and Sally's ears.

John and Sally stood at the door, waiting for someone to seat them. "Maybe we should find another place to eat," John said. Sally shrugged slightly.

Moments later, a gravel-tinged voice came from the corner with a distinct Texas drawl. "Hey travelers, why don't you join us?"

John turned and noticed a couple from their travel group. The man motioned with his hand for them to come to their table. John and Sally walked over and sat at the table.

"Service is kinda slow and they don't speak English too good but the chow tastes mighty fine," the man said. "By the way, I'm Chuck Bannister," and nodding toward the woman, "and this is my better half, Addy."

"It's a pleasure to meet you," John said before introducing himself and Sally. Chuck's thick silver hair flowed straight back, and his meaty jowls and prominent nose gave him somewhat of an aristocratic air. Addy was petite, with small creases from her tiny mouth and across her rosy cheeks. Her gray eyes sparkled as her face seemed fixed in a perpetual smile.

"Are you enjoying the trip?" Addy asked.

"Very much so," Sally said. "There's so much to see. How about you?"

"Just wonderful."

"So where are you from?" John asked. "We're from Kentucky."

"Guess," Chuck said.

"Hmm, I'd say Texas," John said.

"You guessed right, young man. From Midlothian. Ever heard of it?"

"Can't say that I have."

"We're about twenty-five miles southwest of Dallas."

"I've been to Dallas but never to Midlothian."

"It sounds like an English town," Sally said.

"Some people think that when they hear it," Addy said. "And that's close. Local lore has it that it's named after a Scottish county by a Scotsman who was homesick. I'm not so sure about that but it makes for a cute story."

Sally smiled. "I like that story."

"Where are you from in Kentucky?" Chuck asked.

"Lexington," John said. "The Horse Capital of the World. At least we like to think that we are."

"I wouldn't dispute that. Been there a few times and bet on a few ponies at Keeneland."

"I guessed that you were from Texas," John said. "Rancher? Oil?"

"Guessed wrong. Cement."

"Really?"

"Midlothian is a big cement production area. Spent my entire like working in cement. It's a solid job, if you know what I mean." Chuck winked. "How about yourself."

"Newspapers. Retired as a sports editor. Sally was a teacher. Now trying to enjoy life as newly retired."

Chuck turned in his chair and waved at waitress. The young woman approached the table, red-faced for apparently noticing she hadn't taken John and Sally's orders.

"We'll have what they have," John said, motioning toward the Bannisters' golden walnut dumplings, or *aranygaluska*, and lattes. Within minutes, she returned with their order.

"How do you like the life of a retired person?" Chuck asked.

"I'm not sure if retired is a good word for it," John said. "We're retired from work, but we stay busy all the time. Something always seems to be going on. And usually not things I want to be going on."

"I know the feeling. Makes you wonder how you ever found time to work or do anything."

"How long have you been retired?'

Chuck glanced at Addy. "Does twenty-six years sound about right?" She nodded.

"You must have retired when you were young."

"Fifty-six; eighty-two now."

"I wouldn't have guessed you being that old."

Addy tapped Chuck's hand. "He's speaking for himself. I'm not *that* old."

"They can see I robbed the cradle." Chuck smiled and squeezed Addy's delicate blue-veined hand.

"Travel a lot?" Sally asked.

"Not as much as we'd like to," Addy said. "We've slowed down the past few years for health reasons."

"I hope it's nothing too serious," John said.

"This will probably be our last trip," Addy said.

"Now, don't say that," Chuck said, patting the top of her hand.

Addy looked at John and Sally, her glistening eyes beginning to tear but still managing a small smile. "I've got lung cancer."

John cleared his throat. "I'm sorry to hear that."

"I suppose I didn't quit smoking soon enough."

"I didn't mean to pry."

"That's okay," she said. "Chuck and I have traveled the world in our fifty-eight years together. We can't complain. Nothing lasts forever."

Chuck patted her hand again. "We've had a great life's journey." He pressed his lips together, fighting back tears.

"Now settle down, Chuck." Addy turned over her hand and clutched his before glancing at John and Sally. "He can be such a softie."

"When it comes to you."

After they finished their desserts, Chuck and Addy remained at the café, saying they wanted another latte. John and Sally returned to the hotel as they assumed the Bannisters wanted some more quiet time together.

Sally sniffled, lowering her head and holding John's hand as they walked back to the hotel in the quiet of the night.

Thirteen

"Sleep well?" John asked as they nestled in bed the next morning, her head resting on his shoulder.

"Not really. I kept thinking about that sweet Mrs. Bannister. I almost wished she hadn't told us about her lung cancer."

"I assume she wanted to be honest with us. Maybe she was just letting us know to experience as much of the world as we can because it'll all come to an end one of these days."

"Maybe so."

"You have to admire her for getting out and seeing the world, even if it might be for the last time," John said.

"It's still sad."

"I hope we're able to do what they're doing when we're their age."

Sally burst out a laugh. "John Ross, I almost had to drag you out of the house to get you to go on this trip. And here you are saying you hope we're like them in fifteen years."

"You got me there. I'm more of a homebody than I care to admit."

"You know, speaking of home, it seems like we've been gone a month. I don't recall us ever being away from home this long. It's only been eight days."

"I know what you mean," John said. "Back in the day when I was working, I don't think I ever took more than a week off. I don't know why because I wasn't indispensable even though some editors felt that way about themselves. Maybe I was too much of a workaholic."

"You did put in the hours. But that was the sacrifice you made for the family."

"The more I think about it, it was more like sacrificing you and the kids for my job. I made some bad choices along the way."

"You were just being human. Isn't it that way with most working families? We still loved you."

"Can't turn back the hands of time, so I may as well deal with it."

"Remember that time we drove out to Kansas with the kids to see Dodge City and other sites and someone at the paper reached us at a motel in Garden City to ask a question about a story that was going to be published?"

"Wasn't that ridiculous?" John chuckled. "Hey, maybe I *was* indispensable."

"You've always been that way for me and the kids."

"I've tried, but like most parents, fell short in a few categories."

"I wasn't the perfect mother either," Sally said. "Sometimes I got carried away in the classroom. And grading papers at home while you watched the kids."

"That's a reason you were a perfect teacher. You always went the distance for your students. You treated them as if they were your own children."

"Let's not get carried away about being the perfect teacher," Sally said. "But I did love teaching, and the kids. I still miss it at times. Much like you with journalism."

John turned over. "So much for reminiscing. What do you want to do today?"

"I kinda like what we're doing now. How often have we been able to talk without interruptions?"

"That's a good point. Ages."

"We need to do this more often."

"Talk in bed?"

"That's nice but I mean travel more, get away from everyone and spend time with each other," Sally sat up against the headboard. "You know, reconnect."

"I'm all for that," John said. "I'll let you be the travel coordinator."

"No way, Jose! We do it together."

"That'll work."

"Maybe we can each come up with wish lists and compare them."

"That's fine, sweetheart. But let's finish this crazy trip first before we start putting our heads together on the next."

"John, I don't mean today," Sally said.

"That's the deadline mentality I have. I spent too much time working at the newspaper."

"I do hope we can do something on our own today."

"You mean, without the Finsterwalds?"

"Exactly."

"We could go back to the spas. Or take in a few museums. I feel like we've only scratched the surface. There's so many things to do here."

"We don't need to waste our last two full days," Sally said. "We need to concentrate on our time here and enjoy them as much as possible."

"I'm on board," John said.

"First we need to find out what Pauline has on the itinerary?"

"I'm almost afraid to go down and check because of who I might see."

"It's still early so we can take our time. There's no hurry."

Three strong thumps on the door silenced their conversation. John tiptoed to the door, holding his breath, and peered through the peep hole. On the other side were Frank and Dorothy, standing like stone-faced statues. John turned and put a forefinger to his mouth.

"Anyone home?" Frank bellowed. "It's your friendly neighborhood travel companions."

John and Sally held their breaths for twenty seconds, covering their hands over their tight-lipped mouths to avoid letting out even a peep.

"I wonder where they could be," Dorothy said.

"Probably having breakfast," Frank said. "Let's go and see."

John and Sally finally exhaled when they heard footsteps plodding away from the door. They didn't move, simply stared at each other as if in suspended animation, fearful that even a creak in the floor or a squeak from the bed would signal their presence.

Then silence.

"That was a close call," John whispered as air oozed from his lungs.

"At least we know they're out and about."

"We know they're out. Let's hope they're about to go somewhere in the opposite direction of wherever we're going."

"And we know they're going to breakfast so we can avoid them there."

They took their time getting dressed and lolled in the room in quietness for another hour, John perusing local brochures on places to go and Sally reading from her Kindle. John picked up the remote and almost turned on the TV, without thinking about the sound, before Sally pushed his hand down.

It must have been one of her intuitions because seconds later there was a rhythmic knock on the door—knock, knock, knock, knock, knock...knock-knock. John and Sally didn't move, staring at each other as if in a catatonic state.

"Yoo-hoo! Anybody home?" Frank said. "It's the big, bad wolf."

"Frankie, quit being stupid!" Dorothy said.

"I've got little red riding hood with me."

"If you don't shut up, I'm going to—"

As Frank and Dorothy stood outside the door, the stillness almost became suffocating as John and Sally sat motionless in what seemed like minutes instead of seconds.

"Guess they've already left," Frank said.

"You think?" Dorothy said sarcastically.

Moments later, their footsteps clacked down the hallway toward the elevators. John and Sally breathed softly until they were sure the Finsterwalds were out of sight and sound.

"Another close call," Sally whispered.

"No shit," John said. "We need to leave before we're held captive here. There's no telling when they'll return. I wouldn't be surprised if they went back to their room."

The phone rang, startling them as they looked at each other while deciding who should answer. Or if they should answer. After numerous rings, John quit counting after ten, silence permeated the room again.

"I hope that wasn't from back home," Sally said.

"I think it was in-house," John said. "My guess—"

"The Finsterwalds."

Deciding it was time to make their escape if the Finstewalds were still in their room, John and Sally they took the stairs and hurried out of the hotel, catching a bus going to Heroes Square. As soon as they sat down, John noticed someone waving at him from across the aisle in the crowded vehicle. His heart almost stopped, then he let out short breath when he saw Phil Graybar's sunny smile.

Phil and Edna exited the bus in front of the Hall of Art, next to Heroes Square, and John and Sally followed a few steps behind. The Graybars stopped in front of the Greek Revival building entrance and flipped through a thin pamphlet about the facility.

"Going inside?" John asked, tipping his head.

Phil nodded.

"Mind if we tag along?"

Phil gave a thumbs up and they followed them inside the building, taking their time viewing the short-term exhibits of contemporary art. For the first time in several days, they didn't feel rushed or the need for pointless chatter. Edna purchased several prints by Hungarian artists in the bookstore. It occurred to John that in their delayed preparation back in the hotel, he forgot to pack his camera, so he ended up purchasing several postcards.

John pointed to the café entrance and they strolled inside and ordered sandwiches and drinks. Sally motioned to Edna about the prints, asking if she was a collector.

Edna nodded, pointed to herself, and informed her that she was an artist as well, mouthing "watercolors."

"Impressive," John said. "I'm lucky to keep a straight line while painting a wall."

"She's very good," Phil said in a distinct audible. "Her work in galleries."

"And what do you do?" John asked.

Phil made a scribbling motion with his hand before saying, "Writer."

"Have you been published?" Sally asked. "What do you write? I'm an avid reader."

"Novels."

"I'll look for them on Amazon," she said. Phil took out his wallet and handed her a business card that showed his website and email address.

Edna, smiling, asked. "You?"

"We're retired," Sally said. "John was a journalist, a sports editor. I was a school teacher."

"Nice," Edna said with an approving nod.

After eating, they strolled across the square to the Museum of Fine Arts to view its extensive international collection of European and Egyptian art. They spent more than three hours browsing the six departments, with Edna leading the way from room to room.

Phil was more conscientious than John when it came to carrying a camera as John took several photos of the Indiana couple with their dSLR on the front steps of the building. Sally handed Phil her smartphone for him to take a similar photo of her and John, then John used his smartphone to take a smiling selfie of the four of them before they boarded the metro.

Street lamps flickered in the twilight as they walked the two blocks to the hotel. "Thank you for a wonderful day," Sally said as they entered the bright lobby.

"Thank you, too." Phil said, reaching out and shaking their hands. Sally gave Edna a slight hug before departing ways.

John and Sally kicked off their shoes and collapsed on the bed seconds after they entered their room.

"I'm exhausted," John said. "And my feet ache."

"Same here but it was worth it," Sally said. "What an interesting couple. I can't wait to check out his novels. Maybe he's written something that will appeal to my book club."

"Do you think she sells her paintings?"

"Probably so if they're in galleries," Sally said. "We'll have to Google her name and find out where."

"This was certainly one of the highlights of the trip."

John noticed the phone light flashing. "I wonder who that could be."

"I'll let you answer it this time," Sally said.

John listened to the message and put down the handset, chuckling.

"What's so funny?"

"It was Dorothy Finsterwald. She's been worried about us all day. She asked that we call their room and let them know everything's okay with us. I'll let you do the honors."

"Oh, no you don't, mister," Sally said. "You took the message, so you have to make the call. Those are the rules."

"Rules? I don't recall those rules."

"I make them as we go along," Sally said.

"That doesn't sound fair."

"It's fair to me."

"I'm sure it is." John shook his head. "I guess I can be thankful it's not anything serious."

"So are you going to call them back?"

"Later. Let me sleep on it a while."

"Did you want to get anything to eat?"

"I'm not hungry. Are you?

"Not really."

John slipped off his pants and removed his shirt, tossing them on the easy chair, and got under the sheets.

"Are you going to bed for the night?" Sally asked.

"Just resting my eyes. I want to be comfortable."

Sally walked over to the dresser and took off her clothes, folding them and laying them in a drawer. She climbed back into bed, cuddling next to John.

A few seconds later, they heard five taps on the door. They didn't move. After a few more seconds, someone walked away without saying a word.

John and Sally remained silent, their eyes closed, and drifted off to sleep.

Fourteen

"Dare we go downstairs and eat breakfast this morning?" Sally asked as she applied makeup in front of the bathroom mirror.

"Probably should unless you want someone banging on the door again," John said, sitting in the easy chair tying his shoes. "We need to look at today's itinerary and see what the tour has planned."

They entered the crowded dining room at eight o'clock. The 'etta sisters and spouses were already gathered at two large tables in the corner, with two chairs propped up at each end, giving the impression they were reserving the seats for friends. John surveyed the area for a few seconds but didn't see a vacant table.

"Let's go check the message board and see what's up before we eat," John said. "Maybe the place will clear out some in the meantime."

Their group was scheduled to leave at nine for a half-day trip to the Hall of Art and Museum of Fine Art, followed by another free afternoon.

"Looks like we have another free day," Sally said. "Any suggestions?"

"How about the synagogue?" John said. "It's within walking distance. Unless there's somewhere you want to go."

"I'd love to see it."

They returned to the dining area, arriving the same time Frank and Dorothy showed up. They waited at the doorway for tables to be cleared.

"Where were you guys yesterday?" Dorothy asked, arching an eyebrow. "We were worried sick. We hope nothing bad happened."

"We're fine," John said with a quick smile. "Thanks for asking."

"So where did you turkeys go?" Frank asked. "We even went to your room to see if you were around."

"We went for an early morning walk," Sally said. "It was nice and peaceful."

"I wish you would have told us," Dorothy said. "We would have enjoyed that, too."

"I'm sorry," Sally said. "It was a spur of the moment thing."

"And why didn't you call me back last night? I left a message on your phone."

"You did?" John raised his brows.

"I told you, sweetie, that you waited too long to start talking," Frank said.

"You did no such thing," Dorothy said, smacking his hand. "I waited until the operator said to start speaking. I don't understand what happened."

"Must've been a glitch." John turned up his palms. "It's happened to me before."

"Oh, screw it," Frank said. "I'm hungry. Let's grab a bite to eat."

Frank led the way to a table near the buffet tables, where they turned up the chairs, then to the assortment of breakfast and brunch items. He heaved scrambled eggs, bacon, and sausage on his plate, and loaded another with toast and pastries. John opted for oatmeal,

Sally grabbed a banana and yogurt, while Dorothy waited as a server prepared a cheese omelet.

"How have you been feeling?" John asked Frank. "No more GERD?"

"Been a good boy and taking my pills," Frank said as he chewed on a slice of bacon.

Dorothy returned to the table. "Have I missed anything?"

"Just catching up on Frank's health," John asked.

"You guys were sure out late yesterday."

"No later than normal."

"I came by last night and you still weren't in," she said.

"You did?" Frank asked, halfway into munching on toast.

"Yes, Frankie. When you were at the bar."

"Oh, yeah, forgot I had a few brewskies."

"Frankie leaves me alone in the room so he can go drink," Dorothy said. "John, I bet you wouldn't do that to Sally."

"Depends on if she wanted to go have a drink," John said. "We don't drink that much so it's really not an issue."

"I wouldn't mind," Sally said. "If John wanted a beer, I'd stay in the room and read."

"See, sweetie, it's not a big deal," Frank said. "You don't even like beer."

"But you don't even ask," Dorothy bit her lower lip.

"Next time I will, sweetie."

"Oh, forget it," Dorothy said. "You don't understand."

"Huh?" Frank face went blank.

"Are you folks going with the group today?" John asked.

"Only if you guys are," Dorothy said, lifting her fork. "We're not letting you out of our sight. We want to spend as much time with you as we can before we go home. Don't you think we've had an exciting time together?"

"I can't dispute that," John said. "Memorable. Unpredictable, too."

"That's what trips should be," Frank said, taking a bite of a cherry-topped pastry. "You just go with the flow."

"Frankie, close your mouth when you chew," Dorothy said with squinty eyes. "That's so rude."

Frank covered his mouth with a napkin and burped.

"Frankie!"

"I'm not sure what we're going to do today," Sally said. "We're thinking about the synagogue."

"That sounds so damn depressing," Frank said. "I wish we could just forget about World War Two and the Jews and that hollercost thing."

"You mean holocaust," John said.

"Whatever. You know what I mean."

"Frank, maybe that's a reason to go," Sally said. "So we don't forget about the holocaust and all the atrocities."

Frank shrugged. "Whatever. I kinda think vacations should make you feel happy. You know what I mean?"

"Maybe it's the teacher in me, but I think they should be learning experiences as well. Didn't you go to the House of Terror with us?"

Dorothy shook her head. "We planned to, but Frankie had diarrhea that morning. He stuffed his belly, kinda like he's doing now and before we went to the castle."

"Now, honey bun, that's not nice," Frank said. "I had some intestinal bug or something from the flight over here."

"Get real, Frankie." Dorothy eyed at the ceiling. "You ate too much. You always eat too much."

"Don't they have some artsy stuff for us today?" Frank asked. "That might be fun."

"They're going to two art museums," Sally said. "Leaving at nine."

"We'd better hurry up then," Dorothy said. "We don't want to be late."

"We've already been there," John said. "But you folks go ahead. It's very interesting…and fun."

"And it's not depressing," Sally said. "In fact, it's uplifting. There're beautiful paintings, sculptures and other artwork. Yes, you might say it's a fun visit."

"When do you guys go there?" Frank asked.

"Yesterday," John said. "It was, er, fun."

"You should go, Dorothy," Sally said. "I think *you'd* enjoy it since you appreciate the arts."

"Nope," Dorothy said, shaking her head. "We're stuck like glue."

"Since we're in no hurry, I'm going to get another plate," Frank said. "You know, beans aren't bad with breakfast. Never had it until I came here."

"Quite common," John said. "Especially in England, or so I've read."

"Please skip the beans," Dorothy said. "I won't get an ounce of sleep tonight if you do. You'll smell up the room."

"Maybe some pancakes then," Frank said.

"You'll be sorry, lug head," Dorothy said. "Remember our trip to the castle when you puked up everything?"

"Maybe I'll just get some of that fruit," Frank said. "That should be okay."

"Why don't you just get a glass of orange juice and be like a normal human being? Is that asking too much? You wanted to lose some weight on this vacation."

"Sez who?"

"That's another cute outfit you're wearing today," Sally said to Dorothy, who was wearing a pink jogging suit with black piping and matching shoes. "Everything is so color coordinated."

"I just love wearing exercise clothes." Dorothy held out her arms to admire her fashion statement. "They're so comfortable and versatile. And you can wear them practically anywhere."

"I've noticed," Sally said. "I need to buy me several outfits."

"I have some catalogs I'll mail to you once we get back home. I just know you'll love the variety of colors instead of the drab, uh, you know what I mean."

Frank plodded back to the table with a small glass of orange juice, along with a bowl of fruit cocktail, orange slices, and an apple. He gulped down the juice, followed by a booming belch. Dorothy glowered at him. John and Sally lowered their heads as if to hide. Diners at surrounding tables looked over, holding their glares for a few seconds before going back to their meals. It didn't faze Frank as he took a chomp of the apple.

"Frank, I don't recall you telling us what you do for a living?" John asked to break the ensuing silence.

"Oh, I'm a building contractor. Semi-retired but still have my business. My daughters' husbands run it for me. We try to keep it all in the family."

"Stay busy for the most part?"

"It was a struggle for a several years after the market crashed in 2008 but we were blessed by Hurricane Sandy back in 2012."

Sally set her coffee down from her mouth before taking a sip. "Blessed?"

"Oh, hell yeah," Frank popped an orange slice in his mouth and swallowed without chewing. "We got all kinds of work after that. Still doing some odds and ends. Best thing ever happened to my business. We made a killing."

"It was terrible for lots of people," Dorothy said. "But not for us. Frankie was able to retire in 2014 and let the boys take over. He still goes to the office now and then to check the books. You never know if someone might cheat you. Even your own kin."

"Interesting." John took a swallow of water and glanced at Sally.

"You'd be surprised how floating a thousand dollars here and there to the right people can make things happen," Frank said. "That's when everything really took off. I wish I'd known that trick years ago. I could've retired by the time I was fifty."

"I really don't know what to say." John's brows furrowed.

"Shit, we even got involved in tree removal and other debris. I had to hire about ten more guys and we kept them busy for a couple years. Then things started to slow down a bit. But it was good while it lasted. Hired a few illegals on the cheap. Made a bundle."

"And it involved behind-closed-door talks?"

"Come on, John," Frank said with a wide smile. "You tell me you haven't slipped someone some cash for a good table at a restaurant? Or to get into some show? Maybe get your roof repaired?"

"Can't say that I ever did," John said. "Never really occurred to me."

"You're so sweet, John," Dorothy said. "And you too, Sally. Must be a Southern trait. So innocent about things."

"We try to mind our manners and do what's right," Sally said. "I'm not so sure that is being innocent."

"And ethics," John added.

"I hope I didn't offend you," Dorothy said, the corners of her mouth curled down. "I didn't mean to."

"No offense," John said. "Just an eye-opener. Learn something every day from you folks."

"Now don't try and tell me that doesn't happen in the South," Frank said. "Hell, I've read enough about crooked politicians getting paybacks. Even coaches and lawyers. It happens everywhere. All the time. It's part of doing business. Damn, it's practically the American way."

"I didn't say it didn't occur in Kentucky or other places," John said. "I simply said that I didn't do it. I think—"

"Let's get off this nonsense and decide what we're going to do today." Frank lifted the bowl of fruit cocktail and slurped the juice. "Let's have some fun."

John clenched his jaw.

"How about another walk to the Danube?" Sally asked. "I've read about a place where bronze shoes are encased on the banks where people were killed by fascists during World War Two."

"That doesn't sound like much fun," Frank said. "If you ask me, it's depressing as hell."

"Frankie, just be quiet," Dorothy said. "Everything doesn't have to be fun. We're not at Coney Island or Atlantic City. Besides, you need the exercise."

"Can we take a taxi?"

"Hey, maybe we can hop a trolley," John said. "That should be fun. Right, Frank?"

Frank's eyes brightened. "Yeah, I'd like that."

"You would," Dorothy said.

"We can get walk around the area after we get there," Sally said. "There's no sense in overdoing it early in the day."

"That makes sense," Dorothy said. "That should make you happy, Frankie. We sure don't want to overexert ourselves."

"Then how about your sore ass?" Frank glared at Dorothy. "Every night you complain about your hips. It's just not me. Okay?"

"That was uncalled for, Frankie." Dorothy wiped a tear from her eye. "You know what I went through when I had my hip-replacement surgery."

"I'm sorry, honey bun," Frank said, touching the top of her hand. "I didn't mean it that way." She jerked her hand away.

"You folks ready to leave?" John asked, sighing. He pushed back his chair; the others followed in unison to the lobby.

"Hey guys, I need to take a whiz," Frank said, already heading toward the men's room. "Wait for me out front."

"How about you, John?" Sally asked.

"I'm good," he said. "But I will run back to the room. Forgot the camera."

John dashed back to the room and grabbed the camera on the dresser. Then he took Sally's advice and stopped in the bathroom and peed. Better safe than searching around for a restroom. Frank still hadn't returned by the time he rejoined the women in front of the building.

"Where's Frank?" he asked.

"It's his prostate," Dorothy said. "Enlarged. He says he should play on a basketball team."

"What?"

"The way he dribbles. That's his big joke."

John chuckled. "Cute."

"Don't encourage him."

Frank finally showed up, adjusting his jeans' zipper as he stepped out on the sidewalk. "I should play on a basketball team."

"Don't say it, Frankie. I already told them."

"You did?" Frank said, frowning. "Well, then, you guys ready to rumble?"

"Please Frankie," Dorothy said. "Let's just go."

They boarded a trolley that took them near the Parliament Building. They walked to the Shoes on the Danube memorial, about a quarter-mile south on the banks of the river. They strolled among the empty bronze shoes in silence, bringing tears from Sally and Dorothy. John took several photos of the poignant setting. Frank was apparently moved by the site as he didn't make any wisecracks.

"How about we go to the Dohany Street Synagogue?" Sally said. "I've heard it's the largest in Europe. We can ride a trolley again. Unless you want to walk. It won't take that long. There's even a statue of Ronald Reagan along the way."

"Seriously?" Frank asked. "A statue of Reagan? You've got to be fuckin' kidding me."

"They credit him with putting an end to communism," John said. "He's well thought of in Hungary."

"That's cool. He's one of my heroes. Hot damn!"

"Reagan? Seriously?"

"Hell, yes. He set our country straight. We haven't had a decent president since him. He was one of a kind."

"I can't disagree with that," Sally said, pursing her lips. "Certainly one of a kind."

"Well, uh, let's get going then," John said. "It's not far from the Parliament Building. We'll see the American Embassy as well."

"Cool." There seemed to be a little bounce in Frank's usual shuffle. "This is going to be the highlight of the trip."

"For me, too," Dorothy said. "How did we miss this?"

"It was part of the tour after we went to the Parliament Building a few days ago," Sally said. "There was a guided walking tour after that."

"I sorta remember that," Dorothy said. "Frankie was getting hungry so we went back to the hotel with the others so he could eat. Thanks a lot, Frankie!" She whacked his shoulder.

After spotting Reagan's statue in Liberty Square, Frank and Dorothy bolted ahead of John and Sally as if in a race to see who could get there first. John and Sally stopped for a few seconds, watching them savor the moment before joining them. Frank handed his camera to John to take several photos of him and Dorothy next to the statue. Frank placed an arm around the statue's shoulders while Dorothy held a hand.

"I may have to get an enlargement and frame it in the living room," Frank said. "My buddies back home won't believe this."

"I'm glad it made you happy," John said. "That's a reason we explore places. We find all sorts of interesting things."

"Yeah, this is kinda fun."

They stopped in front of the U.S. Embassy, where John had to take several more photos of Frank and Dorothy with the American flag in the background, possibly suited for framing on their living room wall, right next to Reagan.

Frank and Dorothy were so enthralled by the experience that they continued walking toward the Dohany Street Synagogue without mentioning public transportation. They stopped several blocks from their destination for lunch. Frank was talked out and turned his attention to a pork cutlet sandwich and pickled vegetables while the others had soup and salad oliviers, a scrumptious potato salad popular in Budapest.

They spent an hour walking through the synagogue, also known as the Great Synagogue. It ended with the Holocaust Memorial Park, where four hundred thousand Hungarian Jews murdered by the Nazis were remembered on a shimmering sculpture that resembled a weeping willow. The leaves contained the names of the victims.

"That was quite moving," John said as they left the building grounds.

"Yeah, I know what you mean," Frank said. "I used to have some doubts about this hollercost stuff. Thought it was propaganda by the Jews."

"What do you think now?" Sally asked.

"It sure ain't propaganda or fake news."

John and Sally led the way on the crowded sidewalk to the hotel, waiting in the lobby a few minutes for Frank and Dorothy, who stopped along the way to sit on a bench and rest their feet.

"Man, thanks for wonderful day." Frank pumped John's hand. "I'll never forget it."

Fifteen

On the morning of the final day before departing Budapest, the group visited St. Stephen's Basilica, taking a guided tour of the nineteenth-century neo-classical building dedicated to the first king of Hungary.

"They sure like Stephen here," Frank said as they departed the church. "He's always all over the place, like the castle and that place we went to by bus. He's huge."

"Probably because of religion," John said. "He had a big role in the spread of Christianity in Hungary."

"Just shows what can happen when you've got God on your side."

"Or if people think you do," John said.

"It's a shame we don't have time to attend a concert," Sally said. "I imagine it would be something else with the building's acoustics."

"Maybe when we return," John said.

"You guys coming back?" Dorothy asked, tilting her head in surprise.

"Just a figure of speech," John said. "Too many places to visit, not enough time. But, honestly, I would love to come back to Budapest. The more I see, I learn there is more to see. And as Sally said, more to listen to."

"Wonder what the Boss would sound like here?" Frank said.

"The Boss?" Sally asked.

"Springsteen. I know you've heard of him. A Jersey boy. Asbury Park."

"Of course, I've heard of Springsteen," Sally said. "John and I have been to several of his concerts."

"Being the sensitive musician that he is, I doubt if he'd play here," John said. "Maybe an acoustic set for charity. Like Bono."

"That'd be really cool," Frank said. "I'd come back for that. Who's Bono?"

"Lead singer of U2. I would hope you've heard of them. An Irish band."

"Yeah, they're cool, too. But not as cool as the Boss."

"Why are we having this stupid conversation?" Dorothy swirled her forefingers by her ears. "This is ridiculous."

"Just speculating," John said. "Nothing wrong with that. Procol Harum has performed in churches."

"Who?" Frank asked.

"Never mind."

"The mummified hand of St. Stephen was interesting," Sally said.

"I thought it was creepy," Dorothy said. "Why would they do something like that?"

"I read where it has some kind of miraculous qualities," Sally said. "At least that's what Hungarians thought a thousand years ago. I think it's more of a curiosity now. You also learn more about the culture."

Dorothy shrugged. "I suppose so. I still think it's creepy."

"I still think it'd be cool if the Boss was here."

"Oh, shut up, Frankie! Who rang your bell?"

"Speaking of bells, the bell towers are impressive," John said. "The largest bell in Hungary is housed in one of them."

"You think it's as big as the Liberty Bell?" Frank asked.

"It weighs nine tons so it might be a tad bigger."

"That's one big ass bell."

"You could say that."

John pointed to the front entrance of the building where the South Carolinians posed with rare smiles as Pauline took their photo. It turned into several photos as the sisters each handed her smartphones. She turned and headed toward bus in the parking lot.

"I bet she appreciated being asked to do that," John said to Sally. "Isn't that supposed to be a no-no?"

"That's what I've read," Sally said. "Considered rude by most guides. I can't say I don't blame them."

"We need to get a selfie of all of us here," Dorothy said. "Maybe Pauline will take one of us, too."

"I don't think so," John said.

"Why not?" Dorothy said. "She did it for them."

"Because we're not going to ask her," Sally said.

"Oh, she won't mind doing it," Frank said. "She did several of Dorothy and me."

"Because she's a nice person," John said.

"It's not that big of a deal to ask her."

"It is to me and Sally," John said, firmly.

"You guys can be so fuddy-duddy at times," Dorothy pushed out her lower lip.

John spotted Tyrone leaving the church with several others in their group and waved both arms to get his attention.

"Hey Ty," he shouted. "Can I get you to do a favor?"

Tyrone jogged over to them. "What do you need?"

"Would you mind taking a photo of us," John said, glancing at Sally, Frank and Dorothy.

"No problem." He took John's camera.

After snapping several photos, Dorothy handed him her smartphone. "One for us, too."

"Any more?"

John handed his camera to Frank. "Mind taking one of Sally, Ty and me?"

After Frank clicked a couple images, Ty trotted back to the group he was with touring the church.

"That was sure interesting," Frank said. "You don't want Pauline to take photos, but you ask the black guy to do it."

"Get real." John turned and walked toward the building, then stopped and faced Frank. "For your information, we didn't ask her because she's our guide, not our personal photographer. It's a matter of respect. She's got enough to do without snapping photos of everyone. And furthermore, I'm sure she would have done it because she's a nice person. But Sally and I don't want to take advantage of that. Understand?"

Frank backed off a few steps, holding out his palms. "Well, excuse me. I didn't know it was that fuckin' important to you. You need to chill out, man."

"Just letting you know how I feel. Sorry if I offended you."

"Well, I think—"

"Just be quiet, Frankie," Dorothy said. "John is right."

"But—"

"Frankie!"

They paraded around the massive structure, John leading the way and no one uttering a sound, except for Frank's heavy breathing when they were about finished. They boarded the bus to return to the hotel. It was an open afternoon to do as they please.

"What's on our schedule now?" Dorothy asked Sally.

"I really need to do some packing," Sally said. "We leave early in the morning and I've done hardly anything to get ready."

"We thought we'd go to see those communist statues," Frank said. "That should be fun."

"Everything's not fun," Dorothy slapped his arm. "I wish you'd quit saying that. It's embarrassing. Can't you ever be serious?"

"It's a vacation so we should be having fun," Frank said, his arms crossed over his chest.

"Oh, you don't understand. You never had much culture."

"There you go again," Frank said, a vein popping out in his neck. "Just because you were a beautician doesn't mean you understand culture. You only know how to fool with your fake hair."

"Frankie, you better watch what you say if you know what's good for you." Dorothy's face turned a glowing red.

"We've been doing the same things for over forty years so I have as much culture as you do."

"Frankie, I'm warning you!"

"You folks want to get a bite to eat when we get back to the hotel?" John asked, breaking his silence.

Dorothy glared at Frank for a moment before turning toward John with a flip grin spread across her mouth. "That'd be nice, John."

"Yeah, I'm starting to get hungry," Frank said to John. "I hope you're still not mad at me."

"Frank, I was just letting you know how I felt. I apologize if I offended you and Dorothy. It came out a little stronger than I intended."

"That's cool. I accept it."

"Frankie, you need to apologize, too," Dorothy said, giving him a slight shove with her shoulder.

"Uh, yeah man," Frank said. "Sorry, buddy."

As they stepped off the bus, Sally noticed Phil and Edna standing near the entrance to the hotel, hand signing and pointing down the street.

"Why don't you join us for lunch," Sally asked, moving her hand as if using an eating utensil toward her mouth.

They nodded and walked side-by-side with Sally while John led the way with Frank and Dorothy a step behind on each side.

"I was kind of hoping it would just be the four of us," Dorothy said. "It *is* our last day."

"We've spent some time with the Graybars and become friends." John looked straight ahead.

"When?"

"A few days ago. Mr. Graybar also loaned me a camera after we got here."

"We had a camera you could have used," Frank said. "You shoulda asked."

"Thanks, but I didn't know you at the time."

John entered Alexandra Bookcafé, located in a building which once housed a high-end department store. Elegant chandeliers graced a fresco-style ceiling adorned with paintings by Károly Lotz.

"Kinda ritzy," Frank said as they walked up the stairs to the dining area. "No McDonald's near here?"

"There you go again, Frankie," Dorothy said. "Just be quiet."

Phil and Edna drifted to a corner of the room and studied the artistic surroundings in more detail.

"What do they think they're doing?" Dorothy asked Sally as they followed a young waiter to a table.

"Edna's a painter, a watercolorist," Sally said. "She has a keen interest in art."

"Oh," Dorothy said. "I would've never guessed."

Phil and Edna joined them after several minutes and they ordered gourmet sandwiches and cappuccinos.

"How did find out about this joint?" Frank asked.

"Pauline recommended it as a place to stop on a free day," John said. "She has good tastes."

"Part of being a good guide," Sally said.

"Even if she doesn't like taking photos," Frank said.

"Now hold on, Frank," John said. "I didn't say she didn't like taking photos."

"Sure sounded that way to me."

"We simply said that some people consider it rude to ask a guide to do it. It's taking advantage of them."

"Must be nice."

"Frankie, would you just drop it?" Dorothy said. "Let's just eat. A little peace and quiet. I'm sure Mr. and Mrs. Graybar don't want to listen to your gibberish." She looked at them. "Right?"

The Graybars looked at each other for a moment before breaking out in small laughs.

"Oh, I'm sorry," Dorothy said, turning red-faced.

"That's okay," Phil mouthed. "We thought it funny, too."

They ate in silence for the most part. John figured it was because of Phil and Edna, since Dorothy usually had something to say regardless of the time and place. At least it quelled the tension between the Finsterwalds. And himself.

They had pastries and hot chocolate for dessert before going downstairs to browse the book section. Phil and Edna decided to stay longer and told John they would return to the hotel later.

"Let's do a little window shopping before we go back," Sally said. "I need to walk off that dessert."

"Me, too." Dorothy took Sally by the arm and walked ahead of the men. "Now that's my kind of culture."

"We're serious about you guys coming to our place," Frank said, shuffling next to John. "I know you're probably still a little pissed at me but we've got plenty of room. It'd be no problem."

"Like we said, we'll let you know," John said. "We have a few things going on back home that we need to take care of. We can't just pack up and leave. And I'm not pissed off at you. Okay?"

"You packed up and left for this trip."

"It was a retirement gift from my children. But the truth is, we had to cut it short. Too much going on."

"Anything in particular?"

"Just some personal things. I don't want to bore you with them."

"That's cool," Frank said. "I'd really like for you to see my gun collection."

"Gun collection?"

"Yeah, I've been picking up pistols for quite a few years at flea markets and from private parties. It's been my hobby for a long time."

"I can't say I'm really into guns but I'm sure it's an interesting hobby."

"You're not one of those gun-control loonies, are you?"

"I don't consider myself a loony, although that's probably open to debate." John chuckled. "But I do think we need some limits. Don't you?"

"It's a god-given right in the constitution to bear arms."

"God-given?"

"We're a Christian nation, so it has to be god-given."

"Much of a sports fan? Figured you might like the Giants, Knicks, Yankees or Mets."

Frank snickered. "Changing the subject, old man?"

"Do we need to get in a political discussion before we leave?" John said. "I don't think this is the time nor the place."

"Touché."

"Huh?"

"Surprised ya, didn't I?" Frank let out a whopping laugh. "You didn't know I knew some French."

"Funny."

When they arrived at the hotel, John went to the restroom off the lobby while the others proceeded to the elevator. "See you folks later."

They were nowhere to be seen when he came out until he felt a tug on his elbow. Turning around, it was Sally. They walked to the lounge area near the front desk, and sat.

"I told them I had to buy toothpaste," she said. "They went on to their room."

"They didn't offer to let us use theirs?"

"You know they did. I didn't think you'd want to know the details."

"You're right. I should have known."

"Dorothy asked me to call if we want to do something later on."

"Doesn't surprise me. What did you tell her?"

"I said we'd probably be too busy getting our stuff together."

"Good answer."

"You were kind hard on Frank back at St. Stephen's," Sally said. "I haven't seen you that upset since, well, talking to Brody."

John stroked his beard. "I was wondering when you would bring it up."

"He can be irritating. Well, to be honest, both of them."

"That's why I unloaded on him. I regretted it after I said it, but I must admit it made me feel a little better. Sometimes I get tired of bullshit."

"I think there was more to it than that."

"There was," John said. "I didn't appreciate the insinuation about asking Tyrone to take the photos. I thought it was uncalled for."

"Maybe Frank will think twice before he says something like that again."

"I'm not counting on it."

"Now let's go to the room before they show up."

"And pack."

"And nap."

Sixteen

John opened his travel pouch and took the ED pill bottle and held it high for Sally to see. "Since this is our last night here, think you'll be in the mood?"

She winked. "Always for you, babe."

He removed a pill and put it in his shirt pocket to take with their meal before returning to the hotel. Maybe he should save it for dessert, he thought, smiling to himself.

"Think I should call Dorothy and invite them to dinner with us?" Sally asked.

"Are you serious?"

"It's our last night."

"And that's the point. Our last night. Together."

"Let's get going then."

They entered a quaint café several blocks from the hotel and sat at a table in the rear. Besides a degree of privacy in the darkened, if somewhat romantic space, it provided a wide view of those coming and going on the street from the large filmy front windows. They ordered Dreher drafts and studied the menu.

"I don't think I could make it more than another day," John said. "These vacations can wear a person out."

"Because of Frank and Dorothy?"

"They're a big factor but trying to take in as much as you can. It takes a lot of time and energy. There's so much to see. I sorta feel rushed at times. And I'm not as young as I used to be."

"We still did pretty well," Sally said. "For older folks."

"This may sound crazy, but I can barely remember what we did the first few days. Everything seems to run together. It's kind of a blur."

"I know exactly what you mean. I hope you took enough photos so we can relive and remember everything."

"It's funny that you say that," John said. "I probably didn't take as many as I thought I would. I got too busy sightseeing. I hope you don't mind."

"We have our memories. That's what's important."

"Think we should buy a few more postcards or a picture book about Budapest?"

"It's up to you," she said. "We always have the Internet."

"Yeah, but it's not the same."

"Why not? Remember Humphrey Bogart and Ingrid Bergman in *Casablanca*? They always had Paris. We'll always have Budapest."

He placed a hand over hers. "I like that."

"Me, too."

"I may need a vacation to recover from this one."

"Well, we can always go to Jersey."

"Ha, ha," John pointed a forefinger at her. "That's not funny."

"A little of Frank and Dorothy runs a long way," she said. "Kind of smothering."

"Maybe we're just too private. We've never been much into socializing for various and sundry reasons."

"I know what you mean. Outside a few work-related functions, we've pretty much stayed to ourselves."

"I don't know what it is but I have trouble warming up to people I just meet. I always sense an ulterior motive, like they want something in return. It's probably something from my newspaper days, certain people getting friendly with me for news coverage. It happened all the time. About the only people I felt comfortable around were those at the paper. And still, there were limits on some folks."

"I felt that way to some extent while I was teaching. Teachers could confide in each other and share experiences. But there were nosy busybodies as well."

"Makes me wonder if it's not that way with every profession."

"Probably so."

When the waitress returned to take their order, John stared big-eyed at the front window: The Finsterwalds. "Oh, shit."

"What is it?" Sally asked.

"Frank and Dorothy."

The Finstewalds wandered in front of the restaurant, stopping for a few seconds and turning their heads in different directions like hunters looking for game. And John and Sally were the likely prey.

"Turn and cover your face with the menu." John lowered his head. The waitress did what he asked. Sally giggled, spraying a mist of beer across the table.

John glanced at the woman and shook his head, biting his lower lip. "I'm sorry. I don't mean you. There's someone outside we didn't want to see us."

The woman, her puffy cheeks a glowing red, raised her head. "I'll be back in few minutes." She marched away in a huff, shaking her head. John wondered what she thought of these crazy Americans. Sally tried to stifle giggles, placing her hand over her mouth.

The Finsterwalds meandered past the window and out of sight. John rose from his chair and dashed to the entrance, peeking out the door to see if they were continuing down the avenue. He saw Frank standing tall in the crowd, his head moving like a radar dish. Dorothy was nowhere to be seen, even in her bold red-and-white fitness attire.

"I think the coast is clear." John walked back to the table with a broad grin. The waitress returned, this time taking their orders for goulash and another beer for John.

Soothing Hungarian string melodies played in the background as they sipped their beers. They relished the tranquil atmosphere and quiet time, knowing that they'd be back in the U.S. in twenty-four hours. And Budapest would be a far-off memory.

Then a loud, high-pitched voice came out of nowhere with a distinctive New Jersey accent. "There you guys are!"

John froze in his chair; Sally stiffened like a statue. Diners at two other tables stared in disbelief. Even the waitress appeared stunned.by the noisy intrusion. Frank swaggered behind Dorothy, placing his huge hands on her shoulders.

John's head moved like an elfish bobble head with a silly grin. "What a surprise. Look who's here, Sally."

Sally snapped out of her stony stance with a clenched smile. "This is a surprise. Won't you join us? We only ordered a few minutes ago."

"Don't mind if we do, don't mind if we do." Frank took the nearest chair while Dorothy went to the opposite side of the table. The waitress took their drink orders, a tall mug of beer for Frank and red wine for Dorothy.

"This place is so romantic." Dorothy gazed at the rough cast pastel walls adorned with old black-and-white photographs in thick black frames. "I hope we didn't spoil any plans."

"We were out for a walk and just stumbled in here. It looked like a nice place to relax before that long journey back home," Sally said.

"That's what we were doing. We just happened to walk in here and see you guys."

"What a coincidence," John said, glancing at Sally.

"We all must think alike," Dorothy said.

"You may have a point," John said. "Oh well, it'll be a nice dinner before we go back home."

"Yep, we'll be back in those friendly skies before you know it," Frank said. "Heading back to the greatest country on Earth."

"We like to think of Kentucky as God's country," John said with an arched brow.

"God's country?" Frank asked. "Never heard that."

"Just a saying. Anyone can say it about their home state."

"Even their country?"

"Well, I suppose so," John said, squinting. "It's not to be taken seriously. Kind of a joke."

"But it's okay to say we're going back to God's country?"

"Please, Frankie," Dorothy said. "It's just an expression they use in Kentucky."

"Actually, I've heard it in other places," John said. "I was just making a funny."

"I kinda like God's country," Frank said. "It takes in all the states."

John let out a short breath. "Whatever." He looked pokerfaced at Sally. She was tight-lipped, holding back giggles.

"Are you okay?" Dorothy turned toward Sally.

Sally bolted from her seat. "Excuse me for a minute. I really need to go to the restroom."

"She must have been holding it in for a while," Frank said. "I get shaky when I do that."

"Beer does that to her," John said. "This is what happens when she has one."

"That's why I drink wine." Dorothy took a sip from her glass. "It smooths me out."

"Are you folks ready to head back to Jersey?" John asked.

"I suppose so," Frank said. "Unsure what we'll find once we get back."

"You'll see your children? Grandkids?"

"We have four grands," Dorothy said. "Three girls and one boy. Precious. I can't wait to hug them. I've missed them so much."

"And four children?" John said.

"We have three," Dorothy stammered. Frank took a big swallow from his large mug while looking over John's head at the wall.

Sally returned to the table, composed, and took a swallow of beer.

"Better be careful with that," Frank said.

"Honey, I hope you don't mind but I told them that beer kinda runs through you," John said.

"Oh, it does," Sally said. "Only one beer for me. I used to be called two-beer Sally when I was a lot younger, back in my college days. But just one-beer Sally now."

"Sad, but true." John dropped his head, avoiding eye contact with her.

"We were talking about our grandchildren while you were away," Dorothy said. "I told John that we have four."

"As I told you, we have a granddaughter," Sally said. "She's in kindergarten."

"Is she in a private school?' Frank asked.

"I don't believe so. Private schools are rather pricey in New York."

"It's worth it. Kids aren't exposed to all that riff-raff, if you know what I mean." Frank took a gulp of beer and wiped his mouth with the back of his hand.

"I'm not sure I know," John said. "Our children attended public schools and didn't seem to suffer any ill effects. I thought they received a good education. Wouldn't you say so, Sally?"

"Brody and Chloe received excellent educations," she said. "They also went to public universities. Brody got an accounting degree at the University of Kentucky and Chloe studied communications at Eastern Kentucky."

"You know, Sally was a school teacher." John studied Frank's doughy face. "Public school teacher."

"Didn't know that," Frank said. "Learn something new every day about you guys. But we're talking apples and oranges when comparing the school systems. You might say we're a lot more diverse in Jersey."

"I'm not so sure about that." Sally straightened in her seat. "We have quite a diverse population in Lexington. Not in the same numbers as from where you're from but still relative. It's important for children to interact with different ethnicities. It's part of learning."

Frank shook his head. "Whatever." He waved at the waitress for another beer.

"Frankie, let's change the subject," Dorothy said. "This is our last night so let's not go off on one of your tirades about minorities."

"Making a point, sweetie."

"You've made your point. Now let's talk about something else. And not politics."

"Okay, sweetie," he said. "If you don't want us to have an intelligent adult conversation, maybe we can discuss the latest news from your beloved garden club or some celebrity bullshit you watched on TV or read in a magazine."

John turned his head away from Frank. Sally rearranged the napkin on her lap.

"That's uncalled for, Frankie." Dorothy's mouth puckered. "You're making our friends uncomfortable as well as me. So please shut the fuck up. Now."

John and Sally made eye contact, took deep breaths, and lowered their heads.

"I wonder what's taking our order so long," John said to break the tension.

Frank sat tightlipped.

"It is taking a while," Sally said. "They move at a slower pace than what we're used to, even in Kentucky."

"And they haven't even taken our order," Dorothy said, her voice shifting from caustic to sweet.

"I don't believe I'm hungry." Frank pushed back in his chair and stood. "I'm going back to the hotel."

"Oh, Frankie." Dorothy rolled her eyes. "Quit being such an ass. Sit back down. You've been a pain ever since we were at that church. You'd hope that some of that religious stuff would rub off on you."

John and Sally sat stone-faced except for Sally's tapping her foot against his shoe.

The waitress appeared out of nowhere, standing between Frank and Dorothy, holding menus. Her restrained demeanor a giveaway that she heard part of the conversation.

Frank eased his chair back toward the table and took the menu. He held it for a few seconds. "I'll have what they're having," nodding toward John and Sally.

Dorothy smiled. "Me, too."

After a moment of chilled silence, Dorothy said, "What time is your flight tomorrow?'

"At nine," Sally said. "We have to get up early. Pauline said we need to be on the road to the airport by six. What time do you leave?"

Dorothy glanced at Frank. "At the same time. Right, Frankie?"

"You handle those things," Frank grunted. "Don't ask me."

Dorothy puffed her cheeks. "Wouldn't it be wonderful if we were on the same flight back home?"

Sally turned toward John, batting her eyelashes. "I guess it would be."

"That'd certainly top off the trip," John said.

"It would sure make the flight go faster if I had someone to talk to," Dorothy said. "If you haven't noticed, Frankie drops off to sleep at the tip of a hat."

Frank stared at her with narrowed eyes. "Ever wonder why?"

She gave him with a piercing look, opening her mouth for a moment before closing it when the waitress approached the table with John and Sally's meals. The server told the Finsterwalds their meals would be ready in a few minutes. Frank ordered another beer for himself and, after a prickly pause, another glass of wine for Dorothy.

"You guys go ahead and eat," Dorothy said. "It'll get cold if you wait for ours to arrive."

"We're in no hurry." Sally flashed quick grin.

"Have you enjoyed Budapest?" John turned toward Dorothy.

"It's a beautiful city. It was always on my bucket list of places to visit."

"It's very different from Kentucky."

"And Jersey," Frank raised his beer for another swallow. "Ain't nothing quite like it. Maybe Bayonne."

"Bayonne?" John asked.

"Frankie's trying to be funny," Dorothy said, her eyes narrowed. "Don't mind him."

"I've been to New Jersey several times," John said. "The farther you get away from New York, the nicer it is. I always liked Bergen and Maplewood."

"There's a reason they call it the 'Garden State.'" Dorothy said. "Unfortunately, we don't live in the garden part. We're in the weedy part. We're more down the shore. And you know what Hurricane Sandy did to the area a few years ago."

"I remember what you told me," John said. "A blessing."

"A blessing in disguise for us," Dorothy said. "But not so much for those people who lost their homes and belongings. I feel kinda bad about it."

"But shit happens," Frank said. "You take the good with the bad."

"I guess that's a good way to look at it," John said. "God works in mysterious ways, I suppose."

"Like sweetie said, we live in the weedy part of the state," Frank said. "It ain't pretty, but it's home."

"Every state has seedy areas," Sally said.

"We said weedy, not seedy," Frank said. "Ain't the same. Weedy places have all kinds of shit everywhere. Seedy is just a shitty place."

"I think I simply misunderstood the first time, thinking Dorothy said seedy instead of weedy," Sally said with a forced smile. "Thank you for the clarification."

"Now, Frankie, you shouldn't be telling them we live in an undesirable area," Dorothy said. "They won't want to come and visit us."

"Hell, we could visit them instead," Frank said, pointing his elbow toward John.

John took a bite of his food before realizing they were waiting for the Finsterwalds' meals to arrive. He set the fork next to the plate.

"Our home is always open to guests," Sally said. "Just let us know."

"But we're thinking about moving this year," John said.

"Out of Kentucky?" Dorothy asked.

"In Lexington," John said. "Or maybe a surrounding town. A smaller place. The place we have now is too large for the two of us and our dog."

"We want to downsize," Sally said. "You know what I mean? The house almost gets too large as you grow older. And too much to clean."

"We like our home," Frank said. "We have about four-thousand square feet. I never have a problem when I want to hide."

"Hide?" Dorothy said. "Then why are you always under my feet, asking me to do this and that? I'm the one who needs a place to hide. And I have to clean the place too. You sit on your ass and watch TV while I clean up after the kids and grandkids. Maybe we need to downsize."

John sensed another eruption at the table by their taut expressions.

"Excuse me for a second." John rose from his seat. "I need to find the men's room. The beer is beginning to fill my bladder. How about you, Frank?"

Frank shrugged. "You must be like your honey. Two-beer Johnny."

"Go with him," Dorothy commanded. "If you don't, you'll be up in the middle of the night having to pee. And I'd like to get one decent night's sleep before we leave tomorrow. Is that asking too much?"

Frank eased from his chair and followed John to the restroom. It had only one toilet, so John motioned Frank to go ahead and take care of his business. After several minutes Frank stepped out with a blissful look on his face. John dashed inside and unzipped in time to avoid a personal disaster. When he opened the door, Frank was back at the table, digging into his goulash.

"Couldn't wait for you, old buddy," Frank said. "By the way, you sounded like Niagara Falls in there."

"When you have to go, you have to go," John said as he picked up a fork.

"And you had to go. I hope we don't get any flood warnings."

"Oh, shut up, Frankie," Dorothy said, holding her glass of wine. "I don't see what's so funny about it. When nature calls, you have to answer. Right, John?"

"I couldn't agree more," John said, before taking another bite.

"You had to be there to appreciate it," Frank said. "He was pissing the night away."

"You're disgusting, Frankie." Dorothy scowled. "Let's eat. Isn't that why we're here?"

Frank puckered his mouth and lowered his head.

"Delicious dinner," Sally said. "I like Hungarian food."

Frank's head shot back up. "Are you serious?"

"Frankie!" Dorothy's brows narrowed.

"I was going to say it doesn't beat a Coney dog, Philly beefsteak, or a juicy American cheeseburger."

"Because you don't have class," Dorothy said.

"I'm joking, sugar pie."

"No, you're not. Now shut up so we can eat in peace and quiet."

John wriggled his brows at Sally. He decided to follow Dorothy's admonition to eat and be quiet...and hope for peace the remainder of the evening.

When the waitress asked if they wanted dessert, John looked at Sally. "I'm stuffed," she said, placing a hand on her stomach.

"Oh, come on, this is our last night," Dorothy said. "We all need to eat dessert. You can work it off when you get back home. Be sociable."

"Works for me," Frank said, his eyes lighting up.

"Dessert always works for you," Dorothy said in a vinegary whine.

"Why not," Sally said. "We only live once and may never get back to Budapest."

Dorothy asked the waitress what the house specialty was, which she didn't understand. "All is good," she replied.

They decided on a raspberry cream roulade—a rolled sponge cake with raspberry filling and topped with whipped cream.

Frank asked for another beer, but Dorothy terminated that order, raising her hands.

"You've had enough. Furthermore, I don't want to spend our last night taking you to the hospital. Right, John?"

John turned his head in her direction. "No, that wouldn't be fun on our last night."

After dessert, John reached into his shirt pocket and took the ED pill and popped it in his mouth with a swallow of water.

"Got plans for tonight, big guy?" Frank asked, with an exaggerated wink.

"Huh?" John's face flushed and grew warmer. He took another sip of water and avoided looking at the others.

"Looks like you'll be getting another dessert later on," Dorothy said with a devilish snicker.

Sally remained silent, pokerfaced. John could tell she was biting her tongue to keep from laughing. The dinner had turned into a comedy hour for her.

"That was my blood-pressure pill." John looked at the others with a blank face. "I take one each evening with my meal."

"If you say so, big guy," Frank said with an okay sign with his chubby fingers.

"Oh, leave John alone," Dorothy said, patting him on the shoulder. "It's sweet that they plan to have some romance on their last night. I bet it's more than what a lot of those old fogeys in our group will be doing."

Sally didn't come to his rescue, or at least change the course of the conversation. She sat glossy-eyed, staring at a far wall.

"Like those goofy bitches from South Carolina," Frank said.

"Watch your mouth, Frankie," Dorothy said.

"Well, they are."

"They're just kinda snobby."

"How about snobby bitches?"

"If they're bitches, then what are their husbands?" Dorothy asked. "Do you have something nasty to call them?"

"Assholes," Frank said. "Snobby assholes."

"They are a bit different," Sally said.

"They ticked me off the first morning," Frank said. "We went to the have breakfast and they had they fuckin' nerve to tell us we couldn't sit at their table."

"You, too?" John said.

"Hell, yes. I couldn't fuckin' believe it."

"It happened to others so don't feel you were singled out," Sally said.

"We just kept our distance from them," John said.

"And that's what we decided to do, too," Dorothy said. "We found you guys and wanted to spend time with you. So if it hadn't been for them, we might not be sitting here right now."

"I don't know what to say," Sally said.

"Oh, sweetie, you don't have to say a word. It was a blessing for all of us."

John let out a deep breath. "Indeed."

Dorothy crunched her face in a supercilious smile, flicked her brows at John and Sally, and took a sip of wine.

John sensed tension spreading through his body, creating a blood flow that was beginning to swell in his pants. He attempted to reverse the effects by taking short, deep breaths, but it was a futile attempt to stop the growing bulge. Frank and Dorothy stopped their arguing and stared at him, making him more uncomfortable. Sweat dotted his forehead. He sensed they detected the change in him, like a person turning into a werewolf, or a caterpillar, or worse yet, a giant penis.

"Are you guys about ready to head back to the hotel?" Dorothy asked. "I'm sure John must be getting a little anxious." She twisted her neck and smiled, making John more ill at ease.

Sally snapped out of her momentary trance, blinking her eyes several times. "I'm ready. You, John?"

"You folks go on. My leg has fallen asleep." He massaged his right thigh down to his knee, making it obvious to everyone with exaggerated strokes.

"We can wait," Dorothy said. "We're in no hurry."

"I get these cramps and they sometimes last a few minutes," he said. "Right, Sally? Doesn't it last for several minutes? Like I said, go ahead and I'll catch up with you."

"I'll wait here with you," Sally said.

John winced. "No, go on. My foot may start cramping too. You know how that is. I could fall on my rear end. Anyway, I want you to go on and call Brody and let him know about our travel plans."

"Are you sure?" Sally asked.

John leaned over and mouthed with his eyes open wide, "Leave."

"Why don't you gals go and I'll stay back with John," Frank said. "In case he has trouble walking. I can help him along. Okay?"

"There's no need for that, Frank," John said as he continued to knead his leg. "I'll be fine after a few minutes."

"Oh no, you won't," Dorothy said, pushing her chair back. "Sally and I will walk back to the hotel and Frankie will stay with you.

That's final. That's the least he can do after you spent time with us at the hospital."

John let out a short breath. "Okay."

"One more thing, Frankie," Dorothy said, pointing a finger at him. "You pick up the tab. This was our treat for everything you guys have done for us on this trip."

"Are you sure?" Frank said, a crease in his forehead.

"Frankie, you heard me." It sounded more like a warning.

Sally kissed John's cheek and grabbed her purse. "I'll see you in a bit, honey." She followed Dorothy, who was waiting for her at the door.

"How's the leg?" Frank asked. "Still cramping?"

John reached down further and massaged his calf. "Some."

"Mind if I get another beer?"

"Sure," John said with a pretend groan. "We have time."

"Care for one?"

John shook his head, deciding that mixing the pill and booze would be asking for more trouble.

The waitress brought over the Dreher, and Frank took a hefty swallow. "I used to take those pills."

"Blood pressure?"

"Come on, old buddy, I know what that pill was for. Lots of guys take 'em."

"How come you don't now? Don't need 'em?"

"I wish." Frank took another gulp and let out a belch that drew attention of several other diners.

"Health reasons?"

"Dorothy reasons. She lost interest in sex a few years ago. All the sudden, she cut me off. Said she didn't want to fuck anymore. Cold turkey, if you know what I mean."

"Sorry to hear that," John said. "Those things happen."

"At least your Sally still puts out."

John let out a light cough. "Er, yes."

"Do it often?"

"Enough."

Frank smacked his hand on the table. "I don't think I've ever had enough poontang."

"So you're doing without?"

"I take the matter in hand, if you know what I mean." Frank raised a thumb. "Gotta do whatcha gotta do."

John stroked his beard, taking a second to decide he didn't want to follow the course of the conversation. "About ready to head back to the hotel?"

"Let me settle up with that pretty gal." Frank glancing at the waitress. "Unless you want to."

"I need to go to the men's room for minute. Wait for me outside the restaurant. It shouldn't take long."

"Just don't piss another river like you did last time."

John stood, turned from Frank and readjusted his pants before going to the restroom. He peeked back at Frank chugging the rest of his beer and summoning the waitress with his hand.

When John stepped out of the restroom, he noticed Frank standing outside with his hands stuffed in his pockets. He half expected the waitstaff to grab him by the arm, but Frank apparently had picked up the tab.

What should have been a five-minute walk to the hotel took triple that time because of Frank's meandering gait after the beers. John wondered if Frank had chugged another beer while he was in the restroom. They rode the elevator together, with Frank getting off first.

"Thanks for dinner, Frank." John shook his hand. "We enjoyed it."

"I hope you enjoy dessert, old buddy."

"Huh?"

"When you get to the room," Frank said with a puckish grin and wink.

"Thanks." John forced a smile as the doors closed.

He heard Sally talking on the phone when he opened the door to the room. He tiptoed to the other side of the bed, slipped off his shoes and jacket, and sat in the chair. He closed his eyes.

From Sally's short responses—"Yes, Mother," No, Mother," and "Please, Mother,"—he knew the person on the other end.

When Sally replaced the handset, her exasperated appearance brought a teasing smirk to John's face. "Ready to go back home to Mother, dear?"

"Could we stay another week or two or three?" Sally plopped on the bed and slapped the mattress. "I was all ready to go but now I'm not so sure."

John touched her knee. "What's up with her this time?"

"Brody isn't home that much. Whiskers pooped in the hallway. She feels like a prisoner. And she can't wait to go back home."

John snickered. "So what you're telling me is nothing's changed?"

"And it seemed weird talking to her, like someone was in the room with her," she said. "Almost eerie, if that makes any sense."

"What do you mean?"

"I don't know." She raised her hands in frustration. "No television blaring in the background. No barking from Whiskers. Just her voice. Kinda strange."

"I suppose we'll find out what's going on when we get back."

"That's what bothers me." Sally raised herself up by her elbows. "I'm not sure I want to know. I don't think I'll be in the mood for any surprises."

"Did you have a pleasant walk with Dorothy after dinner?"

"She didn't say a whole lot other than being aggravated with Frank for how he acted today. Especially about schools. She apologized several times."

"It's funny how you can travel across the ocean to get away from things." John rubbed his temples. "And then you encounter folks like the Finsterwalds."

"Oh, Dorothy did say she hopes we have fun tonight."

"That was thoughtful of her," John said. "Frank did the same."

"Are you in a hurry?"

"No."

"Will it wear off?"

"It doesn't last forever, thank god. But I still feel alive and well in my pants at this very moment. Wanna see?"

"Would you quit acting silly? You sound like Frank."

"Now those are fightin' words, little lady." John raised a fist. "You just don't want me to smell like Frank."

"Mother kinda took me out of the mood."

"We don't have to," John said. "It's not a matter of life or death. At least, I hope it's not. Dr. Riley never mentioned that to me."

That brought a laugh from Sally.

"Would you mind if I call Chloe?"

"Of course not. Why should I?"

"I don't want to leave you frustrated."

"Honey, it's not that big of a deal right now."

"Is that a pun?"

"Huh," John tilted his head. "Oh! You're making a funny now."

"I couldn't resist."

"At least you have a sense of humor in your time of distress."

"You bring that out in me."

John eased beside her on the bed. She snuggled next to his shoulder.

"Regardless of what's happened on this trip, it's been exciting. I regret we couldn't travel more when we were younger. And I hope we get to see more places in the future."

"Even New Jersey?"

John poked Sally's side, causing her to flinch. "You're being funny again."

"I couldn't resist."

"I guess Frank and I are in the same boat tonight."

Sally looked at him and squinted. "What's that supposed to mean?"

"He confessed to me that he hasn't had sex in quite some time. Or, as Frank says, not getting any poontang."

"What brought that on?" Sally raised up on an elbow. "You discussed our sex life with him?"

"I couldn't help it," John said straight-faced. "After those beers, my mouth was a fountain of confessions. But to save face, I lied and told him it was your fault."

Sally punched him in the shoulder. "You didn't."

John howled and covered his face with his hands. "I wanted to make Frank feel better."

"You're teasing me!"

"Yep," John said, rolling on his side and facing her. "Had you going."

"I know you better than that, John Ross."

Without any prompting, they both began tossing their clothes to the foot of the bed. Before long, their bodies became entwined as one. They caressed, fondled, and kissed before reaching the pinnacle of their lovemaking.

"We forgot to shut the curtains," Sally whispered, resting her head on John's chest. "And the lights are still on."

"I guess we may have given someone a show tonight."

John climbed out of bed and turned off the overhead light. The curtains remained open as moonshine cast a velvety glow on Sally's delicate figure.

"We should stay here a few more days," Sally said. "In bed."

"That would be nice." John pecked her cheek.

"I hope we can do this again?"

"Return to Budapest? Make love?"

"Both."

Sally flitted out of bed and closed the curtains. "I need to do a few things before we leave in the morning."

"Damn, I forgot to look at the board downstairs to double-check on our departure to the airport," John said. "You take care of your stuff while I'm gone. And by the way, don't forget to give Chloe a call."

John slipped on his pants and shirt while Sally headed to the shower. He went to the lobby, where he saw Pauline writing notes on the poster board.

"We missed you at the departure dinner tonight," she said. "Did you forget?"

"Oh, my goodness." John smacked his forehead. "I apologize. That completely slipped our minds."

"I do hope you had a memorable evening."

"Quite frankly, we would have preferred being at your dinner. It was our loss."

"About ready to return home?' she asked.

"Yes and no," John said. "There are some things Sally and I need to take care of back in Kentucky but we're sure going to miss Budapest. This has been an unforgettable vacation for us. In many ways."

"Budapest is one of my favorite cities. I've lived in Europe my entire life, and each city has its own distinct charm. I never tire of seeing places again and again. There always seems to be something new or something I missed on previous trips."

"We do hope to return some day," John said. "We'd be fortunate to have you as a tour guide again."

"That's awfully sweet of you to say, Mr. Ross." A blush radiated across her oval face.

"I guess we'll see you around six in the morning," he said.

On his way to the elevator, John peeked in the dimly-lit bar to see if any of his fellow travelers were enjoying a final drink before hitting the proverbial road back home. He wished he hadn't. Frank sat at the far end of the bar, a solitary figure lifting a half-empty mug of beer.

"Hey there, Johnny boy!" Frank slurred. "Get any?"

John stuck his hands in his front pockets and sauntered toward Frank in the near-empty room. "Where's Dorothy?"

"Packing our luggage." Frank motioned for John to sit on the stool next to him. "She didn't want me under her feet. I obliged and came down here."

"Dorothy's doing the same."

Frank pointed at the large TV screen mounted on the wall at the corner of the bar. The channel was on CNN International. "That's one thing I haven't missed since being here."

"CNN?"

"Fuck no! You've got to be kidding me."

"I have no idea what you're talking about, Frank."

Frank finished his beer and raised his hand at the bartender for another one. "That liberal news bullshit. That's the only English-speaking station I could find here. You'd think that they'd have some real news here instead of that fake crap."

John glanced at his watch. "I need to get back to the room and give Sally a hand."

"Oh, don't rush off, old buddy," Frank said. "Let me order you a beer. Be sociable with a fellow traveler. It's our last night, pal."

"Thanks, but no thanks." John held his hands palms up. "It's getting late and we have a busy day tomorrow. Plus, I'm bushed. It's been a long day."

"Be a pussy then." Frank sneered. "Or do you want to get some more pussy."

John's legs bounced against the barstool brace. "I need to go."

"Be that way."

"I guess so." John eased off the stool. "It's getting late."

"We've enjoyed our time with you guys. You're not bad for hillbilly rednecks."

"I beg your pardon?" John felt his face flush.

"Hey, I'm kidding with you, old buddy."

John's neck tingled. "Kidding or not, that's considered rude from where I'm from."

"I didn't mean anything by it. You're too thin-skinned, old buddy."

"I don't think so," John took a step backward. "See you in the morning."

"Aw, come on, John," Frank said. "Don't leave. I need someone to talk to."

"You've already said enough. Good night."

John pressed his lips together and ignored Frank's pleas to return, including a faint "fuck you" as he left the room. Instead of waiting for the elevator, he took the stairs to his floor, taking two steps at a time.

~ * ~

With the phone cocked against her neck, Sally chatted while sorting clothes and travel items into open luggage on the bed, seemingly oblivious to John returning to the room. He sat in the chair, gathering bits and pieces from the conversation, that she had reached Chloe.

Sally, wearing a short pink nightshirt, put down the phone. "Nothing new with Chloe."

"That's good to hear," John said in weary voice.

Sally stopped her packing and turned toward him. "Everything okay?"

John, slumped in the chair, recounted the conversations with Pauline and Frank. Sally sat on his lap and kissed his forehead. "It'll be over tomorrow."

"And it won't come soon enough."

"Don't forget we're on the same flight."

John closed his eyes. "Thanks for reminding me."

"I know you've had your fill of him. Or should I say them. Me, too."

"I've really tried to keep my cool with him. It hasn't been easy."

"I know it hasn't but there's no reason to get your blood pressure up over them."

"I've had to bite my tongue several times," John said, shaking his head. "He ticks me off and seems to know what buttons to push. Like at the St. Stephen's and his remark about asking Tyrone to take our photos."

"Honey, you did say something to him about it."

"I know, but I still feel somewhat bad about it. I feel like I let him get the best of me."

"You didn't. I thought you handled it well."

"Thanks for saying that." John shrugged. "I don't want to come across as spineless or whatever. I just feel that if I lash back at him I'm stooping to his level, and it's not worth it, especially since we may not see them again. Hopefully."

"John, you've handled it very well." She kissed his cheek.

"Thanks for understanding."

"Ready for bed?"

"Whenever you are. Don't let me rush you."

"I think we're packed and ready to go." Sally pulled back the covers and climbed into bed. John undressed and snuggled beside her.

"There's one thing we forgot on this vacation," John said.

"Forgot?"

"Pauline said we missed the departure dinner."

"Oh," Sally said with a long face. "I hate that. I wanted to say goodbye to some of the people. We may not see them in the morning."

John knitted his brows as he shook his head. "All the folks we met, like Ty and the Wilsons, Flynns, Bannisters and others and we end up with a farewell meal with the Finsterwalds. It figures."

"Flynns? You mean the Chens."

"Yeah, the Chens. George and Lei. Right?"

"Yes, dear."

"At least I was half right," he said with a loopy grin.

"Maybe we can get emails from Pauline and send them notes after we get back."

"Let's don't forget to ask her."

"There's one thing I've really enjoyed about this vacation."

"What's that?' Sally asked, her head resting on his shoulder.

"Probably sounds a little corny, well, it is corny, but we've been able to rediscover each other while discovering another part of the world. We need this time by ourselves, so to speak, to reconnect with each other. We've been pulled in so many ways the past year or so that we lost some of our intimacy. I don't think we've been taking each other for granted, but maybe we've been doing things out of habit."

"I know what you mean." Sally wrapped an arm across his chest and squeezed. "We were empty-nesters for so long and then everything seemed to happen at home. I'm glad we've found some time to talk about things, even with all the distractions."

"Let's really try to make time for each other when we get back home. Maybe some short trips. Or even long walks."

"That may be difficult with Mother and Brody."

"Probably so, but we need to make sure we have some time to ourselves. I think it's important. Okay?"

"Yes, honey."

John lowered his head and they kissed.

"Love you."

"Love you, too."

Seventeen

The hotel provided pastries, fruit, coffee, and tea for the early departures since the dining room was closed. Sally followed John to a table in the corner, obscured by a large planter. Half of the overhead lights were on, casting a milky glow throughout the room. They drank their coffee in silence, as did most of the other travelers. Everyone appeared a bit worn out and sleepy-eyed but prepared for the long trip to their homes.

"Wouldn't it be nice if the Finsterwalds overslept and missed the flight?" John said as he buttered a croissant.

"Now that's not nice." Sally creased her nose. "For all their faults, they've tried to be pleasant."

"I'm being selfish, but he pissed me off last night. I don't know who in the world he thought he was speaking to. He hardly knows me. To be honest, he's somewhat of a mean drunk."

"Now calm down, John," Sally said in a soothing voice. "We discussed this last night."

"Thanks for reminding me."

Moments later, Frank burst through the doorway flapping his arms like an aroused rooster, breaking the predawn quiet saturating the room. "Coffee! I need coffee!"

Several travelers chortled, then resumed their light breakfast. John maneuvered his chair to keep out of Frank's view, imagining his annoying acquaintance surveying the room to find him. He stared at Sally in stony stillness.

"There you guys are!" Frank walked toward them, wearing baggy khakis and a garish loose-fitting orange sweatshirt with Mets emblazoned across the front. "For a moment, I could swear that you guys were hiding."

"Now why would we do that?" John said, raising his cup. "Have a seat and join us. We're only getting caffeinated for the long day."

Frank pulled out a chair. "Don't mind if I do."

"Where's Dorothy," Sally asked.

"She still back in the room, fixing her pretty face," Frank said. "You know her. She has to look perfect in public. As for me, I could care less."

"I see," John said, bringing the coffee cup up to his mouth.

Frank rose without saying a word and went to the pastry tray. He returned with a plate stacked with a variety of squishy sweets and a handful of napkins. John and Sally watched as he carefully wrapped five pastries in napkins and deposited them in his carry-on bag.

"Goodies for later on," Frank said. "Have you seen how expensive food is at the airports? And what they give you on the airplane isn't enough to satisfy a piss ant."

"Never thought about that," John said. "But I'm not much into sweets."

"Hey, buddy, I'll be taking a few of those fruits over there with me as well." Frank nodded toward the fruit platter. "Keeps me regular."

Dorothy arrived in a lavender jumpsuit and sequined purple athletic shoes as Sally poured coffee from one of the dispensers. Dorothy got herself a cup and followed Sally to the table.

"Did you guys sleep well last night?" Dorothy asked. "I didn't. I get restless before big days."

"Oh, I'm sure they slept fine." Frank slapped John's shoulder. "Right, old buddy?"

John sensed a light bump against his foot and glanced at Sally. "Like a baby."

"Must be nice," Dorothy said. "Besides tossing and turning, I get to listen to Frankie serenade me with his snoring most of the night. I can't wait to get back home and get in my own bed."

"Something to look forward to," Sally said. "I prefer sleeping in my bed as well."

"You guys have separate beds, too?" Frank asked. "We haven't slept together in several years."

"Frankie!" Dorothy said, giving him a dirty look. "That's nobody's damn business."

"We sleep in the same bed," Sally said. "I was saying that I like sleeping in the bed back home. I suppose I should have said our bed." She placed a hand over John's.

"Maybe that's the reason I haven't slept that well," Frank turned his gaze to Dorothy. "Having to sleep with you the past week or so."

"You should have asked for double beds," John said.

"Now you tell me."

Doretta, Loretta, Moretta and Noretta made their grand entrance, their husbands lagging, pulling their oversized luggage on two carts. The women pushed two tables together in the nearly empty room and waited for their spouses.

"I'm not going to miss them," Dorothy said to Sally, holding a hand over her mouth.

"Did you see the Graybars after we left the restaurant yesterday?" John asked Sally.

Sally frowned. "No, and I guess they're not flying out this morning. I wanted to say goodbye to them."

"At least we have Phil's business card. We can send them an email later."

"Maybe we can go to Indianapolis and visit them." Sally's eyes brightened. "That'd be a nice overnight trip."

"Not until you guys come to Jersey," Dorothy said, raising her forefinger.

"Yeah, we've got first dibs," Frank said. "You guys better remember that."

"How can we forget?" John said.

Pauline entered the room and announced that the bus would depart for the airport in ten minutes.

"I got pastries to take with us," Frank said to Dorothy. "I'll grab some fruit on the way out."

"No oranges," Dorothy said. "They're too messy."

"You guys better get something," Frank said, pushed himself up from the chair. "It's a long flight."

"We'll pass," John said. "We prefer traveling on a light stomach."

"Suit yourself." Frank walked to the breakfast spread while Dorothy went to the lobby to make sure their luggage was loaded on the bus.

John glanced at his watch. "We've got a couple more minutes."

"We learn something new about them every time we talk," Sally said. "Even things I don't care to know."

"I hear ya," John said. "And like Frank said, it's going to be a long flight."

Sally leaned over, placed a hand over her mouth, and whispered. "Are you going to take some items from over there?"

"No, honey." John chuckled. "It's going to be a long flight because they're on the same plane."

~ * ~

At the appointed time for departure, Noretta dashed outside the hotel entrance and lit a cigarette, taking deep drags as travelers lugged their luggage to the rear of the bus for loading. Moretta stood on the opposite side of her sister in a drab gray sweatshirt and pants, arms outstretched doing knee bends, arms outstretched.

Frank and Dorothy took the first seats on the right side of the bus, behind Andras, the driver. John heard his sonorous voice giving a "good morning" to each passenger as they boarded the small transit vehicle. The Carolina contingent ignored him. Dorothy held a small mirror, smiling at herself from different angles.

John and Sally sat midway, holding hands as the bus whisked past other vehicles in light traffic to the airport. Subdued conversation wafted in the dark cabin as passengers gazed out the windows, catching a final glimpse of the illuminated Buda Castle in the fading distance.

"I do want to return someday." Sally's eyes were moist. "This place really grows on you, for some reason. I can't explain it."

John squeezed her hand. "I'd like to come back as well. Just the two of us. We know the city rather well, so we could probably get around on our own. Don't cha think?"

"Maybe," she said.

"Maybe? What do you mean?"

"Remember when we walked back from the castle? I seem to remember someone getting lost along the way."

"We'll use a map next time."

"Whether we return or not, we still have our memories."

John snickered. "Both good and bad."

"People tend to forget the bad things over time. And the bad on this trip wasn't completely bad. Just different and unpredictable."

"I agree," John said. "Bad like a pain in the ass. But never a dull moment."

The bus parked outside the main terminal. After retrieving their belongings from the back of the vehicle, Pauline directed the passengers toward the airline check-in desks. She received several hugs as they handed her small, white envelopes with monetary tips.

"You made our trip special," Sally said, hugging her. "Thank you so much."

"I try my best," Pauline said. "I do hope you return someday."

John shook her hand. "Safe travels."

"I almost forgot, but did you get the emails of everyone?" Sally asked.

Pauline pulled out a sheet from her clipboard and handed it to her. "Some people didn't give me their email addresses."

Sally glanced over the list, noticing blank spaces from the South Carolinians. "Doesn't surprise me."

"I got the same reaction from a few others."

John wasn't paying much attention but assumed Frank had given Pauline a tip as well. But it reminded him that he still had an envelope for Andras and hurried over and gave it to him.

The 'etta sisters gave her envelopes but made one last request. Doretta handed Pauline a camera for a group photo, standing in front of their stacked luggage with glowing grins, before entering the terminal. Pauline's genial smile quickly faded as she headed back to the bus.

"Pauline's got a long day ahead of her," John said.

"Why's that?" Sally asked.

"She'd mentioned in the lobby before we left that she has to bring five others here at noon and the remainder of the group around four. She won't be able to return home to England until tomorrow morning."

"She's been worth every penny we've spent on this trip and more."

"You mean forint?"

Sally crinkled her nose. "You know what I mean, John Ross. Quit being a smarty."

~ * ~

Boarding the plane, John nudged Sally when he noticed their seats about ten rows behind the Finsterwalds. They slipped past them without hearing any unsolicited comments. Frank munched on a crumbling pastry from his carry-on bag as Dorothy grumbled about a missing item as she sifted through her oversized purse.

Several bounces and bumps along the way to Amsterdam resulted in some passengers clutching armrests. A few minutes later, John glanced up the aisle when saw two stewards rushing to Frank and Dorothy. Moments later, they guided Frank, hunched over and clutching the back of each seat, to the lavatory.

John nudged Sally, unaware of the commotion as she flipped pages in a flight magazine.

"What?" she asked.

"Something's going on with Frank," John said.

"I hope it's not a heart issue." Sally stuffed the magazine in the seat pouch in front of her and raised her head to see what was going on.

John stepped into the aisle. "I'll go ask Dorothy."

John found Dorothy staring out the window when he tapped her shoulder, causing her to recoil. Expecting her to be upset, her eyes flared with anger.

"What's up with Frank?" he asked, leaning toward her. "Anything serious?'

"Better watch where you put your hands." Her jaw jutted.

"Huh?"

Dorothy pointed to splotches of yellow vomit on Frank's seat and the back of the seat in front of him. "Frankie got sick."

"Airsickness?"

"You could say that." Dorothy pressed her lips together for a few seconds. "And those damn pastries he got at the hotel. He couldn't eat one. He couldn't eat two. He ate three. So, yes it might have been from the flight. But more likely, it's from being a damn pig. And now I've got to sit here and smell this puke."

"Can I do anything?"

"I wish you could get me in another seat but that's not possible. There's not a vacant seat on the flight." Her face turned a bright red. "A stewardess said she'd be back and wipe up the damn mess. I wish she'd hurry because it's making me sick just looking at it and smelling it. But thanks anyway."

John noticed Frank step out of the restroom, wet spots on his sweatshirt and pants where he'd patted off the pastry spew.

"He's on his way back," John said. "Let us know if you need anything. We're a few seats back."

"Oh, you can do one thing." Her eyes glared like lasers.

"What's that?"

"Take Frankie with you."

John popped a grin, then hurried to his seat to avoid speaking to Frank lumbering down the aisle.

"Is he okay?" Sally said as he refastened his seat belt.

"Too many sweets," John said. "And Dorothy wasn't one of them."

"What do you mean?"

"Frank got sick on the pastries from the hotel and threw up all over the place. She's not a happy camper."

"Poor Frank."

"And poor Dorothy."

Several minutes later, the stewards rolled a coffee and snack cart down the aisle. John watched as it stopped next to Frank's seat. Everyone within earshot heard Dorothy's shrill voice, "Oh, no you don't Frankie. You're not getting sick on me again!"

Frank leaned to his left and raised his hands over his head; Dorothy turned sideways and flailed her arms at him. The stewards stood speechless at the encounter. The cockpit door opened moments later, and a crewmember dashed toward the altercation. English-speaking passengers sat in stunned silence as the Hungarian words spewed from his mouth. Scattered snickers came from the Hungarians seated near the feuding couple.

"Yeah, poor Frank," John mumbled.

~ * ~

The layover in Amsterdam lasted two uneventful hours, from stepping single file through security to sitting in the lounge before boarding the sleek jetliner for the eight-hour flight across the Atlantic. Dorothy refused to speak to Frank, using John and Sally as buffers throughout the airport. In the boarding area, John and Sally sat in the middle, with Dorothy next to Sally and Frank next to John. The Finsterwalds were so put out with each other they had little or nothing to say to anyone. For John and Sally, that was a silver lining around the storm clouds.

John went to the men's room, and Frank tagged along. They did their business and walked over to a window for a view of the tarmac.

"You feeling better?" John asked.

Frank shrugged. "Could be better, but what the hell? She can be such a bitch at times. But she'll get over it. She always does."

"I think we're all tired. We've had a busy ten days or so. It'll be nice to be back home."

"You got that right, old buddy."

After they returned to their seats, Sally walked to a snack bar with Dorothy to purchase a bottle of water. John cringed when Frank removed a pilfered pastry from his carry-on and devoured it in three bites before they returned.

A sense of relief flowed over John when the boarding announcement came over the speakers. Looking at Sally, he knew she felt elated as well.

The Finsterwalds asked to be moved to the same row as John and Sally but a steward told them to stay put until after takeoff. Any changes depended on two other passengers willing to switch places. John wanted as much distance as possible from the feuding Finsterwalds. And it was reinforced after witnessing Frank gobble the pastry in the waiting area.

As luck would have it for the Finsterwalds, a young couple next to John and Sally agreed to change seats. John stiffened as Frank moved to the aisle seat and Dorothy sat next to him.

As John raised in his seat to switch places with Sally, Dorothy tugged his shirtsleeve. "You stay here, John. I haven't had much time to talk to you."

John turned Sally as if to seek her approval, then back at Dorothy. "Are you sure? You know I'm not much of a conversationalist."

"I'm going to watch one of the movies," Sally said. "I haven't seen any of them. Spend some quality time with Dorothy."

John turned to Sally and mouthed: "Thanks a lot."

Sally placed two fingers over her lips, then over his, and then began scrolling the list of movies on the tiny screen.

"I may do that, too," John said as he clicked on the screen.

"You can wait on that, John." Dorothy brushed her hair back with her hand. "It's a long flight. There's a lot we can talk about."

John leaned forward and observed Frank furtively retrieve a large chocolate-glazed pastry wrapped in a napkin from his carry-on. With Dorothy's head turned toward John, he must have figured it was safe maneuver. But Dorothy must have noticed John's eye movement, or smelled the chocolate, and twisted around.

"Oh, no you don't, Frankie." Dorothy pushed Frank's guilty hand toward the carry-on. "I'm not going to have you puking again."

Several passengers turned their heads toward the Finsterwalds with bewildered expressions. Frank, his lips pinched, recovered the napkin over the mushy pastry and shoved it back in the bag like a shame-faced child.

"Have you thought I could be getting hungry?" Frank asked, bumping his knees into the seat in front of him while stowing the carry-on.

A petite white-haired woman craned her neck around the seat. "Excuse me!"

"Uh, sorry, ma'am," Frank said, the corners of his mouth curled downward. "Tight squeeze here."

"Just be more careful," the woman admonished. "You made me spill some of my tea."

"Again, sorry 'bout that. I'll be more careful."

The woman shook her head, tight-lipped, and turned back around.

"I hope you're satisfied," Dorothy said.

"But I'm hungry."

"You won't starve before the snack carts come around." Dorothy sounded more like a mother admonishing an unruly child. "And we'll have dinner here as well. So wait. Understand?"

Frank scowled for a moment, then pushed in the earplugs in the entertainment console. He clicked on the menu without saying a word.

Dorothy turned to John as if nothing had transpired. "What do you and your sweet wife like to do for fun?"

John took a dry swallow. "For fun? We don't do a lot of fun things, like you and Frank. You folks are the fun couple. We do more regular things like reading, going out to eat, being with friends. You could say we're kinda boring."

"I thought you had children."

"A son and daughter. Our daughter lives in New York and—"

"New York? Sally never mentioned that to me. How often do you visit her?"

"Not often," John said. "We have busy schedules."

"From what you said about you and Sally, it doesn't sound that busy."

"I just retired last year," John said. "We're still adjusting. But we stay in touch with her on a regular basis. She visited last Christmas. How about you and Frank? How long have you been in retirement?"

"He's been for about four years. I've never been. I've been a housewife all these years after I left the beauty business, raising four kids and you know who. And living with him, I'll never retire. Sometimes I'd go to the office and answer the phone. Frankie needs constant attention, which I'm sure you've noticed. Lord help me, it's a full-time job."

They glanced at Frank, hunched over, mouth partially open, and still clicking away at the entertainment options on the screen pad. They looked at Sally's screen showing a movie starring Tom Hanks.

"You need to do some things by yourself," John said. "Sally sometimes goes with her friends on trips."

"I could visit Kentucky." Her eyes brightened.

"I guess that'd be an option," he said. "I know there's a lot of places I'd like to travel to in your part of the country."

"When you visit us in Jersey, we'll take you to several sites," she said. "It'll be a lot of fun. I can't wait. We'll have so much fun."

John strained a smile. "That's something to look forward to."

John experienced a small measure of relief when the stewards showed up with the snack cart. Frank ordered two cocktails and drained them as though dying of thirst. Dorothy bought a Bloody Mary while John and Sally chose coffee.

The alcoholic drinks turned out to be a blessing. Frank dozed off within a few minutes, his double chin resting on his chest and letting out occasional snorts. Dorothy closed her eyes and tilted her head toward John's shoulder, drifting off to sleep. Sally was oblivious to anything going on as her eyes fixated on the tiny screen.

John inched closer to Sally, bumping his knee against hers twice to get her attention.

"Can we trade places?" he whispered.

She removed her right earplug. "What?"

He repeated his request and motioned his head at Dorothy. Sally put a hand over her mouth, shook her head, pushed back in her seat, and returned to watching the movie.

"Thanks a lot," he said to himself.

John eased his seat back a couple inches, not wanting to disturb the person behind him. He clasped Sally's open hand and closed his eyes. The next thing he knew, Dorothy nudged him in the side, holding a food tray to pass down to Sally.

Frank wolfed most of his food before the others opened their plasticware. "Let me know if you're not going to eat everything," he said, turning toward John and Sally. "I'm famished."

"Will do," John said. "But I must warn you that I'm a bit hungry myself."

"This stuff doesn't look that appetizing to me," Dorothy said as she picked at a small pasta salad. "You'd think they could provide better meals for the money we pay for tickets."

"Lots of passengers," John said. "I don't see how they manage to do what they do."

"You don't have very high standards."

"Don't forget, honey," Frank said. "They're from Kentucky."

John glared at Frank. "I beg your pardon?"

"Only kidding, old buddy," Frank said, holding up a hand. "You take things way too seriously."

"Maybe so," John said as he unwrapped a vegetarian lasagna.

"You have a lot of room to talk," Dorothy said, turning to Frank.

"I married you," Frank said with a beaming smile. "Doesn't that count for something?"

"For you," she said. "I'm not so sure about me."

Dorothy covered plastic sheets over the containers of the food she'd hardly touched.

"You're not throwing that away, are you?" Frank asked. "Can I at least have the chocolate cake?"

"No," she said. "You don't need it." She turned toward John and Sally. "How about you guys? Would you want it?"

"Thanks, but no thanks," John said while Sally shook her head and smiled. "It is a bit dry."

"See what I mean?" Dorothy said.

"Huh?"

"The food quality. It's not fit for anyone to eat except for Frankie."

"Oh."

Dorothy picked up the container and set it on Frank's tray. "Go ahead, honey, if it'll make you happy."

Frank unwrapped the container and consumed the small chocolate square in two bites.

Dorothy looked at John and Sally. "See, it doesn't take much to please him."

Eighteen

For the rest of the flight, Dorothy watched a movie, Frank snored, Sally read from her Kindle, and John listened to music. It ended with a smooth landing at Newark Liberty International Airport.

"Back in God's country," Frank said as the plane taxied to the terminal. "I love that phrase."

"It'll be nice to get our feet back on the ground," John said. "My legs feel crampy."

"You should've gotten up and walked during the flight," Sally said. "That's what health providers recommend."

"Thanks for telling me now." John stood on his tiptoes several times. "Anyway, it'd been too much trouble."

She looked at Frank and Dorothy. "You're probably right. Just remember to do it on the flight to Lexington."

"I've got a better idea," John said.

"No, John, we're not going to get a rental car and drive to Kentucky."

John held up a hand. "Let me finish, sweetheart."

"Go ahead. I'm listening."

"How about making a short trip to New York and visit Chloe, Whitney, and Sam?"

Sally's eyes sparkled.

"Oh, honey, are you serious? That'd be wonderful. She's been on my mind the entire trip."

"You guys are welcome to stay at our place," Dorothy said. "We're only forty-five minutes from the city."

John and Sally looked at each other with furrowed brows.

"Thanks for the offer, but we'll go on to Chloe's apartment," Sally said. "It'll be much easier."

"You've never mentioned Sam," Dorothy said.

"Oh, Sam's her partner."

After being corralled in security for half an hour, John and Sally made their way to claim their two pieces of baggage. The Finsterwalds were nowhere in sight, disappeared among the mass of humanity swarming in all directions.

They hustled to an airline representative about exchanging their tickets. Sally explained that it was for medical reasons. They gained quick approval. They learned later from the loudspeaker the flight to Lexington was overbooked. That was the likely clincher.

"Free at last," John said as they made their way in the congested exit ramp toward the bus terminal that would take them to the Port Authority in New York.

"Shouldn't we call first?" Sally asked. "Chloe may be at work or busy doing something. I don't want to drop in unannounced, especially since she's not feeling well."

"Never thought about that," John said. "My days and hours are all turned around. But you're right."

They sat on a bench as Sally rifled through her purse for her phone, taking longer than expected. John yanked out his phone from his coat pocket just as she found hers. She got Chloe's voice mail and left a brief message about their plans and that they were about to leave the airport. As they approached the ticket booth, they heard a familiar booming, jovial voice: "You guys look lost. Need a lift?"

"Oh, shit," John muttered. "They found us."

Frank and Dorothy stood off to the side, next to a cart loaded with their six pieces of luggage. They smiled like proud parents at a graduation party.

"You guys almost got away before we could say goodbye," Dorothy said, tilting her head. "And we haven't even exchanged emails and phone numbers for when you visit us later this year. Did you forget?"

John and Sally wandered toward them, weary looks on their faces like marathon runners.

"I apologize," John said. "We got so wrapped up in going through security and changing flights that we lost sight of you folks. Easy to do in this place."

Dorothy handed Sally a sheet of paper with their home address, email addresses, and phone numbers, then gave her a blank sheet and pen. "Write down your information," in what sounded more like a demand than a request.

"Can I email the info?" Sally asked as she glanced at her watch. "We're in kind of a hurry. Don't want to miss the next bus."

"I'd like to have it on paper," Dorothy said. "It's more permanent. We can transcribe it later to our cell phones and I can put it in my little file box."

"Don't worry about the damn buses," Frank said. "Hell, they leave about every ten minutes or so. You've got plenty of time."

Sally sat on a bench and began scribbling the information. John looked at his watch while tapping a foot on the glossy granite floor.

"Need to take a leak?" Frank asked.

"Huh?" John said.

"My feet do the happy dance when I have to take a leak."

"We'll stay here with Sally and watch your bags," Dorothy said.

"I saw a restroom little ways back there."

"I'll do that," John said of the opportunity for a brief break. "Don't leave without me."

Sally raised her brows. "Don't worry. I'll wait, honey."

The trip to the restroom took longer than expected as he had to wait in line at the urinal. Washing his hands was fast as most of the men opted out of cleanliness and hurried out the exit to their next destination. On his return, John saw Sally waving for him to hurry. He picked up his pace in the crowded corridor despite jet-lagged legs.

"Our bus leaves in two minutes," she said.

After they grabbed their luggage and were about to board the bus, Dorothy stopped them. "Aren't we going to get a hug?"

John and Sally dropped their baggage in unison and gave their unsolicited friends quick hugs.

The exchange included a kiss on Sally's cheek from Frank and Dorothy, an extended handshake between Frank and John, and a wet kiss from Dorothy to John.

Seconds later, John and Sally broke free and boarded the packed bus headed toward the Holland Tunnel.

"Is that lipstick on your mouth?" Sally asked.

"Don't ask." John ran the back of his hand over his mouth, leaving a red smear from his wrist to the middle knuckle. "Good grief."

"I knew I needed to watch her around you."

"At least it's not on my collar."

"You know, I heard that New Englanders don't like to hug," Sally said after they squeezed onto the bus. "It's more of a Southern thing."

"Are we in south Jersey?"

"Maybe it's their little rule with casual acquaintances?"

"What difference does it make now?"

"I just think it's curious."

"I'd just as soon forget about it."

They sat solemnly the rest of the way to the city, their luggage on the floor tucked between their legs. Coming out of the tunnel into Manhattan was like entering another world—the tall buildings, the bumper-to-bumper traffic, and the streets teeming with pedestrians.

They took an Uber from the Port Authority to Chloe's apartment. She lived on the second floor of a three-story brownstone on the lower west side in Manhattan. They buzzed her apartment several times, but no answer.

"That's about par for the course," John said, staring at the door. "Did she ever get back with you?"

"Why are you asking me that? I would have told you if she had."

"I suppose we'll have to wait on the steps until Chloe or Sam arrive," John shrugged. "At least we can rest our feet."

"And rest our nerves. I'm sorry for snapping at you. I'm just worn-out. From everything."

"We're both exhausted. I could use a nap. Wake me up if I fall asleep."

Sally pointed to a bench next to the street, under an oak tree. They gathered their belongings and sat in the shade, amid assorted bird droppings, and dog poo. They jerked when Sally's cell phone rang.

"I bet that's Chloe," John said.

Sally shook her head, frowning.

"Hi Brody." She clicked on the speaker phone.

"Where are you?"

"New York," Sally said. "We decided to spend a couple days with Chloe."

"Thanks for letting me know." They heard Brody let out an enormous sigh. "I thought you'd be at Blue Grass Airport by now."

"Since we landed in Newark, and so close, we thought we may as well pay her a short visit," Sally said. "Especially since she hasn't been feeling well. Have you talked to her?"

"Been too busy."

"We're outside her apartment now, waiting for her to come home."

"You didn't even let her know you were going to visit?"

"It was a spur-of-the-moment thing."

"I hope she's not too surprised. I know I wouldn't like it if someone dropped in on me with no notice."

"She can handle it," Sally said. "I'm not worried."

"Most children welcome their parents," John said, leaning toward the phone.

"Oh, hi Dad. Didn't realize you were eavesdropping."

"Hi son," John said dryly. "And I wasn't eavesdropping. We're on speaker phone. Okay?"

"When are you coming home? Grandma's still bugging the crap out of me. I wish I could go ahead and put her on a plane to Arizona and get her out of my hair."

John nodded his head and grinned. Sally gave him the evil eye, tapping him on the leg.

"We should be there in two days if everything goes well. Are you doing all right?"

"Getting short of cash again."

"Can you make it two days?"

John's eyes opened wide when noticed Chloe and Whitney walking toward them. "Look who's here!"

"I need to go," Sally said to Brody. "Chloe's home. Talk later."

"But I could use—" Brody blurted as she ended the call.

Nineteen

Whitney scampered to John and Sally with outstretched arms and a beaming smile that lit up their hearts. Chloe lagged, a drained smile and deep circles under her eyes. She'd probably be unable to keep up with her energetic four-year-old if she wanted to.

"Papa and Granny!" Whitney dropped her backpack on the sidewalk. John swooshed Whitney into his arms and lifted her, bringing forth a shower of giggles. Sally kissed her forehead and gave her a gentle hug.

"Didn't you get my call?" Sally asked as Chloe tottered toward them, picking up the backpack, and nearly out of breath.

"I've been busy," Chloe said as she trudged up the steps. "I guess I wasn't paying close attention. I thought you were letting me know that you were back in Kentucky. I'm sorry."

"Don't worry about it," Sally said, patting Chloe's shoulders. "Are you feeling okay?"

Chloe didn't answer as they entered the building and plodded up the steps to the apartment. Chloe unlocked the door, using three keys for the deadbolts. The living room was neat except for an empty bottle of red wine in the middle the walnut coffee table and two smudged goblets, one at each end.

"I apologize for the mess," Chloe said. "I haven't been able to do much cleaning the past week or so. And Sam's been busy with work."

"If my house was this messy, I'd receive a Good Housekeeping Award for cleanliness," Sally said. "You don't need to apologize."

"You know me."

"Come here," Sally said, motioning with her outstretched arms. Chloe took a few steps to her mother, who wrapped her arms around her in a warm embrace. "It's so good to see you again. I've been worried sick about you."

John walked over to them, spreading his arms around both and kissing Chloe's pale cheek. "You've been on our minds, princess."

Chloe stepped back with a teary smile. "I've missed you, too." She walked to the adjoining kitchen, wiping a hand across her eyes. "I need to get a tissue."

Sally smiled and followed her to the kitchen. Dirty dishes filled the sink, papers cluttered the table, and crumbs and empty food containers littered the compact counter. These were not the signs of the neat freak that Chloe revealed in recent years. Certainly, no housekeeping awards for the untidy room. Chloe leaned against the counter, dabbing her eyes with a paper towel.

Seconds later, John trailed Whitney to the kitchen. "Can I have my snack, Mommy?" she asked, climbing into a chair.

Chloe opened a cabinet door and sorted through several boxes before taking out a granola bar. Sally gave a baffled gaze at John, who was standing at the doorway.

Sally cleared off the small table in front of Whitney while Chloe poured a small glass of milk. Chloe sat next to Whitney, unwrapping the sweet snack.

"Have a seat," Chloe said. "If you can find one." The other two chairs were stacked with magazines and newspapers.

"I'm good," John said. "I've been sitting for so much the past twelve hours my butt feels deflated."

That brought a light laugh, the first from Chloe.

"Me, too." Sally pressed her lips together, her blue eyes focused on Chloe's gaunt appearance. "But I could afford to lose some of the padding."

"You look great, Mom," Chloe said with a paltry smile. "I wish I looked as good as you."

"Sweetie, is there something you haven't told us?" Sally asked. "I feel like you're keeping something from us. I've felt that way since we were in Budapest."

Chloe bolted from the chair and yanked a paper towel off the cabinet, sobbing, and covered her eyes. Sally hurried to her side, wrapping her arms around her Chloe's bony shoulders.

"Mommy cries all the time," Whitney said, her mouth puckered.

"Eat your granola bar," Chloe said, fighting back tears.

"What is it?" Sally said.

Chloe's voice trembled. "I have cancer. Ovarian cancer."

John moved to their side, his arms embracing his wife and daughter. Whitney rose from her chair and squeezed her arms around Chloe's thin legs.

"Why didn't you tell us?" Sally said, her eyes welling.

"I didn't want to spoil your vacation." Chloe wiped her nose.

"You should have said something," John said. "No vacation is more important than you."

John guided them to the table, where they sat in silence for several seconds. Whitney sat on Chloe's lap, nestled against her chest.

John grabbed the roll of paper towels and placed it on the table. Sally took one, wiping her eyes and blowing her nose.

John leaned against the counter. "Where's Samantha?"

"Work," Chloe said. "She should be home soon."

"Has she been here to help you?" Sally asked.

"Yes, Mom. She never left the hospital."

"What can we do?" John said. "We told Brody we planned to be here a couple of days, but we can stay longer. You let us know."

"You need to go back home," Chloe said. "Grandmother and Brody need you. I'm all right now."

"No, you're not." Sally squeezed her daughter's slender pale hand. "I'll stay here as long as you need me. John can go and check on things back home."

Chloe lowered her head against Whitney and wept. John eased over and placed his hands on her shoulders, massaging several times before bending over and kissing the top of her head.

"Are you going to have surgery?" Sally asked.

"I already have," Chloe said.

"When you were in the hospital last week?"

Chloe nodded.

"I can't believe you didn't you say something?" Sally raised her voice. "How come?"

"Like I told you, I didn't want to mess up your vacation. Besides, Sam was with me. Everything was under control. I didn't want you worrying about me."

"I wish Sam had said something to us. I'm going to ask her why she didn't."

"Mom, it's not Sam's fault." Chloe mustered a firm voice. "I told her not to say anything to you. She wanted to, but I made her promise. Don't blame her. Blame me."

Sally let out a heavy breath. "I understand but I wish she had."

"I had my first chemo two days ago," Chloe looked around the kitchen. "That's why this apartment is such a disaster zone. I haven't had the energy to do much of anything."

"You're not working?" John asked.

"I'm off for six more weeks," Chloe said. "I can get more time if I need it. I've got a ton of comp time built up."

"I wish we'd known about this." John bit his lower lip as a tear trickled down his cheek. He tore off another paper towel and patted his eyes.

"How was your vacation?" Chloe said. "I've heard Budapest is beautiful. Tell me about it."

"Let's not change the subject, sweetheart," Sally said. "We can talk about our vacation later. We need to focus on you."

"Can I have some more milk?" Whitney raised her glass.

John tapped Chloe's shoulders to stay seated. He poured Whitney some milk and sat at the table after removing papers from a chair.

"It's not that serious, Mom," Chloe said. "The doctor said I'm fortunate they found it so early. It's stage one. It hasn't spread."

"Mommy says she's not going to die." Whitney beamed.

Chloe ran her fingers through Whitney's wavy hair. "That's right, darling. Mommy's going to be all right."

Sally turned her head and wiped her eyes again. "Can we discuss this later?"

"That sounds like a plan." John rose from the chair. "I'm getting hungry. Are there any places around here to eat?"

"Millions, Dad," Chloe chuckled. "This is New York."

"Within walking distance?"

"Everywhere. It's not Lexington."

"Can we wait until Sam comes home and go out together?" Sally asked. "It's been ages since we've seen her. And I need to rest up a little. It's been a long day."

"I'll text her in a bit and see how things are going. She's still putting in a lot of extra hours at work," Chloe said. "Up early and home late."

"Any hotels nearby?" John asked. "Or bed and breakfast?"

"Daddy, you and mom are staying here. No need to do that."

"We don't want to intrude. We showed up unannounced so it's not a big deal for us to stay somewhere else."

"It is a big deal," Chloe said. "I want you here. I haven't seen you since Christmas. We have lots of things to talk about."

John grinned. "Okay, that settles it."

"The couch is a hide-a-bed."

"I didn't know they still made those things. Mom and I had one right after we got married. The most uncomfortable bed I've ever slept on."

"John!" Sally said, her brows furrowed.

"This one isn't great, but it's probably better than what you had," Chloe said. "We have a thick foam pad we put on it. It sleeps okay."

"We'll be fine," Sally said. "After sitting up on cramped flights for nine or ten hours, we can sleep anywhere. Even the floor. Right, John?"

John nodded. "No problem. We've done that before."

"Do you mind if I go to my room and take a short nap?" Chloe asked. "My stamina isn't what it used to be. The doctor said it'll be that way for several months, especially with the chemo."

"Take your time, honey," Sally said. "We'll look after Whitney."

"And let us know about Samantha," John said. "No hurry, though."

Chloe eased up from the chair and wobbled to her bedroom. Sally pressed her lips and wiped a tear, fighting an urge to weep in front of her granddaughter.

"Mommy doesn't feel good," Whitney said. "She cries."

"She's going to get better, sweetie." Sally tapped the tip of Whitney's nose. "We'll take good care of her, so don't you worry."

"Can I go watch TV now?"

"Of course, sweetheart. Let Papa go with you while I put things away in here."

Whitney slid off her chair, took John's hand, and led him to the tidy living room. She sat in a small foam pink chair, monogrammed with a W, her legs stretched on the floor. Soon she was engrossed in *Sesame Street*.

John found a magazine from a wooden rack and flipped through several pages. After seeing two women in a tender embrace, he realized it was a lesbian-oriented periodical and put it back as if he were intruding on a private matter.

The front door to the apartment clicked open and Samantha stepped into the living room. She flung a bag to the corner and kissed the top of Whitney's head. She noticed John seated on the couch and placed her hand on her chest as if she'd seen an intruder.

"Oh my goodness, I didn't see you sitting there," she said, eyes wide. "When did you get here?"

Before John could reply, she rushed over and hugged him around the neck and kissed his cheek, startling him for a moment.

"An hour or so, I guess." John held one of her hands as she stood next to him. "We wanted to check in on you folks before going on to Lexington."

Sally stood at the kitchen entry, smiling and holding a damp washcloth. Samantha turned and scurried to her, giving her an embrace. Tears filled their eyes as they stepped away from each other.

"Chloe told you everything?" Samantha asked, brushing tears off her cheeks.

"For the most part," Sally said.

"I wanted to tell you when you were in Europe, but she made me swear not to do it. Forgive me."

"We understand," Sally said, glancing at John. "It's not your fault. And she told us as well."

"I'm so glad you're here."

"She's napping right now. We thought we'd all go out and get a bite to eat after she wakes up. If she feels up to it."

"She's been awfully weak," Samantha said. "I've tried my best to make her take it easy. But you know how she is. Always has to be doing something. But not this time. I've tried to do more things around here, but it's hard taking care of her and Whitney."

Sally didn't want to discuss Chloe's condition in front of Whitney, and motioned Samantha to follow her into the kitchen. Samantha poured a glass of water from the sink and sat at the kitchen table, recounting everything that had transpired while John and Sally were away in Europe.

"I'm thankful they discovered the cancer before it got any worse," Sally said. "I had a friend from high school who didn't find out about her condition until it was stage four. She managed to live another three years or so, but it was difficult for her and her family."

"We were lucky," Samantha said. "At first she resisted going to the ER but the pain got so bad she relented. She can be so headstrong at times, always wanting to do things by herself. It can be frustrating at times to get her to listen or do things. Of course, you know that."

"I'm glad you were persistent," Sally said. "You were a lifesaver."

Tears filled Samantha's dark brown eyes. "We can only hope."

Twenty

They ended up staying in the apartment as Chloe's short nap lasted more than three hours. John and Sally even found time to doze on the couch while noise from the TV filled the background. Sam retreated with Whitney to her room to review her schoolwork, and probably sneak in a catnap as well.

When Chloe finally padded into the kitchen, the others were at the table talking about international places they'd like to visit. Whitney was occupied with a coloring book. Chloe's puffy eyes were a sign she should have remained in bed.

John rose from his chair and motioned with his hand for Chloe to sit. "I'm not much of a hostess," she said with a stifled laugh.

"Are you hungry?" Sally asked.

"No, but I know I should get something in my stomach. I need to keep up my strength, however little it is."

"How does breakfast for dinner sound?" Sam asked. "I can whip up some scrambled eggs and hash browns. We have some biscuits, too."

"That'd be okay," Chloe said. "But not much. You know how my stomach is."

"Can I have pizza, Sam?" Whitney asked.

"No problem, sweetie," Sam said. "We have some of your small ones in the freezer. Why don't you go watch TV and I'll let you know when it's ready."

Whitney scampered to the living room and changed the channels on the TV. She couldn't find anything of interest, so she put a *Moana* disk in the Blu-ray player, a movie she had watched countless times. Sam peeked in and asked her to turn down the volume.

"I've never asked you this so please don't take offense," John said, "but why does Whitney call you Sam?"

Sam, cracking eggs into a bowl on the counter, laughed. "No offense taken. Before we adopted her, everyone at the agency was calling me Sam and she picked up on it. She's always called me that. And it might be confusing for her to call me mom, mommy, or whatever. It doesn't bother me. In fact, I think it's kinda cute. The main thing is that I know she loves me and that's all that matters."

"Thanks for clearing that up," John said.

"You know, my mother had a problem with that," Sally said. "I never gave it much thought either."

"It wouldn't bother me if Whitney called me by my name," Chloe said. "It's whatever she's comfortable with. She's always known me as 'mommy' so I guess that'll stick with her. Sometimes I think we get carried away with nicknames like that."

"Is that so?" Sally said.

"You know what I mean, Mom," Chloe said.

"Did you call me Mom? Would you prefer Sally?"

"Okay, okay, I see your point," Chloe said, letting out a light laugh.

"And I'd prefer Dad to John," John said, grinning. "I hope that isn't a problem."

"It's Daddy, not Dad. You'll always be Mom and Daddy, so don't worry about it."

"Forgive me for saying this, but your mother gives me bad vibes," Sam said to Sally while whisking the eggs in a bowl. "Whenever I've called your house, she's been short with me. I wouldn't say she's rude; just not friendly."

"She can be that way," Sally said. "Even with me."

"She's impolite with you because of our relationship," Chloe said to Sam. "It's not you."

Sam turned toward Chloe. "I know I'm being a little sensitive about it, but I've tried to treat her with respect."

"Please don't worry about it," Sally said. "Mother has a lot of opinions about things. It's her problem, not yours."

"She's short with everyone," John said. "We don't like it but we're kinda used to it. She's gotten worse the past few years. We really don't pay it much attention. Or try not to."

"She still upsets me at times, but I've learned to get over it and move on," Sally said. "At least I try to. It's not easy at times. But she's my mother so I have to be understanding and considerate."

"How's Brody these days?" Sam asked. "Still in rehab?"

"We sure hope so," John said. "We'll find out for sure when we get back home. But he claims he's been going three times a week."

Sam walked to the refrigerator and took out a large bag of hash browns and a small pizza, then turned on the oven. "He hasn't asked me for any more money."

"What?" Sally asked, turning her head, eyes opening wide.

"Last year he called a few times for Chloe and I talked to him because she wasn't here. He said he needed some money to cover a few expenses. It seems like he mentioned something wrong with his car. He promised to pay me back."

"Did you give him any?" John asked.

"A few hundred dollars," Sam said.

"Did he pay you back?"

"No, but that's okay. I'm glad I could help him."

"You should have told us." Sally shook her head in disdain. "I can't believe he'd do something like that."

"I do," John said, sitting back and crossing his arms.

"Why didn't you tell me?" Chloe asked Sam. "He shouldn't have done that."

"He asked me not to. And besides, we're all family and I was trying to help. I know you'd do the same for mine. It's not a big deal."

"I'm curious how many people he approached for money," John said to no one in particular.

"As long as he's trying to get better, that's the main thing," Sam said. "Addiction is something a person never recovers from. It's a disease. Like cancer."

Everyone in the room froze for a second, eyes lingering on Sam.

"Oh shit," she said, bending over and hugging Chloe. "I didn't mean it that way."

"I know," Chloe said, patting her partner on the back. "We want to become survivors."

Sam kissed her cheek. "I love you."

"You, too." Chloe pressed her lips together to fight back tears.

~ * ~

After finishing the late dinner, Chloe and Sam put Whitney to bed. John sat in the living room while Sally loaded the dishwasher. They returned a few minutes later, about the time Sally finished the kitchen chores.

Chloe cuddled next to John, bringing back memories of when she was his little girl. Sally sat on the other side of Chloe, touching her curled under leg. Sam sat cross-legged in front of the muted TV, twisting her body in various yoga positions, reminding John of Moretta's impromptu calisthenics in Budapest.

The silence ended when Sally's cell phone buzzed. "That has to be Brody," she said, reaching to pick up the phone on the end table before the sound disturbed Whitney.

She stared at the phone, then let out a deep sigh.

"Who is it?" John asked.

"Dorothy Finsterwald."

"You've got to be kidding me."

"Who in the world is Dorothy Finsterwald?" Chloe asked, cocking her head.

"We'll tell you later," John said.

Sally clicked the receive and speaker buttons. "Hi Dorothy."

"I wanted to check on you guys to make sure you made it to your daughter's place," Dorothy said.

"We're here," Sally said with embellished cheerfulness. "I hope the same for you and Frank."

"We hit a massive traffic jam but that's par for the course living here. Frankie's exhausted and was out like a light on the recliner after we got home. He's still there, snoring his life away." She laughed.

"I appreciate you calling and checking on us," Sally said. "We're tired as well and plan to go to bed soon."

"Can you believe our kids haven't called to check to see if we made it back?"

"My goodness."

"Not even the queer one. He sometimes will send me a text message. Frankie doesn't know that and would have a conniption fit if he knew I was still in contact with Andy."

"It's good you've maintained a relationship with your son."

"You don't know how difficult that is. Your children are normal."

Chloe and Samantha covered their mouths to muffle snickers. John shut his eyes as if in deep meditation.

"Babs, Jill, and Junior only call when they want something, like for me to babysit. They know better than to ask for money because we don't have any to give away. You know what I mean?"

"I'm sorry to hear that."

"Children can be so ungrateful. You know? They don't realize all the sacrifices we make for them when they're growing up. We change their dirty diapers, buy their clothes and food, send them to college and everything else. But do they remember all those things? Hell no. Except for Andy. He's such a sensitive boy."

Sally twirled her free hand for Dorothy to finish her rant.

"Thanks so much for calling."

"Are you guys going back home in a couple days?" Dorothy asked. "It would be so nice if we could see each other again before you leave. We had such a wonderful time with you in Budapest. We've been on other trips and others have ignored us. Do you think it's because we're from Jersey? I don't know. What do you think? But you guys were so nice. Are all Kentuckians as nice as you and John?"

Sally chuckled. "We've got our share of ornery ones. Well, it's been nice talking to you."

"Maybe Frankie and me will go to Kentucky this summer. Wouldn't that be nice? I don't think we've ever been there. At least I don't remember. Is that where they have the Kentucky Derby?"

John, Chloe, and Sam emitted light snorts while Sally bit her forefinger. Sam jumped up and dashed to the kitchen, clamping a hand over her mouth.

Sally cleared her throat after regaining her composure. "It's in Louisville. The first Saturday in May."

"I knew that," Dorothy said. "I don't know what I was thinking. I must be getting tired or I've had too much wine."

John and Chloe nodded.

Before Dorothy could utter another word, Sally said, "I really need to be going. I'm tired as well. We'll stay in touch."

"Promise?"

"I promise. Good night."

Sally put the phone back on the end table. "Wasn't that insightful?"

"Now we know why she was gabbing so much," John said. "Wine. She did seem to enjoy wine on our trip."

"You can look forward to seeing them this summer," Chloe said. "And you can show them where they hold that horse race. Isn't it called Churchill Downs?"

"I'm not sure I'm ready for that," Sally said.

"Do you think they'll let Andy tag along?"

"I wish you hadn't heard that," John said.

"Dad, gays and lesbians don't live in a vacuum," Chloe said. "We hear stories like that all the time. It's not easy at times being who we are but we try to accept it. Life's too short to get caught up in those things."

John pulled her close and kissed her temple. "You're my daughter and that's all that matters to me."

"By the way, I think I know all I want to about Dorothy Finsterwald," Chloe said. "She and her husband, uh, Frankie, must have been interesting travel companions."

"Sweetie, we'll tell you about our adventures with them one of these days, probably after a few glasses of wine," Sally said. "They made the trip unforgettable in more ways than one."

Sam stepped back into the living room. "I hate leaving good company, but I've got an early assignment in the morning. Can I get you anything before I crash for the night?"

"We're good," Sally said.

"I need to go to bed as well," Chloe said, swinging her bare feet to the floor. "Thanks for the evening entertainment."

"Entertainment?" Sally turned her head.

"Your friend from Jersey."

"We'll invite them over tomorrow, so you can meet them."

"Thanks, but no thanks," Chloe said. "Tonight was enough. And like you said, I need my rest."

Chloe leaned over and kissed John and Sally on their cheeks. She took Sam's extended hand and followed her to the adjoining bedroom. All was quiet except for occasional creaking footsteps on the floor above them.

John pulled out the top of the hide-a-bed. Sheets were between the folding rails. John and Sally stood on each side, spreading and tucking in the sheets.

"I don't see a quilt," Sally said. "Or pillows."

"Should we ask Chloe?"

"She's tired," Sally said. "We'll be okay."

"I'll keep you warm," John said. He placed his hands on her waist and pecked her on the tip of the nose.

"I'm glad we decided to come here rather than go home," Sally said softly. "I'm not sure when she would have ever told us about her condition."

"Maybe after she finished chemo?"

"Probably because she wouldn't want us to worry."

"You're the reason we're here."

"Me?"

"Because of your mother's intuition."

"Like I told you in Budapest, I knew something wasn't right."

"And I'm glad you sensed that."

"Oh honey, I'm exhausted," Sally said, resting her head on his shoulder. "Let's turn out the lights and go to bed."

John clicked off the lamp on the end table. A golden glow from a street lamp filtered through the half-open drapes on the tall windows. They slipped out of their clothes and snuggled under the sheets.

"Are you as tired as me?" Sally whispered.

"Bushed."

"Love you."

"Love you, too."

Twenty-one

John awoke at daybreak, a faint light trickling through the windows as he put on his pants and shirt. Sally stirred on the couch but continued to slumber in the serene surroundings. He crept barefoot to the kitchen to make a pot of coffee but couldn't find the grounds in the chockablock cabinets.

Sam came to his rescue, already dressed for work in khakis and denim shirt, when she grabbed a bag of coffee from the refrigerator.

"Chloe swears that refrigerating coffee keeps it fresher," Sam said. "I'm not so sure about that but it's not worth arguing over. And with space at a premium in this tiny flat, the fridge is as good as place as any to store it."

John watched as Sam spooned coffee into the Mr. Coffee basket. She took two cups from a metal holder on the counter and liquid creamer from the refrigerator, setting them on the table.

She plopped down across from him and smiled. "I envy you not having to work. I get so tired of this same routine each day, and knowing I have to do it another thirty years or so. Or longer. I don't want to have to work my life away."

"Believe it or not, it does come to an end," John said. "Sooner than you may realize. The key in the meantime is doing something you enjoy."

"That's easier said than done."

"I was fortunate in that I found a career I enjoyed. And if the company hadn't started buyouts and downsizing, I'd still be working. I'm not sure what that says about me."

"But didn't you want more in life than going to work and putting in eight, ten, twelve hours or more a day and bringing home a paycheck? There has to be more to life than that."

"I'm sure there is, and it's something I regret to some extent because I wasn't as home as much as I wanted to be or needed to be. But I had a family to support so the paycheck was important. You make sacrifices. You can't undo things, but you can learn from what you've done."

"Even the money doesn't seem that important any longer."

"You've got that right. It pays the bills, which is important, but it doesn't necessarily buy happiness."

"Can't buy love either."

"Ah, the Beatles. You like them?"

"Love the Beatles."

"I saw them in concert back in sixty-six."

"No way. You're kidding me."

"In Cincinnati."

"I'm really jealous now."

"Saw them with the Remains, the Cyrkle, Bobby Hebb, and the Ronettes. Really can't remember much of it now except for all the screaming girls. They only played for about thirty minutes."

"Did Sally go with you?'

"Didn't know her back then. Just me and a few buddies from high school."

Sam rose from the table and poured coffee into their cups. She sat and chewed on a fingernail for a few seconds.

"I went off the subject," John said. "I apologize. Was there something else on your mind, Sam? Something you want to discuss?"

"I don't know what's going on with me. I'm antsy most of the time, like life is slipping away from me. I don't know what I want, though."

"Is that why we discussed work?"

"Kinda. That's part of it."

"Are things okay between you and Chloe?"

Sam ran a forefinger down her nose. "For the most part."

"We know you and Chloe had some problems around the holidays. Are they still lingering?"

"I suppose so." Her eyes began tearing. "I can be such a bitch. Pardon the language. Here she is with cancer and my mind is racing in all directions. I can be so selfish."

"Do you feel helpless?"

Sam's brows furrowed. "Helpless?"

"Because you can't handle what's happened to Chloe."

"John, I know what you're saying but I hate to admit this. I was having some heavy thoughts about leaving again. Then we found out about the cancer. I feel awful about it."

John stroked his beard. "I didn't realize it was getting back to that point."

"But I'm not going to leave her, especially with the way things are now. I'm not that bad. And I hope this is only a fucking phase I'm going through. Or maybe it's a full-blown midlife crisis."

"Could be. But I hope you're being honest with me, yourself, and especially Chloe. Whitney, too."

"I just feel trapped."

"Have you been to a doctor? It could be something physical."

"Like menopause?'

"Why don't you discuss it with your doctor? You might want to talk to Sally about it." He rubbed his neck and chuckled. "You know you're not going to get an expert opinion from me."

"I'll do that." Sam stirred her coffee.

"And please don't say anything to Chloe. I know I'm being protective, but she doesn't need to deal with your feelings now. She has enough on her mind. We all have enough on our minds."

"I'd never do that. Believe it or not, I love her. I'm conflicted and confused about everything."

"We all experience different emotions in our lives."

"Even you and Sally?"

"We've had our differences. Every couple does, no matter what they may say. We've never wanted to leave each other." He laughed. "At least I haven't. Don't know about Sally. But we've learned through the years to compromise. You take the bad with the good. And if you're fortunate, there's a lot more good than bad."

"When Chloe gets over this, I think we're going to take a short trip, maybe even to Europe, and discuss where our relationship is going. We need to get our feelings more out in the open. We need to compromise on things, especially me. And she likes to hold things in so others won't worry about her, like she's been with the cancer."

"Communication is the first step."

Sam rose and carried her nearly full cup to the sink. "I need to get to work. I apologize for dumping this stuff on you. I shouldn't have. I don't know what I was thinking."

"I admit I wasn't expecting it but it's good to get it out in the open. None of us needs any surprises right now. And let me or Sally know if you need to discuss it more. We don't ever want to intrude but we're always available to help. Okay?"

"I really do appreciate everything you and Sally do for us. I want you to know that." She wiped her eyes on a paper towel and left the room.

A few minutes after Sam departed for work, Sally sauntered into the kitchen, rubbing her puffy eyes. Her short hair was sticking out in the back and mashed on top. She headed to the coffee maker, but John directed her toward a chair and eased her down. "I'll pour you a cup."

"Were you talking to Sam a while ago?"

John placed the coffee in front of Sally. "More or less."

Sally clutched the cup in both hands. "What do you mean?"

"She still has a wanderlust. She confided about her unhappiness with life."

"Including Chloe and Whitney?"

John leaned against the door frame. "Perhaps to some extent, but more so with the direction of her life."

"Anything specific?"

"She feels conflicted about her feelings. She really didn't go into a lot of detail. I don't think she really knows."

"Has she told Chloe?"

"No, and I asked her not to say anything. She said she wouldn't."

"What has brought that on again?"

"I told her to see a doctor, that it could be something physical."

Sally shrugged. "Could be."

"She mentioned menopause."

"She discussed that with you?'

John covered his mouth and let out a single cough. "Only mentioned it. I told her to discuss that with you or a doctor. Gimme a break."

"What are we going to do?"

"Nothing, for the most part. I told her to feel free to discuss her feelings more with you and me. Our priority is to care of Chloe."

"Did someone mention my name?"

John turned around as Chloe padded barefoot toward him in a wrinkled pink bathrobe and matching pajamas.

"We were talking about your care." John kissed her on the cheek as she sat at the table. Sally poured her a cup of coffee.

"Don't worry about me," Chloe said. "I've got everything under control. My calendar is already marked for the chemo. Sam says it won't be a problem taking me to the treatments. Only five more to go."

John glanced at Sally. "That's good to know you're on top of things."

"I don't want either of you worrying about me. You've got enough going on with Brody and Grandma, and who knows what else could be going on."

"You're our daughter," Sally said. "I don't care how old or independent you are, or think you are, we're going to be here for you. Like you are with Whitney. Accept it."

"I understand your concern, Mom. I want you to realize I've worked out everything. Please don't worry about me."

Sally touched the top of Chloe's hand and smiled. "No. End of discussion."

"Any plans for today?" John asked.

"I have to take Whitney to school," Chloe said. "It's about five blocks from here."

"Why don't you let me take her? I need a breath of fresh air. I don't think I'll get lost if the school's that close."

"That's fine, Dad," Chloe said. "Mom and I can do a few things around the apartment while you're gone. The bathroom's a mess. The bedroom's a mess. Everything's a mess. I'm a mess."

"Are you saying your life is a mess?" John chuckled. "Well, join the club. That's what life is all about."

"I don't know if that makes me feel better or what."

"I hope a little better. I'm just saying that life is unpredictable, and you've got to be ready for whatever comes your way."

"I've tried."

"That reminds me of something a relative told me a long time ago," John said. "I think it was my Uncle Mort."

"What's that?"

"He said that we make a mess when we come into the world, and we generally leave a mess when we leave."

"That's funny and true," Chloe said. "Did old Uncle Mort leave in a mess?"

"Somewhat. He didn't have a will, had bank accounts at seven or eight places, and made investments he didn't tell Aunt Myrtle about. It was a big mess for her and my cousins trying to track down everything. You want to know what Aunt Myrtle said?"

"What's that?"

"She said if Uncle Mort was around, she'd kill him for what he did."

Chloe let out a big laugh that seemed to bring some color to her face. "That's hilarious."

"You'd better not have any surprises for me, John Ross," Sally said.

"Wait and see." John looked at Chloe and winked.

"Can we change the subject?" Sally said.

"Oh, Mom, quit being overly sensitive," Chloe said, touching Sally's hand. "Because I have cancer doesn't mean I'm dying. I've got a whole life to live with Sam and Whitney."

"You've done a great job in handling the adversities," Sally said as her eyes began to well. "I've always been proud of you."

"We'll see how well I do it this time," Chloe said.

"Should we be getting Whitney up?" Sally asked.

"Yeah, we don't want her to be late for school," John said.

"I'll wake her up in a few minutes," Chloe said. "It won't take long to get her dressed, eat breakfast and be out the door."

"I'll explore the neighborhood after I drop her off," John said. "So just take your time."

"Trying to get out of work, eh?" Sally asked, raising her brows.

"Hey, you know I make more work when I'm around."

"Thanks for reminding me," Sally said. "You take all the time you need."

"But I can stay if you really want me to. I love work. I could sit around and watch it all day."

"You're full of funnies this morning," Sally said.

"Must be the jet lag because I still feel a little silly."

"I won't argue with that."

Chloe finished her coffee and left the room to get Whitney dressed for school.

"I hope things go as well as Chloe thinks they will in the coming weeks," John said.

Sally clutched her cup with both hands. "Me, too."

~ * ~

Whitney finished a bowl of cereal and scampered to the living room, eager for another day of school. Chloe strapped a Disney-themed backpack on her and kissed the top of her head. Whitney ran to Sally for a hug and kiss.

"Ready, Papa?" She took John by the hand.

"Let's go," John said as she led him out the door. When they reached the bottom step to the sidewalk, they turned around and waved at Chloe and Sally. Whitney tugged John's hand to start walking as they headed toward her school.

John held his cell phone in one hand, using the GPS to make sure they reached their destination. Whitney took all the proper turns as they reached the front entrance of the gated school. Parents, grandparents, nannies and others gathered to see the children off for six hours. John leaned over and Whitney pecked him on the cheek. She grinned and dashed into the brick building, holding hands with two pint-size classmates.

John journeyed in the opposite direction of Chloe's apartment and the school. As usual on this vacation, he forgot to bring his camera. He thought about using his smartphone but realized the risk of running down the battery. He didn't want to lose the GPS function and get lost like they had in Budapest.

He walked for nearly three hours, taking in the cityscape, going up and down narrow side streets, and stopping once at a sidewalk café for coffee and flipping through a *New York Times* someone had left behind. The more he strolled, the more he wanted to sightsee. He viewed statues, building facades, and peeked into the windows of curiosity shops. The exploration ended when traffic became more congested and noisier with the blaring horns, shrill sirens, and booming building equipment coming in all directions. Pedestrians raced in every direction, almost knocking him down if he dared to stop. And then he noticed a weak GPS signal on his phone.

After wandering for another forty-five minutes, John recognized a bakery, a book store, and a deli. The phone's GPS came back to life as he got closer to Chloe's place. It was almost one-thirty in the afternoon, about time to go back to Whitney's school.

John walked into the living room and sat on the couch, extending his legs, and kicking off his shoes. He rested his head on the back of the couch and closed his eyes.

"Where in the world have you been?" Sally stepped out of the kitchen. "We thought you'd be back around eleven or so. We weren't sure if we should call the police."

"Taking in the scenery. And I wanted to give you a lot of time to do your chores. You told me to take my time. Remember?"

"I bet you got lost along the way. Right?"

John sighed. "Never mind. Can I have a glass of water?"

Sally went to the kitchen and came back with a large glass of ice water. John took a big gulp and handed the glass to Sally.

"Are you going to be able to go after Whitney?" Sally asked. "She gets out at two forty-five. Chloe's been napping for the past hour or so."

"No problem." John turned toward her with tired, burning eyes from the polluted air on the streets. "I just need to rest my eyes a little longer."

"You look like you need more than that."

"Don't let me oversleep. Give me about thirty minutes. A power nap. I'll be okay."

Sally went to Whitney's bedroom where they were kept their luggage. She changed clothes, putting on black leggings and a lavender tunic top. She applied makeup in the bathroom and returned to John's side, tapping him on the shoulder.

"Time to wake up, sleepyhead," she said. "We need to leave in about ten minutes."

John rubbed his eyes before sitting up. He slipped on his shoes and stood. "Ready?"

She handed him a small bottle of eye drops they had used to moisten their eyes on the flights to and from Europe.

"You're the best." He squeezed two drops in each eye and blinked several times.

They arrived at the school with five minutes to spare. Adults stood around the perimeter, some chatting with each other, when the bell rang. A minute later, children swarmed out the front door like bats leaving a cave.

John walked to the other side of the school while Sally remained near the entrance. They had difficulty picking out Whitney from the mass of kids, who stood about the same height, all wearing backpacks, and moving about in search of their guardians.

John and Sally spotted Whitney at the side of the building, looking in all directions with wide-eyed innocence. Sally reached her first and gave her a comforting hug.

As they were about to leave, a young teacher rushed over to them and took Whitney's hand.

"Do you have permission to take her from the premises?" she asked, lifting a brow.

"We're her grandparents," Sally said. "We're here to take her home."

"I need to see a permission slip."

"I beg your pardon?" John said, feeling his face beginning to get warm.

"We can't have just anyone come here and pickup children." The teacher squeezed her lips together.

"We're not just anyone," John said. "We're her grandparents, and we're her mother's parents. Just ask Whitney."

They all glanced at Whitney, who looked up at them with puckered mouth. Sally touched the top of her head. "It's okay, sweetheart."

A moment later, a stout older woman in a blue blazer and gray skirt, strolled up to them. "Is there a problem, Ms. George?"

"This couple claims to be Whitney's grandparents, but I don't see a permission slip for them to pick her up." The young teacher stood erect and stern-faced, tapping her shoe on the concrete walk.

"I'm Mrs. Dinsmore, the school principal." She shook hands with John and Sally. "Let me make a quick call to Chloe. We must do this for security purposes. I hope you understand."

Mrs. Dinsmore took a cell phone from the side pocket of her coat. After pushing a couple buttons, she put the phone to her ear.

"She was napping when we left," Sally said. "She may not pick up the phone in time."

Mrs. Dinsmore gave an understanding nod, then a second later began talking on the phone to Chloe.

"It's okay now." She nodded to the teacher. "They're Whitney's grandparents."

A quick grin came and went on Ms. George's face. Without saying a word, she pivoted and headed toward a group of children milling around the playground equipment.

"I know about Chloe's condition," Mrs. Dinsmore said. "She alerted me several days ago that there might be others beside her and Samantha to pick up Whitney. I guess she forgot to give us your names. We must take precautions because there've been abductions in the school system. They usually arise from child-custody disputes. Ms. George was doing her job."

"Not a problem," Sally said. "We arrived yesterday afternoon. It must have slipped Chloe's mind after John walked Whitney to school. I'll mention it to her when we get back to her apartment.

We'll pick up her one more time before we go back home to Kentucky."

John and Sally each took one of Whitney's hands and walked back to the apartment. They listened as their granddaughter recounted everything that had happened during the day.

Chloe stood at the kitchen counter when they returned, preparing a light snack for Whitney. She hadn't changed clothes, still wearing a robe over her pink pjs. Whitney ran up and gave her a hug around the waist. Chloe smiled and kissed her forehead.

"Sorry for not notifying the school," Chloe said as John and Sally sat at the table. "It totally slipped my mind."

"Those things happen," John said. "The teacher wouldn't budge but that's okay. Just doing her job. Better safe than sorry."

"Ms. George is a caring teacher, but she goes strictly by the book," Chloe said. "Kinda like me when I'm on top of things." She laughed.

"We had the same rules when I was teaching," Sally said. "Better safe than sorry when it comes to children."

"It's a crazy world out there," John said.

"Mom, everything looks so nice in the apartment," Chloe said.

"I cleaned the bathroom and dusted Whitney's room and the living room while you napped," Sally said. "I would have done some laundry but didn't know where the washer and dryer were. Are they hidden in a closet somewhere?"

"They're in the basement," Chloe said. "But don't worry about doing that. Sam usually takes care of it."

"We have a flight out of Newark tomorrow afternoon," John said. "If you need us to stay, I can cancel. It wouldn't be a problem."

"No, Dad," Chloe said. "You've already done enough. You need to get back to Brody and Grandma and everything."

"Would you want me to stay?" Sally asked. "There's no hurry for me to return. Your dad can go back and take care of things, and when everything is back to normal here, I'll go back."

"Are you sure?" Chloe lowered her shoulders.

"We're sure," John said. "I'll go back tomorrow, and Mom will come when you're back at full strength."

"But Mom, you don't have many clothes." Chloe looked at Sally.

"I don't need much," she said. "After being in Budapest for ten days, I learned to live with less. And if I need anything, I'll buy a few things at a thrift shop."

"That settles it." John thumped his hand on the table.

Chloe placed a peanut butter-and-jelly sandwich, with the crust removed, and a small glass of milk on the table for Whitney. "She's picky," Chloe held up the bread crusts.

"I wonder who she gets that from," Sally asked.

"From school," Chloe said. "She also doesn't want her food to touch on the plate. And her clothes have to be laid out in a certain way the night before school."

"That sounds more like you." John laughed.

Chloe grinned. "Maybe."

Chloe followed Whitney to her room after the snack to work with her on reading, writing and other things. It was a daily ritual that had begun many years earlier when Sally would spend an hour with her to review classwork. Brody wasn't so amenable.

After clearing Whitney's leftovers on the table, Sally retreated to the living room couch with John.

"Are you sure you don't want me to stay with you?" he asked. "There's no hurry for me to return."

Sally jabbed his side. "You don't want to deal with Mother and Brody."

"You read my mind."

"I'll go back home after she has a couple treatments. Right now, Chloe needs our support and needs to get her strength back."

"I agree." John patted her leg. "Stay as long as needed."

"I'm very concerned about her. She's so lethargic. I've never seen her this way."

"It may get worse before she turns the corner."

"That's what I was thinking."

"And we don't know what Sam is going to be up to. She could bail out."

"I hate to think she'd do that, but you never know."

The apartment door opened, and Sam stepped inside, flinging satchel to the corner. "Hey."

"Aren't you home early?" Sally asked.

"This is my regular time but I'm usually putting in several hours overtime. How's Chloe?"

"She took a long nap," Sally said. "She's with Whitney now."

"If you don't mind, I'll join them," Sam said as she headed to Whitney's room.

"That's fine," John said. "We're just discussing our travel plans."

They heard Chloe and Whitney's raised voices when Sam entered the room and closed the door.

"She seems eager to be with Chloe and Whitney," John said.

"Let's take it one day at a time," Sally said. "These are difficult days for everyone."

"How about we all go out for pizza tonight if Chloe feels up to it? I noticed a pizza place a few blocks from here, on our way back from school."

"You're more observant than I am."

"You're just figuring that out?"

"I think we just notice different things."

"If you say so."

"Are you sure you won't get us lost?"

"Funny." John scowled.

"Anyway, we'll let her decide. If not, you can get a carryout."

"Whatever's best."

Sally's cell phone vibrated. "Who that could be?" She scooted over to the other end of the couch and grabbed it on the end table. "I'm not answering it."

"Your Mother?"

"I wish."

"Brody?"

"Not even close."

"Who?"

"Dorothy Finsterwald."

"Again?"

After several whirrs, the phone went silent. They stared at each other, then jumped when the phone buzzed again.

"That woman doesn't give up," John said. "I sure hope they're not somewhere in the neighborhood."

"Don't say that, John! That's not even funny."

After silence returned to the room, Sally held the phone in front of John to show a voice mail.

"Don't you dare listen to it," he said. "We can pretend you never received it."

"Do you think I should call Mother or Brody and let them know that you'll be flying back tomorrow?"

"I've been thinking about that." John rubbed his chin. "I could surprise them."

"You know that you might be the one surprised when you get there."

"I never thought about that. Why don't you call later tonight or tomorrow morning?"

Twenty-two

A light drizzle began two blocks after they left the apartment, dampening the sidewalks and streets leading to the pizza parlor. Sally asked Chloe if she wanted to go back but Chloe gestured with her hand to proceed.

"Do you know how long it's been since I had a good pizza?" she said. "I've been craving a loaded pizza ever since my surgery. Nothing's going to stop me now."

"I hope this place is decent," John said.

"Kinda slow but excellent," Sam said. "It's owned by an Italian family. No cardboard pizza."

The gray overcast skies rumbled and a streak of lightning popped before a cloudburst sent them scurrying to a covered bus stop. Other pedestrians pushed and shoved their way into the shelter as John picked up Whitney to protect her from the stampede.

"We have a couple umbrellas by the door at the apartment," Sam said. "I don't know why we didn't grab them on the way out."

"I can go back and get them," John said. "It'd only take a few minutes. I don't think I'd get lost."

"That's okay, Daddy," Chloe said, leaning against the plexiglass enclosure. "We can make a run for the restaurant after the rain lets up. It shouldn't be very long. At least I hope not."

The rain cascaded in waves, drenching everyone from the knee down in the shelter. And those outside got soaked to the bone.

"This is ridiculous." Sam pursed her lips. "Let's make a run for it."

Without waiting for a response from the others, she bolted from the shelter and dashed the hundred yards toward the restaurant, splashing through puddles and somehow avoided running into people in reaching the destination.

"Why not?" Chloe said as she watched Sam waving in front of the diner's metal overhang. Sally and Chloe took off, arm in arm, while John carried Whitney, holding her close and bouncing along behind them. Sam stood with the door creaked open for their arrival. Chloe was nearly breathless, leaning with her hands on her knees.

"This wasn't a smart thing to do," Sally said. "Are you going to all right?"

"I'm fine, Mom," Chloe said. "Just out of shape. I'll be okay. You worry too much."

"That's what mothers do."

As they waited inside the doorway to be seated, wet and shivering in the air-conditioned establishment, the rainstorm abated as quickly as it had begun. Moments later, the sun sent a shimmering glow across the wet pavement, releasing a steamy vapor.

"Isn't that the way it always works out?" Sally said, shaking her arms as if it would help her get dry. "It stops raining after you get soaked."

"I almost feel like we should go back to the apartment before it starts up again," John said.

"We're here, so let's go ahead and eat," Chloe said, her chin trembling.

"Are you sure, sweetie?" Sally asked. "You don't need to catch a cold."

"I'm fine, Mom. I've got a little chill. I'll be okay."

A waiter arrived and sat them near the front of the room, across from a long bar where several patrons were sipping draft beers and probably chatting about the weather.

"Why don't you gals go wipe off in the restroom and I'll order the pizzas and drinks," John said. Chloe reminded him about the loaded pizza while the others informed what they wanted on their pizza and to drink. They scurried past the crowded tables to the rear of the restaurant, where they stood in a long line as others apparently sought refuge from the rain to dry off or answer Mother Nature's call.

John glanced at himself in a large mirror on the wall behind the bar and exhaled. He looked like a homeless person, haggard in appearance with his saturated clothes and stringy hair that needed more than a comb over. He needed a makeover.

The waiter set drinks on the table when the others returned, damp dry but better than being drenched. By the time the pizzas arrived twenty-five minutes later, their appetites quelled from the wait. They hardly spoke while picking at the oversized feasts, more concerned with the outside conditions as a light, steady rain began to fall. They ate half of each pizza before asking the waiter for carryout containers.

John told the others return to the apartment while he waited at the table to pay the bill. Chloe crossed her arms over her chest, quivering, and followed Sam and Whitney out the door. Sally stayed with John for a few seconds.

"Better get Chloe in bed," John said. "She's not looking too good. She doesn't need to get pneumonia."

"I know," she said, nodding. "And you be careful and don't get lost." She kissed his cheek and hurried out the door to Chloe's side, placing an arm around her shoulders and guiding her toward the apartment.

The waiter returned with the boxes five minutes later, and after another five minutes, took John's credit card. It was another five minutes for him to return with the receipt. As John stepped out of the restaurant, he secured the cardboard boxes in his hands and jogged to Chloe's apartment. He double-stepped to the front door as the dark clouds unleashed another torrential downpour. He stepped inside, leaning against the wall for a minute to catch his breath, a physical reminder that he wasn't twenty years younger, or in shape.

Chloe was already in bed. Sally was in the kitchen preparing a pot of tea, while Sam was getting Whitney out of her clothes. John placed the pizzas on the end table and removed his light jacket, hanging it on a hook above two umbrellas.

"It sure took you long enough," Sally said, walking into the living room holding Chloe's green tea. "Did you order another beer? Or get lost again?"

"That's not funny." He slipped off his squishy shoes and placed them by the front door. "I know what a New York minute is, but that place goes by another timetable."

Sally carried the tea to Chloe and returned to the living room, holding an armful of hangers and damp clothes.

"How's Chloe?" John asked.

"I got her to take a hot shower after we got back. She's over the chills. She seems to be better. At least I hope she is."

"I may take a shower." He bent over and removed his water-logged socks.

"You'll have to wait in line. Whitney's next, and then Sam."

"So I'm after Sam?"

"Unless you plan to cut in front of me," Sally said.

"I can go last. I'm used to it."

"And Sam said no long showers. They limit them to three minutes."

John's forehead puckered. "Whatever."

"Sam also said we have to wait about fifteen minutes between showers because of the hot water heater. It's old and can't handle the demands from all the tenants."

John let out a deep breath. "Sounds like me."

Sally grinned. "But I can make you some hot tea in the meantime."

"That'll do." John straggled behind her to the kitchen. "And after that I'm going to bed."

Twenty-three

John awoke early the following morning and began sorting through his clothes in a piece of luggage. He sniffed several Henley shirts, deciding on one that didn't have any distinct body odor. He went to the bathroom, where the socks he wore during the rainstorm dangled on a towel bar. He gave one a squeeze. "Ah, dry, semi-clean socks."

Returning to the living room, he found the hide-a-bed folded back into a couch and Sally busy in the kitchen. The aroma of fresh-brewed coffee wafted in the air as he sat on the couch and put on the stiff socks.

Sally peeked out the kitchen entry. "Toast and eggs this morning?"

"Sounds great." John rose from the couch and stretched his arms. "Don't want to leave on an empty stomach."

Sam padded into the living room wearing Chloe's pink bathrobe over a white nightshirt, yawning. "You guys are sure up early. What time's your flight?"

"Eleven. Trying to get everything together so I won't be so rushed."

John followed Sam into the kitchen, where they sat across from each other at the table. Sally set cups on the table and poured their coffee.

"How did Chloe sleep last night?" Sally asked.

"I don't think she moved," Sam said. "I felt her forehead before I got up and she didn't seem to be running a fever."

"That's good to hear," Sally said as she joined them at the table. "I was afraid she'd catch a cold, even pneumonia, after being out in the rain. I know I felt I little clammy when we got back."

They sipped their coffee for a minute in edgy silence, making little eye contact with each other.

"How long to do you plan to stay?" Sam asked Sally.

"As long as she needs me here. And you, too."

"I appreciate that. I can't get away from work to be with her. We don't have a policy that I can take time off to be with her. It only applies to heterosexual couples. Go figure."

"That's the way things are now so we have to deal with it." Sally tightened her lips.

"I'm not so sure about that. I've been talking with several advocates for gay rights in the workplace. We may take the company to court over it because it's not fair and it's not right. Our union is looking into it."

"I hope you have success," John said, raising his cup. "But it's difficult in today's political climate. Corporations kinda rule nowadays. I'm sure you've noticed."

"If the company had a compassionate leave policy, then you could be flying back home with John," Sam said to Sally.

"I wouldn't be going back home and leaving Chloe right now," Sally said. "She needs me with her. That's out of the question."

"I didn't mean it that way." Sam's face turned a pale red. "I was just making a point about the leave policy at work."

Sally went to the refrigerator and took out a carton of eggs. "I'm making breakfast for John," she said. "Can I fix you anything?"

"No thanks," Sam said. "Coffee's my morning mainstay. I'll grab a banana from a fruit vendor on the way to work."

Sally stood by the stove, cracked two eggs and put them in a semi-hot iron skillet. John went to the coffee maker and poured another cup in his and Sam's mugs.

Sam looked at John. "Remember the conversation we had the other day?"

John sat and nodded. Sally turned around at Sam. Silence saturated the room for several seconds.

"I don't know why I said what I said," Sam said. "I apologize for saying those things. I had a lot on my mind. It just spilled out of nowhere. Please forget and forgive me."

John stirred creamer in his coffee before looking at her. "We want the best for you, Chloe, and Whitney. But I will confess that what you said kinda threw me for a loop. And Sally."

"I don't blame you." A tear trickled down Sam's cheek. "I guess I was using you as a sounding board and I shouldn't have. That was stupid on my part. You have a wonderful relationship with Chloe."

"She's our daughter," Sally said. "No matter how old she is, we'll be there for her."

"That's not what I mean," Sam said. "I don't have that kind of relationship with my parents. I've been cast out by my family, for the most part. You and Chloe have a warm, loving mother-daughter relationship. I envy that."

She looked at John. "And she worships the ground you walk on."

Sally placed the fried eggs from the skillet to a plate with the buttered toast. After handing it to John, she reached down and hugged Sam.

"I'm so sorry to hear that about your parents," Sally said. "Your mother doesn't know what she's missing."

"Mom tries to be civil, but that's usually on the phone. She'll ask about Whitney and mention Chloe. That's about it. I don't remember the last time Mom and Dad visited."

"Do they still live in North Carolina?"

"Near Fayetteville."

"Things can change over time." Sally embraced Sam's shoulders and sat down. "I've seen it with other families."

"I hope so." Sam wiped the tears with a napkin. "I'd like for them to get to know Whitney. And Chloe."

"Perhaps you, Chloe, and Whitney need to make a trip to Fayetteville and spend some time with them. That might change their attitude."

"I've given that some thought. I've been leery about my Dad's reaction. He's retired military and rather rigid about things."

"He might surprise you," John said. "He's been exposed to diversity throughout his career."

"I never really thought about that, but you're right," Sam said as stood. "He just doesn't say much. I'll give it some more thought."

"You do that," Sally said. "And we can discuss it more while I'm here, if you'd like to."

"I would." Sam beamed. "But for now, I need go to work. I hope you have a safe trip back to Kentucky."

John hugged her. "Try not to work too hard and come visit us after Chloe is up and running at full speed."

"I'll do that. I'll see you later, Sally. Call me if anything comes up with Chloe or Whitney."

"Oh, one more thing," Sally said. "Wait a minute." She went to the living room and returned with a sack containing several items. "We got you something in Budapest."

Sally handed her a small rectangular box. Sam snapped it open to find a silver necklace.

"Oh, you shouldn't have," Sam said. "It's beautiful."

"I found it in my suitcase this morning," Sally said. "It had slipped my mind in all the commotion of the last couple days. I hope you like it."

Sam held it up by her neck, turning her body toward Sally and then John for them to see the glistening jewelry. She put it back in the box, then gave them both tearful hugs.

Sam was dressed and out the door in twenty minutes. Sally warmed John's coffee and sat on his lap.

"You know I'm going to miss you," she said. "It's been nice being together despite all the calamity of the past few weeks."

"I'll miss you too, through thick and thin," he said, putting an arm around her waist. "But Chloe and Whitney and Sam need you and that's what's important right now. You'll be back home in no time."

She kissed his cheek. "I'm sure I'll stay busy."

"And if you do get lonesome, you know who you can call."

"You?"

"Dorothy."

Sally balled her hand in front of his face and laughed. "You better watch it, mister!"

"Speaking of phone calls, have you told Brody or your mother that I'll be back this afternoon?"

"I'll call in an hour or so, when I think Brody is awake. I'm not in the mood for Mother."

Twenty-four

Chloe coaxed Whitney out of bed earlier than usual so she could see John leave for the airport. As Chloe and Whitney ate breakfast, Sally sorted through John's luggage to make sure he had everything and didn't include anything she needed for her stay.

He took out his blue pills from the toiletry bag and waved them in front of her. "I guess I won't be needing these for a while," he said.

"You better not," she said with a laugh.

He curled his upper lip and snarled. "I'll wait until you get back home, baby."

"Hunka, hunka."

They burst out laughing before falling into each other's arms. She rested her head on his shoulder for a few seconds as they savored the moment in the stillness, ending with a passionate kiss and prolonged hug.

Chloe opened the kitchen door, then closed it when she saw them in a loving embrace. She turned and put a finger to her mouth, signaling to Whitney not to make a sound.

Sally led John to the kitchen, fingertips to fingertips, where Chloe sipped her coffee and Whitney munched on cereal. As John sat, Sally walked to the counter and picked up the bag of gifts from Budapest.

"Here's some souvenirs we bought for you," she said. "I hope you like them."

She gave Whitney the handmade Hungarian girl doll in colorful folk clothes, and a small square box containing earrings to Chloe.

"You shouldn't have," Chloe said, holding the earrings up. "But they're gorgeous. I love them."

"Me, too," Whitney said as she examined the footlong figure unlike anything in her collection. "Can I take it to school with me?"

"That'd be okay," Chloe said. "You can tell everyone in your class it came from Europe."

"We bought Sam a necklace," John said. "We gave it to her this morning."

Sally handed John the bag containing the money clip for Brody, brooch for Geraldine, and candy for Bert and Wilma. "You can pass these out when you get home."

"It's about that time to hit the road," John said as he stood, sadness clouding his face. "I need to call Uber and get my ride."

"I wish you didn't have to leave but I understand," Chloe said.

"I just want you to get better," John said. "Understand?"

"I will, Daddy," she said.

"And I want you to continue to do well in school," he said to Whitney. "Okay?"

"I will, Papa."

John made the call and an Uber driver was in front of the apartment in less than ten minutes. There wasn't much time for anything other than a hugs and kisses before picking up his luggage and going to the vehicle.

John waved goodbye from the rear passenger window of the late-model sedan that would take him to the Port Authority. He pressed his mouth together as a lump swelled in his throat. He glanced at them one more time from the rear window as the vehicle traveled down the narrow street as the sun was edging up on the horizon.

"It ain't easy leaving family," the driver said, looking in the rearview mirror. "I cry my eyes out every time I have to go someplace. Even makes me sad when I have to pick up people like you going someplace. Tugs at my heart."

"It's only temporary but it's still difficult." John puffed his cheeks.

"You don't sound like you're from around here."

"Kentucky."

"I thought I could pick up a Southern accent. I was stationed at Fort Knox before I went to Iraq a few years ago. Cool place. Kentucky, that is. Not Fort Knox. I couldn't wait to leave that place."

John chuckled. "I hear ya."

"You headed that way now?"

"Going to Lexington."

"I love them Kentucky Wildcats. I got to be a big fan of the Cats when I was there. Go Big Blue! Always wanted to see them in Rupp Arena. Still follow 'em."

"They have lots of fans across the country."

"I did go see them at Barclays Center in Brooklyn a few years back. I hope they play at the Garden one of these days. That'd be something."

"If you're ever in Kentucky again, let me know and I'll try to scrounge a couple tickets."

"Oh, man, they'd be cool."

When they pulled in front of the Port Authority, John handed the driver a five-dollar tip and an old business card from the newspaper with the work number marked out and personal e-mail and cell phone number written in.

"Listen, man, whenever you're in the city, or if you're family needs a ride, tell them to contact me. My name's Earl." He gave John a glossy business card with a photo that looked more like a mug shot with a dour expression.

John glanced at the card. "I'll try to remember that, Earl." He reached over the seat and shook the driver's hand, smiled, and hurried inside the building to purchase a ticket to Liberty International Airport. The ride was uneventful other than traffic jams at every exit sign. Didn't he read somewhere that the locals joked about that, saying they lived in "exit" because of the proliferation of the markers?

After going through security, John found a seat in the lounge and picked up a day-old New York *Daily News* someone had left behind. He spent about five minutes with it, then went and got an overpriced cup of coffee, returned, and sat looking out the window at the tarmac, with the nonstop coming and going of jets.

It dawned on John after thirty minutes that he hadn't called Sally to let her know he made it safely to the airport. She told him of a contentious conversation with her mother after he left, informing her that Brody came home late and left early in the morning. And something strange about the brief conversation that bothered her. He'd find out what was going on, if anything, and let her know.

It was on to Detroit, then Lexington, and home. He wasn't sure what to expect other than another new horizon.

Meet Michael Embry

Michael Embry is the author of 13 books including nine novels, three nonfiction sports books, and a short-story collection. He spent more than 30 years in the news media, working as a reporter, sports writer, and editor for two newspapers, a national news service, and a regional magazine as well as a book editor. A U.S. Air Force veteran, he is listed in *Who's Who in America*.

Embry lives in Frankfort, Ky., with his wife, Mary, and two rescue dogs, Bailey and Belle. Among his interests are travel, hiking, writing, reading, music, and family activities, especially those involving his four granddaughters—Lily, Lola, Ellie Cate, and Olivia.

www.michaelembry.com
www.michaelembry.blogspot.com
www.facebook.com/kentuckyauthormichaelembry
www.twitter.com/MichaelEmbry
www.wingsepress.com
www.linkedin.com/in/michaelembry/
www.instagram.com/michael_embry/

For book signings, book clubs, interviews, speaking engagements, media enquiries, and other book-related activities, contact Michael at michael.embry@gmail.com or www.michaelembry.com/contact.html.

Other Works From The Pen Of Michael Embry

Darkness Beyond the Light - John Ross and his wife Sally learn their self-centered son Brody has been leading a double life and must navigate uncharted territory during the Christmas season to lead him out of the darkness of drugs.

Old Ways and New Days - Retired sports editor John Ross discovers there are many adjustments he must make in this coming-of-old-age novel.

The Bully List - Dealing with bullies isn't an easy thing to do, so Josh and Sam try to come up with a list of things to do to get even with a gang of bullies.

Shooting Star - Basketball standout Jesse Christopher finds most of his challenges away from the gym as he tries to fit in as the new kid in school.

A Long Highway - A random act of violence in the workplace forces sports columnist Micah Stewart to hit the road in search of meaning to his life.

The Touch - Sports editor Blake Williams, a widower trying to raise three children, is careful to open his heart to another woman, fearful of the pain he might suffer again.

A Confidential Man - Sports columnist Chase Elliott is known as a trustworthy friend who can keep confidences. But can keeping some confidences prove to be deadly?

Foolish Is The Heart - Sports columnist Brandon Wilkes discovers there are important things going on in his life other than covering the big games.

You *can* make a difference!

Independent publishers like Wings ePress, Inc. do not have the financial or advertising clout of the larger publishing houses.

We depend upon another precious resource: our dedicated base of loyal readers. Please help us get the word out.

What can you do?

Take a few minutes and post a review on this book's Amazon page.

You can post a review on our Wings ePress, Inc page at:

https://wingsepress.com/making-tracks by clicking on the User Reviews tab located in the Review section below the author biography.

Seriously, even a one-line review is helpful.

Thank you!